The Machine

JAMES SMYTHE

blue door

Blue Door
An imprint of HarperCollinsPublishers
77–85 Fulham Palace Road,
Hammersmith, London W6 8JB

First published in Great Britain by Blue Door 2013

1

A catalogue record for this book is
available from the British Library

HB ISBN: 978-0-00-742860-1
TPB ISBN: 978-0-00-749147-6

Set in Minion by Palimpsest Book Production Limited,
Grangemouth, Stirlingshire

Printed and bound in Great Britain by
Clays Ltd, St Ives plc

THE MACHINE

Also by James Smythe

The Testimony
The Explorer

THE MACHINE

PART ONE

Memory is the greatest gallery in the world and I can play an endless archive of images.

J.G. Ballard, *Miracles of Life*

1

She opens the door to a deliveryman, and the Machine, which has come in three parts, all wrapped in thick paper. Each of the parts is too big to get through the door.

We'll have to try the window, the man says.

She shows him which one it is, along the communal balcony. It's already at its widest, to let some air into the flat, to try and counteract the invasive heat from outside. Still not wide enough, so the men – the first has been joined by another from the van, having just heaved another thick cream-paper wrapped packet the size of a kitchen appliance from the van, and left it leaning against the bollards – tell her that they'll have to take the window out.

We've got the tools for it, this other man says.

Beth stands back and watches as they unscrew the bolts on the attaching arms, and then lift the whole sheet down. Others in the estate have stuck their heads out of their windows, or come out of their front doors to watch. Next door, the woman with all the daughters stands and watches, and her girls run around inside. The littlest one stands at the woman's legs, clutching onto her skirt.

Gawpers, the first man says. Always wanting to know what we're up to.

The deliverymen don't know what's inside the packages. They're just paid to deliver them. Beth wonders if she's going to be able to assemble it herself, or if she's better off asking them for help. Slip them a fifty, they'd probably stand around with her for an hour and figure it out. She doesn't know how easy it will actually be: if there will be wires, or if it's just a case of plugging the pieces together. The man she bought it from said it would be simple. They struggle up the stairwell with the first piece, stopping to mop their brows. They still wear dark-blue overalls, in this weather, and their now-sweaty palms leave dark-brown prints on the paper wrapped around the Machine's pieces. The first piece makes it through the window maw, twisted in the frame as if this is one of those logic games. Manipulate the pieces.

Right, the first man says. Where do you want them?

In the spare bedroom, Beth tells him. She indicates it through, pointing the way past the living room. The room is light and airy – or as airy as it can be nowadays – and decorated like it's a master, with an expensive-looking bed. Wallpaper not paint, with a different dado rail, a thick yellow colour contrasting with the impressed patterned cream of the walls. The room looks untouched, like nobody's ever lived in it. The bed is made, the sides of the duvet tucked in below the mattress. There's potpourri on the dresser in a simple golden metal dish, but not enough to stop the faint smell of dust. The sunlight, through the window, hits the dust, a cone of it floating in the air.

Anywhere?

By the back wall. I've cleared a space for it. She rushes past, ducking down in front of him, making sure that the space is still clear, then helps him lower the first package.

What the bloody hell is this thing? the man asks.

Exercise equipment, Beth tells him. That's an answer suggested by the man who sold the Machine to her. In his email, he told her that he would write that on the form for the collection, and on the customs form. He was French, and Beth had had to translate his email using the internet, only the occasional word making her stumble. Still, she got the gist.

Jesus, the deliveryman says as he puts it down – the French seller has marked the packages with arrows, showing which way up they're to be carried and stored – and stretches his back. He's wearing a thick black harness around his waist, which he pats. Lifesaver, he says. They make us wear them now, for the insurance. We take them off in the van, when we're done. Fucking hot though, wearing this along with the rest of the get-up. He stretches again, more exaggerated this time. His friend shouts from the window, where they see he's positioned the next piece – this one long and thin at one end, bulbous and clunky at the other, meant to stand tall, taller than any of the people in the flat – halfway through the window. He's straining to hold it up. Beth sees that the arrows (marked with thin, shaky writing that says THIS WAY UP) are horizontal. She wonders if that'll affect it in any way.

Come on, the man says, can't hold it. The other one takes the inside end and they work it through.

Same place? the first removal man asks. Beth nods, and then he asks for something cold to drink, which she prepares – iced tea, in the fridge – as they both struggle with it through the tight doorways and narrow corner into the room. She's got two glasses on the side ready by the time that they're done with that piece, but the first man – clearly the superior of the two, older and wiser and with a company t-shirt on under his rote blue overalls – waves them aside. Last piece, then we'll have them, he says. Beth watches them both at the van, which they've parked at the bottom of the estate, by the bollards that prevent cars driving right up to the buildings themselves. They look at the last piece, which is nearly the same shape as the first, only somehow wider, more unwieldy, and they both laugh. She knows that they're talking about what it is. Speculating. They'll know it's not exercise equipment. They've handled exercise bikes before. They do this for a living, and the wool can't be pulled over the eyes of those who will know the weight and shape of an exercise bike or a rowing machine. She watches as they finally heave the last piece up between them, up the stairwell and into her flat through the window space. Their sweat drips from their heads and onto the concrete slabs, and the Machine.

It needs to be a certain way, she says. Would you mind? They shrug, and she tells them. The pieces have been labelled with numbers showing where they connect, drawn on the outside of the wrapping.

This is like Tetris, the first man says. The younger man laughs. They back up and look at it when they're done, and the wall is essentially filled by the wrapped packages. The light that came through the small window is totally blocked now, and the room is suddenly darker, thrown into the shade of the still-wrapped packages. You all right with this now? the older man asks. He hands Beth a sheet from his back pocket, and a pen. Sign this and we're all good. They gulp their drinks back as she signs her name three times, and then leave the glasses on the side. They replace the window back in minutes. These things are all designed to be taken apart and put back together so quickly now, the first man says. Everything's a bloody prefab, right? He smiles at Beth as if she doesn't live here, as if she'll be in on the slightly snobbish joke with him. To her surprise she laughs, to back him up.

I know, she says. Thanks for everything. I really mean that.

No problem. She waits until they're back in their van – they stand at the rear of it for a few minutes examining what they've got left on their sheet of deliveries, and where they're heading next, wiping their foreheads on their sleeves and on a towel, gasping for air – and then watches them drive away. Then it's just her and the flat and the Machine.

2

The paper pulls away from the Machine with relative ease. She's surprised that it didn't tear during the move. A few bits she has to attack with scissors but most of it rips away easily, and then she's left with the Machine itself. She stands back, on the other side of the bed, against the far wall. She sizes it up. This one is bigger than she remembers.

The pitch-black casing is grotesque, she thinks. It seems so vast. She hasn't joined it together yet, not where the clips and bolts require, but she can see it as if it was complete. On its side, a coiled power cable waits, like an umbilicus. The Crown has a dock above the screen, in the centre, and the whole thing seems unreal. She looks at it for too long, at how black it is. It almost fills the entire wall, and the shadow it casts is deep enough that she can't see the wallpaper past it. This was the only place it could go, because of the shape of the room. She tries to move as far back as possible and take it all in, but it isn't possible. It's like a cinema screen when you sit near the front: never entirely encompassed by your vision.

She knows, to the day, how long it's been since she last saw one of these. The last one was very different in some ways: it was smaller, she thinks, and the Crown wasn't docked as it is in this one. It was wireless, where here there's a thick cable that looks like it's got sand stuffed inside it to keep it taut, and other lumps and bumps along the length of the pale-coloured rubber. The Crown itself is less flashy as well. This is definitely an older model, but she wasn't looking for a new one. In the newer models, you couldn't change anything. Firmware updates were automatic. The guides on the internet told her that she needed one she could change, and this was all she could find. Even then it was hidden away amongst useless husks and books and videos. She had to email the man directly to ask if he had any working Machines, and it took four emails (making her jump through hoops) before he trusted her enough to tell her his prices. This one was the oldest of the old. She still paid through the nose for it. But it was the only one she had found in six months of searching, and she hadn't spent any money for the last few years beyond the essentials. This was a long-term plan, and she had saved accordingly. The email where he wrote the figure she would owe him made her cry: not from the enormity, but the relief.

She goes closer to the bulk of it. She remembers the one that Vic had during his treatments, and the way that it used to vibrate. They explained to her, once, about the power needed to run it. It's one of the most powerful computers in the country, they said to her. (She supposes that, were they to be invented now, they would be put into a smaller package: something the size of a briefcase, maybe even as small as a telephone.) It used to vibrate right through the floors, and Vic would sit in the chair next to it and his teeth would chatter as he clenched them together, because he was bracing himself. The early sessions were the hardest. This Machine here isn't even plugged in yet, and yet Beth puts her hand on it and would swear that she can feel the vibrations. The metal itself – that's what it's made of, some thick alloy that she couldn't even name, that isn't like anything she's got in the house, not aluminium cans or the wrought-iron picture frame or the steel of that lampshade, but something else, like the material that the thing is made from was this shade of black to begin with – is coarse and cold, and she would swear carries some sort of residual shudder. She takes the plug from the side and uncoils it, and runs it to the base of the bed, where the room's only sockets are. So much is wireless now and yet this needs hard-wiring. The ones that Vic used before were actually attached to the wall, part of the complex that they had to visit. They were monitored.

She goes to work on the bolts. They're all hand-driven, none requiring custom tools, which is good. Some of them have connectors that need to be touching, but the deliverymen got them mostly lined up for her. All the insides are driven by conductive metal rather than wires, which makes them easy to assemble. Foolproof, even. The pieces sit perfectly flush when they're connected and lined up, and it takes a bit of effort – heaving them a centimetre this way, a millimetre the other – but they satisfyingly click together. She can't even see the lines between pieces when it's done: it's like a solid lump of black metal from the front, no seams, like something carved from the world itself. It looks, she thinks, almost natural. Like rock.

She drags the plug from the side and plugs it into the wall, and then strokes the screen. Doing this is like instinct. The screen flickers to life. There's the familiar triple tone of the boot noise – ding-ding-ding, ascending and positive, full of optimism – and then the screen is awash with light. Beth hadn't realized how covered in dust it was. She doesn't know when this thing was last turned on, but the clock has reset. She pulls her sleeve down over her hand and wipes the screen off. She'll do a better job later, but she wants to check that this all works before she gets her hopes up. The interface is exactly as she remembers, all big colourful buttons and words driven by positivity. Nothing negative. Even in the act of taking away they were reinforcing. PURGE, COMMIT, REPLENISH. She presses a button, through to sub-menus. There's a button that offers her the chance to explore the hard drive, which she presses, but the drive is clear. That's what she'd hoped for. She didn't want somebody else's memories lingering here. She heads out of the room and into the other bedroom, her bedroom. Compared to the Machine's room, it's chaos. Clothes everywhere, on the floor and bed, – she sleeps around them, making nooks in them where her body lies – and the walls stacked high with vacuum-packed bags

10

full of clothes that she hasn't worn in years, or that she kept of Vic's. She keeps the hard drive under her bed, because that seemed like the safest place. If she got burgled, she didn't want them to take it thinking that it would be worth anything. Pulling it out – it's been in a box with remnants of who she was before, old library cards and birthday cards and childhood photographs – she walks into the room and sees the drive appear on the screen as she gets closer. It's a first-generation capacitive wireless device, able to pick up on other wireless items in the vicinity and read their drives. A new option appears on the screen: a cartoonish image of a hard drive. She presses the button – her hands are shaking, because she's worried that the drive might have wiped itself or corrupted over the past couple of years (ever since she backed up the contents from an older drive one New Year's Day as she worried about it, worried about the life-span of these things) – and there it is: a folder named after her husband. She presses his name and waits as it loads.

3

There are hundreds of files inside, all date-stamped, and all under an umbrella of his name. She presses the first one, which she can barely remember being recorded because it was so long ago, and waits as it loads. A bar appears on the screen and an icon of a play button. She presses it and the Machine starts thrumming. The file starts loading. The technology isn't there with the size of these files: the pristine nature of exactly what they've recorded, and how long they are. The amount of data that they contained inside the packets of the audio files themselves . . . Everything important. The audio is essentially worthless. It's wrapping paper. But the files are enormous, and streaming them all is impractical. It would take far too long; too much waiting for them to load. She should be using the hard drive of the Machine itself, but she wants to check it works first. That, and she wants to hear him. She's too eager.

Then the first file is done queuing itself up, and it plays automatically, and she hears somebody clearing their throat in the background, the click of something. Somebody sitting down. She doesn't know where the speakers are in the casement, but they're somewhere, or it uses the metal itself as a speaker. Maybe that's where the vibrations come from: internal sound channelled outwards. She saw that once, when she was a teenager: something you could plug your iPod into and it would turn any glass table or window into a speaker. She remembers being impressed by it: as the boys that she knew ran around her parents' house plugging it into everything they could find, dancing in their room full of art pieces as the glass covering a statue that her father described as priceless vibrated with the sounds of trilling keyboards and squawked singing. They danced on the rugs, because of the novelty of not being able to hear their own footfalls.

The first voice she hears is that of a stranger. It must be one of the doctors who had worked with him.

We're ready? Can you say your name for us? it asks.

Victor McAdams. His voice is suddenly full in the room. She can't remember exactly how long it's been since she heard his voice talking properly, saying sentences. Long enough that it's become a memory, rather than something tangible. She's forgotten how deep it was. How it cracks at the higher end. The trepidation as he says their surname, and the pause that hangs in the air afterwards. She can hear him breathing.

And could you state your rank and ID number, for the record?

Captain. Two-five-two-three-two-three-oh-two.

Great. Don't be nervous, the voice says to him. You know why you're here?

Yes sir.

Don't call me sir. My name's Robert. First-name terms here, Victor.

Vic.

Vic it is. Beth hears the smile. Shall we begin? Beth stops the recording. The voices hang in the air, like the dust. It works. The files are intact. Her first worry dealt with. She presses the screen and goes back a few stages, back to the central menu, and ticks the box to copy the contents of the drive to the Machine itself. The vibrations start as it accesses its drives. It's older than her tiny hard drive by a couple of years, and she thinks about the information – about the recordings of Vic's voice, pages and pages of entries where he sat in a room and spoke about the things that he didn't want to remember any more – she thinks about it all expanding as it fills the drive of the Machine. It gives her a time-bar for the download, of hours rather than minutes. The slowest crawl. She goes to the main room of her flat and thinks about how she should tidy more. It's become worse since she invested in this project, stealing both her time and her energy. The kids have suffered most: mountains of marking sit by the front door, and she knows that they need to have most of it done before the summer holidays. Her deadlines are theirs. She has six weeks coming up, and she's planned how she'll break it down by the day. She's begun stockpiling food and provisions: the kitchen is brimming with canned foods, and the bathroom has toilet-roll packets stacked behind the door. The plan involves her not leaving the flat for the first week because Vic will most likely need her. He won't be able to be left alone for more than a couple of hours, not for at least that time, and probably much longer. The schedule of how those six weeks will work is punishing, she knows, but needs must. She has printed them out, a week per sheet of A4 paper, and she's put them on the fridge under a large magnet that Vic was given by his parents when he was a child, that he hung onto. She's kept it as well, like a trophy. Proof that he was once real. She can tell that people don't believe her, when she talks about him. It's like he's a ghost. She says, He used to be a soldier, and they smile, and they ask where he is now. She tells them that he's away, serving still. They look at her – or, if she's let them past that barrier, at her flat – and they know that it's a lie. Nobody's away serving any more. Everything where they were is rubble. So she has to tidy, and she has to make sure that she knows exactly how the Machine works. Two weeks before the end of term.

She has videos on the computer, kept on the desktop. They're taken from a forum about these things, where she's nothing more than a username that bears no relation to who she is. Numbers and letters chosen at random, on purpose. She doesn't know if the forums are monitored – or who would be monitoring them – but just in case. She grabbed the videos over one long weekend, determined in case the site ever suddenly disappeared. She's renamed the videos with numbers, so that she knows what order she's learning them in, and she's already watched them tens of times, but never with anything to practise on. It's different when there's a practical application. Plus, there's a difference in the firmware in the Machines, and she needs to know exactly what she's playing with. She thinks that she should check it, so she goes back to the bedroom. It's the first time she's been surprised: before, she pulled the paper off, and exposed it piece by piece. Now she sees how big it is for the first time, and the mass of blackness seems to make its own negative light, casting the rest of the room in a shadow of its own making. And it seems so tall to her. Impossibly tall. The ceilings are high, ten foot, and this wasn't much taller than the first removal man, but it seems to fill almost every bit of the space. She tries to see on top of it but can't, so she idles in front of it. The screen is still active but on standby, the colour and brightness dampened. She presses it and the whole Machine whirs into life. The noise – she hadn't noticed it before, but it must have been there – is like gears, as if this were some nineteenth-century apparatus. Something almost industrial. She knows that this is a computer, and that what's inside is fans and microchips and cables to carry processes from one part to another; and the hard drive, never forget the hard drive, which is both the brain and the heart of the Machine – but the noise is unlike any that she's heard. She supposes that she's forgotten: that things have changed since this was cutting edge. She thinks about the newer models of the Machine, the ones after this. How much one of them would have cost her, even if it could be hacked and updated like this one has been. That she would have been here in a decade still, forming her plan, slowly losing herself, alone for so long, with Vic's body rotting more and more. Less her husband with each passing day, week, month, year.

The screen gets lighter, and she sees the button labelled ABOUT. She presses it, and there, a year and a firmware number. She reasons that this must have been one of the first commercial models, before even her mother started on the programme, and well before Vic was using one. She pulls the Crown down from the dock and the screen changes, updates. PURGE, it invokes, or REPLENISH. Like this is some sort of advertisement. She's seen the language on both beauty products and bleaches. She doesn't put the Crown on her head, because she dare not.

She's thought about it, sometimes: as she's tried to get to sleep, lying in bed, thinking about how easy it would be to wear a Crown, to press the buttons and to talk about Vic and herself, and their old life together. To talk her way through everything that she's lost. To press the PURGE button and feel it all drift away. Vic used to say that it felt like when you take painkillers for a wound. He said that they gave him heavy stuff after the IED went off and put its shrapnel in his shoulder and his neck, and once he'd popped them there was a sense that it had once hurt, but that it was like an echo of the pain was all that was left, or the memory of the pain. Like it's been rubbed hard and then left alone. That's what the Machine did. He rarely spoke about it as time went on, but in the early days, before Beth was allowed anywhere near the process, when Vic still knew what he was doing and why he was doing

17

it, he frequently used to describe it to Beth when he got home. They said it would be two weeks before he'd start to lose what it was he was running from, and it was, almost to the day. After that, Beth didn't like to say anything more. He knew that it was time for his treatments and he didn't question them. Beth looks at the bar for copying Vic's files over, and it's hardly gone down.

Come on, she says, though it's not like she can do anything with it here and now. She lies on the bed next to the Machine, a bed that she's never actually slept in because it felt wrong, somehow, ever since she decorated the room. She watches the bar and shuts her eyes, and thinks about Vic and what he could be.

When the company behind the Machine announced that they were working on a cure – they would put the word in inverted commas, because they were so cautious with how they went about presenting it to the world after the last time – they said that the technology side of things was flawless.

They said, We can take a person and make them whole again.

Beth – everybody – doubted it, but then they showed videos of a man and his progress. In the earliest videos he shuffled like a zombie and needed feeding and changing and his eyes lolled back in his head even as his loved ones poked and prodded him, asking him questions, trying to get a response. In later ones he fed himself and walked, and even responded to his name. They showed old video of him ignoring persistent, insistent calls – Shaun, Shaun! – over and over again. Then they invited him up onto the stage where they were making the announcement: and they did it solely by calling his name. Once. Shaun! He ran up, and he shook their hands. He looked at the cameras, and his gaze was a bit glassy-eyed but he was mostly there. He waved at the crowd, and then they asked his wife up there as well, and they embraced on stage to applause. Standing ovation: he is healed.

And this can only get better, the men from the company promised. Beth saw it in their eyes: the idea that this was somehow their redemption. The thing that might stop their houses being burned and people fighting with them in the streets and the headlines on the tabloid sites. They have destroyed thousands of lives and now they're back, ready to save the day. They said, It takes years of therapy to bring them to this point. It uses our pioneering technologies. The process works best when we've got a full and frank medical history, and when you help us.

Shaun was back in another video. This time, his bedside in some hospice somewhere, where the bed was thin and metal-framed and the bed sheets that yellow colour. On his head was a Crown, or what passes for a Crown now: tiny multi-coloured pads designed by a famous South American designer, to make it appealing, placed on the temples and the forehead, tiny lights indicating that they're all wirelessly connected. His wife talked Shaun through a shared experience from their past that, presumably, had been lost; she's laughing and squeezing his hands.

We found it so funny, she said, and then you opened the presents, and you had another one, from Mark and the kids. A funny story, and when she laughed at the end,

19

so too did Shaun, somehow simpatico to it all. On stage, Shaun watched the video and then spoke to the audience. Slow and measured, careful with his words.

I can hardly believe this is me, he said. Standing here in front of you. The audience whooped and clamoured.

Shaun represents hundreds of man-hours of work, the doctors said, and it's not perfect. Shaun's not perfect. But we'll get there. By the end of this decade, they said, we hope to be able to offer this therapy to many of our ex-patients. Shaun waved again. The end of the decade made Beth's heart sink, because that was eight years away. That was so far away that, by the time it arrived, she would have been apart from Vic for more time than they had been together. And that was two years ago. They were asked, over and over, how long it would be before the public could have access to the tech. We don't want to rush things, they said. They – everybody – wanted to avoid a situation like the first time around: rushed to market, and then thousands damaged, seemingly irreparably. They were cautious, and their 'end of the decade' became the start of the next decade, in the post-Shaun interviews. They wanted to wait until it was right.

The internet didn't want to wait, though. People who knew things, people who worked for the company and hated what they had done, people with vested interests: they all stepped forward under the internet's veil of anonymity, and they told others how to do it. They leaked firmware, software, instructions; things that somehow they had got their hands on, that they shouldn't have had. Cloak and dagger, they explained that the Machine could be used to create a new persona in the damaged. It could build them up again, as they were, based on who they were. It could be achieved through talk, through photographs and videos. It was better if you had the recordings of their original sessions. They got together in clandestine meetings, organized themselves to do work for this: on the technology, the software, the work itself. Eventually they had their own case study, their own version of Shaun: a lady called Marcela. She was from Eastern Europe, and Beth didn't understand what she was saying but she got the gist. Marcela was herself again, in that she smiled and she waved at the camera and the person behind it, and they bent past the lens and leaned in to kiss her and she kissed his bearded face back, and he gave a thumbs-up to the camera.

We used the original recordings to help Marcela, the video said, and that sold it to Beth. Because she couldn't wait. This was too important to her, and to Vic. When Beth opens her eyes, the on-screen bar is finished: only it says that the files have been moved, not copied. She looks at the hard drive and it's empty, but it doesn't matter. Vic's memories are in the Machine now, and where they should be.

4

The window of her bedroom opens onto a view of what used to be thought of as a field, but now it's just scruff, cracked dry soil and scuffed-up anthills. They called them the Grasslands when they built this place. The area between the flats and the cliffs isn't huge, because that was the only way that they could get planning permission, and the most-desired flats had been the ones with the eastern-aspect view: looking out onto all that grass. The residents would remark that they lived in the greyest building on the island, but it didn't matter, because the view was what you saw every morning. You weren't looking at the walls. It was meant to be for new overspill from Portsmouth, because the mainland couldn't expand any more. That was the trick with it being so enclosed: there was no more land to build on. The developers moved across the water, assuming that people would want to live there, but they didn't. Apart from Beth, that is. The

Grasslands themselves were protected because they were so close to the new cliffs, far too fragile to build on. The local council had decided that those flats that had the spectacular views – out to the sea, to the mainland across the way, to freedom – would be put up for sale, and the rest could go to whoever needed them. Back then, when the first proposals for the construction of the site went through, the Grasslands were still green, and the trees dotted around the landscape were all green as well, their leaves almost constantly present. When Beth moved in she didn't know the names of them, but it helped her, being able to see them so unfaltering: when she was at her lowest, they survived. The trees are still there, now bare or getting there, but the grass is almost entirely gone: it's now a sickly yellowing orange, almost burnt. It looks the way that lawns used to look in the summertime after kids had played on them: hard, dry soil patches, like liver-spotted scalp peering through thinning hair.

Beth spends the day waiting for the files to copy, staring out of her window at the Grasslands, and by the time she's remembered that she hasn't eaten it's dark outside. She looks at the tins piled in the kitchen and thinks about how many of them she'll be eating in the weeks – months? – to come, baked beans and spaghetti hoops on toast, and she looks out of her living room window – past the rest of the estate, over towards the street of shops and takeaway restaurants that leads towards the main road – and decides to chance it. She opens the front door and looks around for people, but she can't see anybody out this side. There's noise (rustling and cackling) from behind the block, from the Grasslands, but that doesn't worry her. The only creatures that she ever sees out on the Grasslands are cats, from all around the neighbourhood: a glaring of them masses, like a congregation. They're not watching her or the flat or anything in particular. They just seem to mass. If there are kids out there – or worse – she can never see them. They've become excellent at staying in the dark. She locks the door behind her, and then checks it's locked, shoving it with her shoulder. When it doesn't budge she checks the window where the men took it out, pushing it as hard as she can to check it's secure. Satisfied, she walks down the bridge path, towards the stairwell. The doorway's open – some of the residents collectively decided to take the door off, because there were times that trouble had waited at the bottom of the stairs, and they wanted to make sure that they could hear it in future – and the lights are on, which buoys Beth. She runs down them, really pelts, and then out into the estate, past the bollards, to the street. She wants something hot. A curry, maybe, or spicy Chinese. She can smell the Indian Palace from the edge of the estate: the restaurant opens their back windows and doors, trying to entice people down. Some nights the whole estate can reek of food, and some nights that's the last thing that Beth wants to think about. But tonight it's enough.

Inside the restaurant they're playing music that Beth recognizes, but in some water-chime musical form. Songs from when she was a child, that she still knows the words to: huge ballads, slow-dance pop songs that once soundtracked hit movies. The waiters all sit around a table at the back, all with half-pint glasses half-filled with lager. Two of the four stand up when Beth walks in.

All right love, one of them asks.

Hi, Beth says. I wanted a takeaway?

Sure, sure. What can I get you?

Chicken korma and a pilau rice, she says. The man nods. He leans back and peers through the door to the kitchen, then nods at the solitary chef Beth can see in there, who's been leaning against the cookers.

It'll be a few minutes, the waiter says to Beth. Want a drink?

I'm fine, she says.

She sits at a table by herself to wait, near the window, and she watches the few other people out for the evening, all of them going to get takeaways or hurrying forward by themselves, collars up and eyes down. A group of kids – heads shaven into a step around the back and sides, suddenly popular again, and ripped jeans with smart-looking cheap shirts – walk past: they see her peering out and they spit at the window. One of them undoes his fly and rushes up to her, and she flinches backwards, away from the window. One of them stands at the back and doesn't do anything but stare, a fixed gaze that won't break. They all laugh.

Ignore them, the waiter who took her order says.

Bunch of pricks, one of the others says. He doesn't look up from his beer.

I know, Beth says. The waiter walks towards her table and leans over it. There are curtains that she hadn't seen, only half-height ones, but he pulls them across, blocking her view of the street, and the kids' view in.

Better when they can't see the customers, he says. Beth sits and stares at the curtain for the next few minutes, because she can hear them still out there on the street. They're laughing about something, down at the kebab house, and there are occasional bangs where they're throwing something, or hitting something. She thinks about standing up to see what they're doing, but knows that if they see her it will only antagonize them. She nearly asks the waiters how many times their front glass has been broken. It always looks new, she thinks.

When the waiter comes back with her food (which smells amazing, she thinks, cooked freshly because she's the only customer they've had all evening) he loads it into a plastic bag and throws a few poppadoms in.

You going to be all right? he asks.

Yes, she says. I only live up the hill.

In the estate? He inhales and laughs with the other waiters. I'll walk you.

Don't be silly, Beth says.

What else am I doing?

I'm fine.

Look at all my customers, he says. He opens the door for her and stands back, letting her head onto the street first. The boys outside the kebab shop shut up slowly, one by one, falling into line. They're all some ambiguous age that Beth can't tell, past the hoods and caps, even in this heat. They're looking over at them. Just ignore them, the waiter says. He walks next to Beth, briskly, their pace faster even than when she walked down here, and they don't look behind them. The boys stay quiet, so they don't know if they're being followed. Beth pictures it: them dropping their kebabs and cans, leaving them on the side, and then walking behind them as one. Falling into a pack, a tight unit, rapidly advancing, a cloud of dust ready to swallow them whole. That one who stared suddenly at the front, leading the others.

They make it to the lights of the estate, and the bollards. Beth can see her flat from here. At a dash, it's only thirty seconds away. The waiter stops. You all right from here? He looks back where they've come from. The boys are nowhere to be seen.

I'm fine. Thank you so much.

Pleasure. Want to walk me back to the restaurant now? He grins. Joking, joking, he says. Enjoy your dinner.

He heads back down the path towards the road. There's a bit where there are no lights and he disappears, and Beth waits to see him reappear on the other side of it. When he does she goes into the stairwell, and then along to her flat. She fumbles for her keys, but there's nobody anywhere near her, and no noise she can hear apart from the background murmur of neighbours' televisions, and the occasional rustle of a cat. She locks the door behind her, then goes to the kitchen with the bag and unpacks it on the worktop. She peels the lids from the tubs, takes a plate and turns them both out onto it, then sits on the sofa with the plate on her knees, the greasy paper slip of poppadoms on the table. She puts the TV on and tries to concentrate on it. She flicks through channels with one hand, eating with the other. But there's something else. She can hear it: a buzzing. She mutes the TV, cutting the weather report off midsentence – the symbols all sweating comical suns, not much chance of them saying anything to contradict that – and listens for it. It's like a fridge, but hers is silent, or an old light bulb about to blow, but hers are all energy-saving modern ones. She puts the plate on the table in front of her and walks around the living room, looking for the source. She can't find it in here, so she tries the spare bedroom and then remembers about the Machine. The screen is on – still – and the buzz coming from it. Not the screen: just, vaguely, the Machine itself. She can't pinpoint it, but she's sure of the source. She puts a hand on the casement and there's something, a movement. The most subtle vibration.

I should switch you off, she says to it. She leans down to the plug and flicks the switch and the Machine's screen goes dark. She can still hear the buzz, though, as she goes to leave the room: and as she lies in her bed, staring at the ceiling, thinking about how this is all going to go. And still, even with it this close to actually happening, how she has her doubts.

5

She swims first thing in the morning. Only some mornings – not enough to call it a regime, but more than a habit. Some deep-seated feeling about being so close to – inside, even, beneath and through – something that caused so much destruction and yet is somehow blameless. She gets up before anybody else, when it's still barely light, and she peels her clothes off and swims out against the waves into the water, and then back: and she stands on the beach and waits for the sun to dry her, which only takes minutes, and then she dresses herself. She doesn't get her hair wet – she ties it up above her head, a style that she never used to wear, but that's practical for her, here and now – and she puts her work clothes straight on and then sets off.

Her walk to work takes her along the path that runs adjacent to the coastline. She and Vic had always wanted to live by the sea: they had said that when he retired it was what they would do. (Without him here, she some-times thinks, this feels almost like cheating on him, with this place instead of another man. She is sure that he would – will – forgive her.) The path is hard ground, old mud that's faded and cracked underfoot. It falls just shy of the green grass; as she walks she keeps her eyes on that side. On the other side are the roughest blocks, the ones where the people always seem crammed in. These were the last ones built, designed to take the council housing overspill from Old Portsmouth after the flooding. The people there are bitter that they ended up here. They didn't choose to move: it was their only option, if they wanted to live where they could still keep their jobs. Most of the children from the estate go to her school, and she teaches many of them, or tries to. The worst of her kids invariably come from the worst parts of the island, where their parents have sob stories about how they lost their jobs on the mainland, or their homes. There's a joke around Portsmouth and Southampton, where they call the island Alcatraz and refer to the ferry that runs six times a day as the prison boat. They don't try and hide it. Anybody with real money left the island a long time ago. Before this, Beth would have been one of those people: running before they sank along with the rest.

Beth passes some children who clearly have no inten-tion of going to school today (out at this time already, racing around on their bikes, standing bolt upright on the pedals and clipping their wheels on curbs, trying to make the bikes jump off the ground for even a few inches of air), and thinks about persuading their parents to persuade them to go, or to force them. It's not a cost thing, she knows, because they fought to keep all the schools free when the new Prime Minister took over: it's an effort thing. They circle her as she walks, flitting between the road and the grass verge. Most mornings they ignore her. Today, one of them rides alongside her as his friends drop back, watching from a distance. She thinks she recognizes him; one of the youths from outside the takeaway house, maybe. Or just from the estate. They all blur into one after a while. Beth pulls her bag closer to her body. She remembers being in London when she was much younger, walking down roads where footsteps behind her might have meant an imminent mugging: she remembers how much that feeling holds you back, steps on your toes as it walks alongside you. She breathes and tries to stare past him, even as he nudges towards her, slightly ahead of her. His hair is clipped short on top, longer at the back and sides – looks like a home-job, clippers rather than scissors – and he is slightly boss-eyed, she notices, as he turns his head back towards her, peers at her from under his drooping eyelids. She wonders if he's stoned. He's very young to be getting stoned.

The fuck you looking at? he asks. His friends laugh behind them: she can hear the spokes of their cheap bikes clattering against wheel frames. You looking at me?

She doesn't answer him. Instead, she stares past him – at the boat in the distance, moored up, ready to take people across the water – and carries on walking. He darts in front of her, swaying across her path, forcing her to keep pausing her steps. He's only twelve or thirteen, she thinks, but his voice has broken into a full baritone, making him de facto ringleader.

I asked you a fucking question, he says, but Beth still ignores him. She would have taken him to task, in the old days: the Beth who walked along those streets in London and heard footsteps would have turned, stopped, done something surprising to scare them off. They're all mouth and no trousers, she would tell herself. But here she keeps her head down, because this is how she knows it has to work. No trouble. Every day is exactly the same where this is concerned. Beth carries on walking, heading up some steps and away from the front, even though it's slightly off-route for her, because she knows that they won't follow. They stay at the bottom of the steps and stand on the pedals of their bikes, laughing as if they've won.

Over the hill she sees the school: the gate that needs a fob to get into the playground, and then the door that requires a swipe of her ID card to get inside the building; and the metal detectors, which used to be something that they threw at troubled schools in America and people the world over laughed at as something that they would never need themselves, because our kids just weren't like that. Now, there's two of the turnstiles and a room, to the left of where the security guard stands, which has handcuffs inside and a locked cupboard crammed with mace, tasers, truncheons and a bullet-proof vest, just in case. Because, the Head told them when the decree came to have them installed, you never know.

The classrooms of Beth's school – which swallowed the

other two nearest schools on this part of the island, a primary and a secondary, turning them into one giant institution spanning two campuses – don't have any air conditioning. The school priced them up, worked out how much it would cost, but it was unfeasible. Even the discounted companies priced themselves out of the running, mainly because the school had one of the lowest budgets of any in the county. Instead, they made do with opened windows and cheap desk fans, often two or three in each classroom, blasting off from one wall, pushing the air away from the desks and ushering it towards the outside.

Beth's Year Ten form has forty-one students: twenty-four girls and seventeen boys. The ratio makes the boys excitable. They rock against their chairs and jiggle their legs, their feet tapping furiously on the floors when some of the girls do salacious things: taking off their jumpers, wearing shirts that are paler than the rules allow, fanning their skirts when they stand up. One of the repercussions of the heat is that everything becomes sweat-laden, and the school has rules. Shirts must be of a certain thickness; no thin cotton, nothing that can become too transparent in the heat. The class sit on cheap plastic chairs; every day, no matter who is sitting down, there's a sweat mark on the seat when they leave. Beth hardly sits down at all any more; she leans against the desk, or she paces.

Her class are always late, but it's excused by all the teachers because of the heat-caused lethargy. Everybody's late. The parents – those that care enough to attend the biannual meetings about their child's progress – tell the

Head that the kids can't be expected to be excited.

It's so fucking hot in there, one shrill woman said at the last parents' evening. It's so hot that they don't want to be there. And if you don't want to be somewhere, you don't fucking go there, do you?

Beth sits and sweats and can, some days, barely concentrate herself, let alone expect the kids to. When the children do eventually arrive in her classroom it's in a single gaggle, a tumble of horny adolescence through the doorway. They sit quietly, because they quite like Beth (even though she's quiet: they think of her as particularly fair, for a teacher), and she takes the register.

Abrams, is the first name, and he says that he's there, and she goes down the list one by one. They laugh when they reach Turner, because he's the butt of all of their jokes, the only fat kid (so fat he's actually clinically obese, with medical certificates brandished at every opportunity to excuse him from any chance of accidentally doing exercise) in a classroom of children rendered thin by profuse sweating. Beth tells them all to shut up and get on with it. They respect her for that. She doesn't beat around the bush. And they respect her expectations of them: she only wants them to pass. Anything else is a miracle, a grade above the expected, frankly, because all the kids worth their salt – or perceived to be, at least – have long left the island for one of the boarding schools that sprang up in the wake of the new education reforms. If she can get her class to read a book of their own accord she's happy to call it a win.

It's a Thursday: they have Beth's English class first thing

after registration. She's meant to spend fifteen minutes doing pastoral care, expected to ask them how they are, what's going on in their lives, their hopes, wants and fears. She skips it. They're reading *Lord of the Flies* as a class, taking it in turns to go passage by passage. The boys at the back of the class have the most problems with the language: they stumble and struggle over the words, clumsily piecing them together as if they're a puzzle in and of themselves, breaking down the components into single syllables. At least they're trying, Beth thinks. They ask her about conch shells, and one – a girl called Tamzin that Beth always butts heads with, who's always tapping on her phone, doing something or other – says that her father, who is American, a soldier, calls them *cock* shells, and the rest of the class laugh. Beth hates moments like this: once they're lost, they're lost for the rest of the lesson. She leans back against her desk, her palms sweating onto the old wood, and she tells them to be quiet.

It's not that funny, she says, but already she can hear it: the quiet ripple of jokes about her and a conch – *cock* – shell, what she might do with it in her spare time, why she might need it. Because they think that she's single, even though she wears the ring on her fourth finger, as they've never once seen her with him. Five years and no sign of her husband. Come on, Beth says, we're already behind. She assigns another reader, asking one of the girls at the front, one of the few who are desperate to listen, who sit there scowling every time the rest of the class manages to derail things, and the girl ploughs through the words like they're going to evaporate. Ordinarily Beth

35

would tell her to slow down, but most of the class just titter every time the word *conch* appears, so she's happy to simply get through it.

She spends lunch by herself, in her classroom. Sometimes some of the girls will ask if they can sit in, but most of the time they're outside, desperately searching for a breeze by getting to high points of the playground or skulking in whatever shade they can happen across. Despite the heat they still drape themselves over each other in primitive pre-sex ways. Beth watches them out of the windows and eats her sandwiches.

When she gets home – school ends early, like she'd heard it used to on the continent, because of the heat there – she opens the windows and sticks the fans on. She has four: two in the living room, one in the kitchenette and one in the bedroom. She's never really used the spare room so that's not got one, but she worries about the Machine. She takes the one from the kitchenette, thinking that she'll angle one of the others later to cover it as well, and puts it on the chest of drawers in the spare room. The chest of drawers, like the rest of the furniture, came from their old house in London. This was the stuff that she brought with her when she moved. The flat was already furnished, and she left it piled up and unused in the spare bedroom for years. For a while, she couldn't bear to look at it, so it was easier to leave it buried under vacuum-packed clothes and old curtains still with the rings through their hooks. She places it facing the Machine and turns it on, letting it rotate and swing around the room.

I hope that this weather isn't making you too hot, she

says. She walks to the Machine and puts her hand onto it, and it's cold. So cold, she realizes: colder than it should be. She wonders how it keeps itself cool. No refrigeration component, and it's been off. The fans can't have been running. She assumes that this must be an effect of the metal that it's made from. She moves her hand across the metal, almost sliding it so that her forearm is flat against the cold, and that makes her sigh. This part of the Machine could easily accommodate her entire body – the thing itself is big enough to fit three or four bodies inside, she thinks – and there's no screen here, nothing but metal from floor to ceiling, and the span of her arms. She grabs the bottom of her shirt and peels it up, rolling it to below her breasts and then pressing her back against the Machine itself. It's so cold that the relief is incredible. She peels herself off and looks at the print of her sweat on the metal, then presses her front, her arms spread, like an embrace. I should have a shower, she says. She stands back and pulls her shirt off, and then uses the shirt to wipe down the sweat, cleaning the metal. She undresses more as she walks to the bathroom, and then steps into the shower, throws the dial to the coldest it can be and stands there.

6

Beth sees the weather report, and it's a relief – even in the voice of the weatherman, and the person that they've got out on the streets, waiting to report on the rain as soon as it happens – but it just makes Beth hesitant for a second. When it rains, most of the South Coast gets caught up in celebrating. It still rains a little more in Scotland, but the closer you get to London it almost entirely ceases. It's not a drought any more, though so many people still call it that. The hosepipe ban started and never ended. When it rains, if the kids are in the classrooms, they get more restless than at the end of term. They can't be kept, and sometimes one or two of them have just stood up in the middle of Beth's class and walked out, choosing instead to dance around on the torn AstroTurf outside.

When the rain finally starts, as she's halfway through a lesson about verbs, Beth shuts the curtains. It's a move designed to curb the distraction, but it can only ever fail.

I know it's a big deal, she says, raising her voice over the din, but it'll still be there when you get out at the end of the day. Nowadays they get two or three days of full-on monsoon rain every few months, heavier than she can ever remember it being when she was a child. It doesn't soak into the ground because the soil is so broken and hard to begin with. Instead, it floods everything, coursing down the streets, turning them into run-off sewers. In the classroom, they can hear it: like a river, doubled by the insistent sound of the rain smacking into the windows that line the one external wall of the classroom. It's a completely different sound to the sea. Funny, Beth thinks, that water can do so many things.

When the lesson is done, Beth takes herself to the staff room. She sits at a table by herself, gets a coffee from the machine. She stares out of the window: the grass of the playground is nearly entirely gone, worn down by the kids playing football. There's a cough: she looks up, and a woman is staring at her.

May I? she asks, meaning the vacant seat opposite, and Beth nods. The woman sits. She's only Beth's age, maybe even a couple of years younger, and she reads through sheets of photocopied paper, notes about classes in a nearly illegible scrawl. She looks familiar in that way that friendly people do: smiling with her eyes, not stern, mouth in a half-tilt upwards. She keeps looking at Beth, glancing; nervously fingers something on a necklace that hangs just below her shirt. Eventually, she speaks again. My name's Laura, she says. I'm a sub, only here for a few days. In for . . . She looks at her sheet. Arnold Westlake. Any tips? The woman smiles. It's something she's used to: having to make introductions, having to do this anew every week. It shows, because it's glossy and confident in a way that makes Beth immediately envious. Apart from, you know: don't let them eat you alive. Beth laughs gently.

No, they like change. No chance of you being eaten, not yet. They're good kids, mostly. Some pains.

Any in particular I should watch out for?

Which classes have you got?

Laura looks at her notes. Nine-C first, then 10-B, 12-C. She thrusts the registers over towards Beth, who scans the names.

Two C-tracks? Lucky. She smiles at Laura sympathetically. They've all been there. Well, Jared Holmes, Beth says. She points to his name on the register. He's got a reputation. I've never taught him, but I've seen Arnie – that's Arnold – going mad over him. Amy Lancer – Amy Chancer, some of the teachers call her. And these. Both the Decker boys are nightmares. Laura nods with each name, mentally filing them away. Where have you come from?

Horsham. Take the work where you find it and all that.

You're commuting?

Staying in a guest house over in Ryde. Apparently I could be here until the end of term, which is why I took it. Couldn't come this far for a day. Do you know what happened to Mr Westlake?

Not a clue. I didn't even know he was off.

Well, I hope he's all right. There's a silence as they both sit; then Laura quickly stands up, grabs her things. I should get my classroom ready. I'm sorry, I didn't get your name?

Beth. They shake hands.

Beth spends the rest of her lunch walking the Black Pitch. It's what the school unofficially calls the main playground: a patchwork of tarmacs, laid at different times to cover holes and cracks that could prove near-fatal, then covered with a thick coat of gravel from end to end. The noise of the children's shoes on the gravel is ever present: a scraping, thin and frantic. The pitch needs to be watched at all times. It's a rare lunch hour that one of the kids doesn't fall and hurt themselves. Beth walks around it by herself, because when it rains like this, the pitch is empty: none of the kids want to brave it. They hang around the grassy fields or the slick tarmac at the back of the art block, under whatever cover and overhangs they can find. She can't hear anything over the sound of the rain on her umbrella. It's quite peaceful, she thinks, watching the water hit the gravel as it does, almost nudging it around to make immediate puddles. It's relaxing. As the break comes to a close she stands in the central doorway to the Black Pitch and waves the children in. They're all drenched, which is a hazard. The school used to trap them inside when it rained, to stop any chance of them getting sick. The kids used to be more trouble than that was worth. Now they get drenched, and they ride through the final two lessons of the day in damp clothes. They're always too exhausted to cause any trouble at least, those afternoons.

When they're all inside Beth still stands there, in the door frame. She loves the smell.

Petrichor, says Laura from behind her. That's what you call the smell of rain on hot ground.

Thanks, Beth says. Good word.

No problem.

Did they go all right? Beth asks, catching her just as she's off to her next class.

The bell rings over her reply, which she repeats. They went fine, yeah. Better bunch of kids than in many places.

Beth thinks that might be a compliment. Her class, a year-seven one, doesn't listen to her telling them about some semi-tragic novel where an Inuit child befriends a husky that saves its life and, tragically, inevitably, dies.

7

Beth can't sleep because of the rain. It's so heavy that it sounds unholy: the windows shaking, the beating of it against the ground outside. Looking down from her bedroom window to the Grasslands she can see that they've become a slop, as the run-off from the hard ground has caused the water to accumulate there. It's puddled around the base of the building – she can lean down and see it, like a trench, and there are things floating in it but she can't see what they are from here, bobbing like dark rotting buoys – because the ground is too hard to take it in. It's easier to watch it than to sleep, so Beth slides open her window and leans out. It's coming straight down, no wind pushing it in any direction. She can lean on the sill and not get even slightly wet, which she does: sitting on the edge of the bed and watching it fall. The cats are conspicuous by their absence. She wonders where they go when it rains like this. If they're young enough to not remember when it rained with any real regularity, and if they don't know what it is, it must terrify them. She remembers being a child and having a small dog, and the first winter it snowed since they got it. Taking the dog out into it and trudging through the foot of whiteness that covered their streets that first morning, and watching the dog licking at it, then jumping through it: trying to make it over the mounds but failing, and ending up leaving pits where its entire body landed over and over again. How it pissed into it, and the cave that the hot urine made, and how that cave made the overlying snow crumble. How she notices that cause and effect, dragging the dog to piles of snow against walls to get it to wee, to make the snow collapse.

When she's done with the window she leaves it open and walks around the flat. She sits in the living room in front of the television, nervous. She checks her bank accounts, which have been all but cleared out by her purchasing the Machine. She's got an email from the French seller. He's ambiguous in the language he uses, but he wants to make sure that it got there in one piece, and that it works. She doesn't know why he cares: probably because he'd likely get in more trouble for selling it than she would for buying it, and if it was broken she would be liable to kick up a fuss. She replies: Everything seems to be fine, and the equipment seems to function. I'm very grateful for all your help. She presses send, and she's barely had time to think before a reply comes.

No problem, it says. It offers her help if she needs it, tells her to email that address. She doesn't reply to this one. She assumes that that's it, the last contact that she'll have with him. She Googles Vic's name, just to see if there's anything new, but there's nothing immediate. There's a lot of articles that mention him as part of some group litigation, and a few people who have studied him, covered him as part of a thesis. Occasionally an article will mention Beth as well: it will say that he was only recently married when he went to war, and that the treatment robbed a wife of her husband, left her practically bereaved only a couple of years past their beautiful union. Purple prose to describe something that was far more simple and crude than it appeared. When it had actually been a lump of shrapnel from an improvised, home-made bomb that robbed her. When she heard that he had been injured – a telephone call from a man whose name she didn't even remember, frantic and desperate where she had assumed that army calls came through measured and calm – she prayed for him to survive. She said, through her atheism, that she wanted nothing more than for him to survive.

Whatever happens, that's all that I want, she said, out loud, to the darkness of her bedroom as she tried to sleep that night. Now, she remembers that night, because – quite deliberately – she never prays. This has been done by her, not some cruel deity. It was an unfair trade-off, to give him his life and then curse him with the dreams that it did, only to rob his life from him again, in all essence. Beth shuts the laptop and walks to the fridge. She takes milk out and drinks from the bottle, standing with the door open, letting the chill run over her body. She can't stop thinking about Vic, so she goes to the spare bedroom. This, in here now, contains a part of him.

You're still here then, she says. She turns the Machine on and presses her hand, all of it, palm fully spread, onto the screen. The whir, the hum. The familiar warmth of the screen as she leaves her hand there, and the print that's left when she peels it away. The start-up tones ring out and she sees the menu there. She chooses to play back a recording. There's a list of them all, each with a date stamp and time count next to it. At the bottom of the list is a total of everything. Just shy of 270 hours of recordings. It's implausible, she thinks, until she remembers that they took it out of him in hour-long chunks, broken down into only a few sessions a week. She can't remember how long it took, not really. How long they lived with Vic having his episodes, and with Beth pretending that it was all right.

She picks one, at random. Vic's voice is first.

I know how this goes, he says. He sounds sick, Beth thinks: like there's a scratch in his throat. He says, What do you want me to talk about, Robert?

I'd like you to tell me your name, like always, the doctor says.

Victor McAdams.

Tell me some other things about yourself, Victor, the doctor says. There's a pause, then he speaks again. Where do you live, for example?

London.

Oh, whereabouts?

Ealing.

Okay. Are you married?

Yeah, Beth. Elizabeth, Beth, he says. Beth presses pause on the screen. Him saying her name, so loud and so clear through the room. She presses the timeline to hear it again. Yeah, Beth. Elizabeth, Beth. Elizabeth, Beth.

Any kids?

No.

Why are you here? Do you know?

Because I have dreams, and because . . . of what I did to Beth.

Good. Do you mind if I start the process?

No, Vic says. On the recording, behind their voices, comes the sudden rumble of the Machine, like a turbine. Beth thinks of sitting on planes and hearing the engines kick in. That lurch of noise. I'm ready, Vic says.

What do you dream about? the doctor asks.

Vic sighs. Mostly about blackness, he says. Darkness. It's like nothing, with noise over the top. It's hard to explain.

What are the noises?

Bangs. Sounds like gunfire, he says. There's a rustling on the recording which takes Beth a few minutes to place, and then she gets it: it's his hair. They decided that he should grow it out, to establish less of a connection with his army persona. And to cover the scar from the bullet. It itched, the scar, and he always ran his hands through the freshly grown hair when he was stressed.

And can you tell why you're hearing them? Why you're hearing gunfire?

No, Vic says. He sounds trepidatious. I don't know.

Beth stops the recording. She wonders if the Machine is like the ones that they used in the labs. Vic was so early on in the run of treatments that he must have had experience with the older Machines. She presses the screen, going to the place she found the firmware number. She writes it down again, on the palm of her hand, along with the Machine's serial number. At her laptop she types them in, but there's nothing. She doesn't know what she expected. Maybe that it would have a list of recalled Machines, and where they originated. Then she remembers the documentary.

8

It's been at least a couple of years since she last watched it, because it was so painful for her to see Vic the way he appears in it. She finds the disc in the drawer, along with everything else she put aside about the Machine, just in case. It's a shop-bought copy, her second. The first she lost after a fight with Vic, during the later days of his treatments, when she pulled it out to show him, to say, This is you.

Fuck you, Vic. This is you.

She puts it into the computer and lets it start up. She still remembers the exact minute and second when he appears, because there was a period that she watched this repeatedly, like a child fixated, so she skips to the first one. It's an introduction of him, only ambiguous, no details offered. They've blurred his face and down-tuned his voice, like he's a criminal or a snitch; only it was so that he himself would never see it by accident, post-treatment, and start to ask questions. They show a blurred-faced Beth walking him into the hospital, where a psychiatrist spoke to them. They made an assessment and offered Vic the Machine.

Beth doesn't care what they're saying in the documentary, because she knows, and she knows that most of it was lies, or ended up being lies. Instead she wants to see him for the first time, wearing the Crown, hooked up. A mock of his first session, staged for the cameras, but she still wasn't allowed to be there.

They told her, It can make things confusing for the patient. So she never went, not until the later stages, during what they termed cleaning up. There was no danger, then, of her messing anything up for him, apparently. So in the mock he's there, in a chair, his face a mess of pixels, with a doctor asking him questions. She knows that the Machine isn't on before they even show it, because there's no noise in the room apart from the murmur it makes when it's merely plugged in. The doctor is asking Vic about the war, and he's answering, and the doctor is fake-pressing buttons. They show the Machine. They have trouble getting it all into shot, but once they've adjusted their field of view and pulled back, there it is. It's the same model, exactly the same as the one in the spare bedroom. Beth's sure of it.

She picks up the laptop and walks it into the spare room. She places it on the bed and changes the angle of the screen. So that she can see both it and the Machine. It's exactly the same model. The same size (she guesses, from the height of it in both rooms); the same width (again); the metal the same pitch black; the screen with the same slightly glossier shine. She knows that it's not the same Machine, not exactly. There were hundreds of them built. But there's something heartening about the fact that it's the model that started this all. The one that took everything away from Vic will play a part in giving him back. It's almost poetic.

She takes the Crown down from the dock and examines it. The pads. She wonders if they got cleaned between patients – she remembers the sweat on Vic's head around where the welts would be, before they turned black over a period of months, permanent bruises that would be hidden by his ever-growing hair – and decides that she needs to take care of that now. From the bathroom she gets disinfectant wipes, and from the kitchen a duster and the handheld vacuum cleaner. She starts with the Crown, wiping the pads down, and the frame that holds them together, and then she lifts it to her face to examine it closely. She brushes apart her hair, taking it back from her face; and then slides the Crown onto her skull. The pads slide into place, like they're meant to be. The perfect size for her. They sit on her temples, where she's got thin hair, like wisps. Vic used to call it her fur. He would sing this song to her – For my flesh has turned to fur, the lyrics went – and she would hit him on the shoulder, telling him to stop it. She looks at the screen. The REPLENISH button is there, on the front page. This is what they took away from future iterations, when they locked it down. Before they withdrew the Machines altogether. She could press it . . . She wonders what it would be like, with Vic's memories in her head. If that is something that she could carry around.

She puts the Crown back in the dock and rubs her scalp. It's tighter than she imagined. She cleans the rest of the Machine's bulk, using the duster to wipe down the metal, then taking the disinfectant wipes and running them all over the screen, into the corners. There's black gunk where the metal meets the glass, which she tries to get with her nails but it won't budge, so she brings a knife in from the kitchen and scrapes away at it, getting it into the vein between the surfaces and reaming the gunk out. Then she wipes it all down again, noticing as she rubs the screen that she's inadvertently cycling through menus. She's managed to end up on a page that's inviting her to wipe the Machine's internal memory. She presses the CANCEL button, suddenly relieved. She had been so close to losing it all. Everything she's worked for, for so long. She turns the screen off, to stop it happening. Puts the thing on standby.

She drags a chair in from the kitchen and places it next to the Machine, and stands on top of it. There's a gap just about big enough for her arm to fit between the Machine and the ceiling, so she runs the handheld vacuum into the gap, watching the dirt and grime that sat on top of it zoom into the transparent container.

She looks at the picture again, the frozen still on her laptop screen. She compares. They really do look incredibly similar. She wonders if it might not be the same Machine.

She unplugs it at the wall. It's nearly light outside. She

dresses for work and sits on the edge of the bed in her bedroom. Now, I could sleep, she thinks. Now, when I have to go to work.

9

At the weekend, one week closer to the end of term, she visits Vic. She packs a bag before she leaves the house, taking biscuits with her, and some of his clothes, pulled out of the vacuum-packed plastic bags where they've been lingering. The walk to the ferry terminal takes her along the coastline, because she goes out of her way to stick to it. It's infuriatingly hot, even this early in the morning. She peels off her sweater and stuffs it into her bag. From the sea, there's a wind, but it barely registers against the heat. She remembers when this was a rarity: when weather like this would have brought the tourists flooding here, and the beaches below where she was walking now would have been crammed. The promenade leading to the terminal is almost deserted. People walking their dogs on the beaches, letting them leap into the waves; some elderly couples sitting in chairs outside the coffee shop. Everybody else is still in bed.

The ferry ride itself is amazing. She calls it a ferry: it's a catamaran, and she stands on the deck and, for a few minutes, it's almost cold. The wind up there, caused by the speed, is biting. She doesn't put her sweater back on, because she wants to feel it. She knows how fleeting it will be. Even as the boat starts to slow she goes inside and rubs a thin layer of suntan lotion onto the back of her neck. They say, on the news, that everybody will get used to the sun eventually. Children born now won't burn nearly as easily. We'll be like they used to be in the south of Europe: naturally tanned. Beth isn't there yet. She rubs the lotion on and then pockets the bottle, in case she needs it later. The ferry docks into what's left of Portsmouth harbour, and they all leave.

She remembers how Portsmouth used to be, back when the Navy was still here, before the collapse of the cliffs and before the flooding of Old Portsmouth. They dredged it, of course, once the waters rolled back a bit, but the damage was done. It's something that people rarely appreciate until it happens: the sense of safety, of not needing to blockade. She thinks about how easily people now put up walls here, after they've been through it. The shops she passes have small steps to enter them and trenches dug along the roadside gutters. Everything seems to have been elevated a few feet. This part of the city, when it was constructed, floated on the water, and there are still the remnants of the parts that were lost when the flood came: the offices that were wrenched away from their moorings, somehow, and collapsed into the sea, toppling onto boats, the masts tearing through the windows and spilling out the guts of the desks and computers and people inside. Even now, that part of the city is bypassed and cordoned off, despite it being years since it happened. Still, in the water, you can see the computers and ruined chairs from the offices under the water, sitting far below the docks.

From here Beth enters the station, where her train is waiting, and she finds a seat and stares out of the window. She's become accustomed to not doing anything on these journeys, because she finds herself too distracted. On the occasions she tried to read a book, she had forgotten about whole characters by the time she boarded her return train. It wasn't worth it in the end.

After the train she fights through Victoria station, and to the underground. The tube is filled with stale air, recycled a seemingly infinite amount of times, pumped out in what is claimed to be cold air, but only *tastes* cold, somehow, and is still warm at its core. She can tell as she walks through the stations: how out of breath she gets just fighting her way to the escalators. Everybody around Beth sweats. By the time she reaches Richmond it's a relief, even just to step out onto the high street. It's busy already, but she turns away from the shops and towards where it looks more residential. Three turnings away and over the bridge and past the little shops and she's there.

The sign in the front garden proclaims it to be a CENTRE, though Beth knows different. It's a hospice, really. She would argue that the patients are all terminal, because they're like this until they die. Any chance of them being treated by this new technique is slim to none; if they're the right patient, and if the company decides that the technology is up to it, then maybe. Probably not, though. Saturdays are visiting days, and she has to sign in. She has to show ID and be scanned, so she places her bag on the table and stands where she's meant to and lets them check she's not dangerous. She has no idea why anybody would want to bring a weapon into this place. The school, that's a risk. Once a year the news rings out with another story about somebody murdering their class-mates. Nobody ever murders the handicapped and dying.

In the hospice itself, Beth knows the way to Vic's room. There are coloured lines on the floor to lead visitors. Green to the gardens; black to the storeroom in the eaves, where they keep old Machines, in case they should ever need them; sandy yellow to the private rooms. Beth follows this last line up the stairs and to the left. She pays for a room of his own, where so many of them are in larger wards, four or six to a room, divided only by thin cotton curtains. There's an argument among the families of those in here that private rooms are unfair, because not every-body can afford the subsidies. They're all in the same boat, goes the argument; and besides, they don't know any different. She pays the subsidy, despite the rising prices, because it gives them privacy.

When he's back to being himself, Beth thinks, he'll appreciate that I did it. What it gave him. That space to be alone, and to be himself.

Vic's room is the same colour as the rest of the hospice. A thin grey paint, a white dado rail, a white skirting. The furniture is hospital standard, with a white wire-frame bed locked to the wall and a table that's high enough to

57

be wheeled over the bed – and over Vic – and a chair in the corner of the room, a soft thing that's low to the ground, impractical to sit in. There's a television (an old-style set, with the bulbous behind and curved screen) on a stand on the wall opposite the bed as well. It made Beth laugh, the first time she saw it. When they brought her into the room, to tell her that this would be where he was staying, and they pointed it out. She asked them if it would be part of his rehabilitation, watching *EastEnders*. They ignored her. She found out later that the building used to be an old people's home, and they simply moved them out and moved the new patients in. In the corner are Vic's personal accoutrements: his monitor, his spare colostomy bag, a collection of kidney-shaped metal trays stacked up like saucepans. There's a bowl of fruit, but it's token, and often the fruit is gone, well past its date. On the wall above the bed, looking directly down at Vic is a security camera, a tiny ball that affords somebody a 360-degree view of the room. A direct line to see and hear whatever Vic is doing at any given point in the day.

Here, Vic is on the bed, shitting himself.

Here, Vic is writhing, managing to push himself onto the floor, his tongue lolling from his mouth.

Here, Vic is in the corner, because he walked of his own accord, which should be a near-miracle, and celebrated, but now he's just standing there and gasping as he faces the walls, heaving his body up and down, his shoulders halfway to a convulsion. Over and over and over again.

Beth always worries what state she'll find him in. She's sometimes been here when there's been an accident, and she's seen it before the carers have had a chance to deal with it, but that's a hazard of their jobs, she thinks. The carers and hers. Even with those paying guests, the clinic is understaffed and underserviced. She could complain, but they've got heading on for a hundred other patients here, and they're all in similar boats. Some are better, admittedly: many of them have kept their day-to-day routine, and they can take themselves to the toilet and feed themselves. Some of them might as well be in a coma for all they're worth. Lying there, calm as anything, barely cognitive when visitors come. Vic is special to the clinic. He's a worst case: not just far less able than the man he once was, but totally out of control of the man he's become. Beth's never seen anybody worse, not in the flesh.

(On the internet she's seen videos of patients who reacted to the initial Machine treatments in other ways entirely. She tells herself that it could have been worse: those patients who, in the early stages of treatment, killed themselves and their families: holding them at gunpoint until they ended it, casually, one by one; or slashing their throats while they slept, disbelieving of the stories told to them to fill in their gaps. Or, when they're vacant – such a cruel word, so suggestive that somebody else will be along in a minute to take their place – they've managed to somehow end it all afterwards. Reduced to something so primal and vague that they're barely even quantifiable as human any more, let alone the men and women that they once were. And they end it, by either just giving up and stopping being any more; or, in worse cases, finding ways to put themselves out of what must be an indefinable misery.)

Today Vic has his back to Beth. She can see the line of his spine, the weight of his skin on it. How it looks almost curved where it follows the too thin mattress, the weak bed frame. His back has spots on it that it never used to have. They never get past red smears, but still. She knows that he's not being bathed enough. The only times she's complained they've told her to be here more, to do it herself. They are understaffed. They aren't, they tell her, paid enough.

They say, Why don't you move closer? They just say it to her, as if they've known her all her life, and who are they to pass judgement?

Because of my job, Beth replies, weakly. She doesn't tell them that it's shame-based: that she doesn't want her colleagues' pity. She tells everybody that Vic's away at war, and she has a photo of him in her classroom. To her classes and workmates, Beth wants Vic to be a hero. Still away and fighting the good fight, even after all this time, even after any war he could be fighting has long ended.

He doesn't stir as she approaches. She has to say his name four times before he even flinches, and then it's not recognition. It's awareness. When this happened they didn't know why, any more than they had when Beth had rushed him to the hospital, telling them that something had gone terribly wrong, Vic's body on the back seat in constant convulsion. He was one of the first to fall apart, because he'd been one of the first to start the treatments, and erase what needed to be erased. He was to be a test case, proudly paraded in front of crowds. But when they let her see him finally without any sedation he was a void. Nothing inside him.

60

They said, We don't know why this has happened. This is an anomaly, it can't be right. They apologized to her straight away, so she knew. You don't apologize if you haven't done anything wrong, and they said sorry so many times.

Vic? Beth says again. He moans: low and timorous, from somewhere other than his throat. From below. It's me, she says.

She puts her hand onto his back and rubs it. Sometimes she's done this and he's reacted to her touch as if she was fire. Throwing her off, writhing around, lashing out with his arms and legs. Today he's more placid. Her hand placed against his shoulder blades, she listens to and feels him breathe.

Some of the other users of the Machine, the doctors said to her when they delivered their final diagnosis, forget the basics, even. They forget the stuff that's innately written into us, deep within us. Breathing, eating. They forget how their bodies work. They told this to Beth as if this should have made her feel better: your husband isn't on a respirator, and we don't have to tell his heart how to work for him. You don't have to make that hardest of decisions yet. He's still alive. And Beth, through her guilt, was even grateful.

Will he ever get better? she asked them. They didn't know. What they did know was that he was ruined.

Sit up, she says to Vic. She moves around to his front, where she can see his face. It's hardly changed over the past few years. He's still handsome, she thinks. He's still an army man, even where he's lost the definition in his muscles. Jowls more than muscle, there, around his face. His hair has grown out, but she can still see the bruises, burned into his skin. They remind her of being a schoolgirl: of Ash Wednesday. All the children lining up to have a cross drawn on their foreheads, big fingers leaving smears that they were all too scared to immediately rub off, even with the slight smell and the stigma of having to wear it. That's what the pad-marks look like to her: ash.

Vic moans again, so she moves her arm underneath him and tries to heave him into a sitting position. Come on, she says.

He says something that sounds like No, but she knows it's not that. He hasn't said a word in years. It's like when parents think that their child says its first word, something random, off the curve. Really, it's just a collection of noises that approximates speech. It's fantasy and hope. She links her arms together, under his armpits and around his back, and she strains to drag him up the bed. He doesn't help her at all. He doesn't fight against it, but there's no compliance.

Come on, she says. When he's nearly sitting – a slight angle to his whole body, like he's on a boat, slanted against the waves – she stands back. Better, she says. She wipes his mouth and then the rest of his face, and she brushes his hair with her hands because his comb seems to be missing. It's usually kept on the shelf at the side of the bed but there's nothing on it today, which makes her think that the cleaners have had off with it. It wasn't a cheap one: part of a set that she gave him for Christmas once. That set went through the war with him, and it was part of the stuff that they shipped back with him after his emergency surgery, that she had to sort through, that she had to choose to keep. The scar – the real scar, not the Machine's burn scars – sits to the left of his forehead. When she stares at it she traces a line to the bullet's exit point, and she wonders how close it really came to ending everything. A fraction of a millimetre, the doctors at the time said. Beth has always wondered if that was an exaggeration.

I don't suppose you've managed to remember who I am, Beth says. She stands back and looks at his face, and tries to make eye contact. You're Vic, she says. Do you remember that? She's not expecting anything. This isn't the point where she gives up: that happened a long time ago.

(She remembers the exact day, because it still sits there as a dream that she has when she's drunk or lonely: Vic bucking as she held on to him, as she tried to console him, and she realized that he didn't know who she was, and he didn't care. She was the only one who cared, and she had the guilt on top of that, and she carried that with her every single day, every single time that she thought about him.)

She changes him. She can't remember what it's like to undress him normally, not like they used to. This is different, a shift in their relationship. The act of pulling down his underwear and replacing it. Wiping him if he's had an accident. The nurses here change him every few hours to prevent them, now. Rubber-lined underwear; rubber sheets on the bed. She pulls the underwear down his legs and past his ankles, and then she takes a bath-wipe and rubs it over him. She doesn't know how often the nurses actually do it.

I hope you're all right in here, she says to him. She sits on the edge of the bed after putting his new pants on, and she turns on the television. It doesn't hold his attention – she isn't sure that he's even capable of paying attention any more – but she watches a daytime cookery show for a few minutes. Sitting next to him is reassuring. She thinks that it won't be that long until she'll have him back with her, back as he was. Sitting with him now makes that prospect feel somehow more real. She can feel his warmth, which hasn't changed at all. His blood still pumps the same way. His skin still smells the same, after she's cleaned him.

He can walk still, sometimes: when she catches him on the right day, when the muscle memory does more than his active brain. Today isn't one of those days. She asks an orderly who passes the room to help her put Vic into a wheelchair. It goes quite smoothly until he's actually in it. He makes himself stiff as a board, back arched, and the orderly straps him in. They forcibly bend him, making him sit.

Safer for you both, the orderly says. He calls Vic Mr McAdams, which makes Beth feel sad. She wheels him down the ramps, pulling him behind her as she walks backwards, because he's so much heavier than she is. At the end of the corridor is a wall of glass that's so reflective and so dark inside as to be almost a mirror. She sees herself with him, her hands on the handles of the chair. She looks older, and his hair has become mussed in the move to the chair. She straightens it again with her hands. He doesn't look at the reflection. She remembers something that she read this one time: how the only animals to recognize themselves are chimpanzees and elephants. You can put a mark on their heads and they will see the reflection and reach for themselves, to rub the mark off. Every other animal tries to find the thing by looking behind the mirror, unable to understand what it's seeing. Vic doesn't even look at the reflection. He sees nothing there; if he thinks it's another person, he doesn't care.

This is how it is, Beth says. She wheels him down the entrance ramps and into the garden, and then across the tarmac path. It's even hotter than she anticipated, and within seconds she can see the beads of sweat on Vic's forehead. She mops them with her sleeve. Jesus, she says.

Around her, other families are attempting to relax. All of this is too demanding. Being with people who are so far gone that they aren't the people that they once were. And some argue that it's like coma patients, and how you would stand by them, but Beth has heard the other side of the argument. That they're more like the dead. There's nothing inside them. They might look the same, and they might smell the same, but they're different. The person that they were is gone. Inside them, the part that made them who they were, that's gone. So what's left? Beth's heard the argument that there's nothing. She's seen the divorce figures for the vacant. Two years ago, a judge in America had annulled a marriage, but that was still an exception.

This is mortality, he said. Life and death. We'd never force somebody to stay married to a corpse. When a person loses this much of themselves, they have lost their soul. And what is left when you have no soul?

Most of the people here with her are parents, looking at their children, all grown-ups. Grey-haired men and women trying to act as if this is normal, because there's a bond there that's indelible. There's no annulment between parents and their children. At their worst the patients are back to the way they were before they walked and talked, when they lay and were inattentive and cried for no reason. She sees the parents trying the same tactics they might have tried then. The snapping of fingers to try and draw their eyes. Calling their name, over and over, in the hope that it will stick. Nobody knows why the brain doesn't work like it should after the Machine's had its way with it. This would be much easier for all involved if it was just a wipe. One doctor who worked on the project wondered if the brain hadn't had its ability to record memories wiped. As in, it had forgotten how to remember. Beth doesn't like to think about it. So she and the parents lie on the lawns with their charges and they treat them like pre-toddlers. She knows that they wonder why she's still with him, because they can't see what she can be getting out of this. Nobody dreams of a vacant shell for a husband.

She wheels the chair out towards the gates, and the road. She wants to see how far she can push it without being noticed, if anybody's going to question anything. There are no security cameras in the grounds because there's no danger of the patients escaping, not when most of them can't even walk. And those who can, can't work door handles, or dress themselves, and certainly couldn't get past the manned security desk. She pushes the chair further down the path, to the gates themselves, and then onto the street. She turns the corner and she stands with him and waits. She can see the people across the road staring at her. Or staring at Vic. It's quite shocking, the first time you see him, because it's not like seeing a disabled man. There's no life in him. When you look at the vacant, there's something wrong, and you can tell. It's immediate. It's what the overly religious factions who oppose the Machine use as evidence: they present the intangibility of the soul as proof of the existence of something less tangible still. The people across the road all turn their heads and stop talking. Beth ignores them. She puts her head down and looks at Vic, and she gently rubs the sides of his head. Apparently they itch, the burn marks; and she used to do this before, to the bullet scar.

After a minute nobody's followed her, and there's no sign of a security guard when she pushes Vic back into the grounds. None of the other visitors notice, even. Too preoccupied with snapping their fingers and whistling as if their offspring are dogs. Beth pushes Vic back the way that they came. She wipes his brow again. Through security with no hassle, and then to his room. She thinks about doing this herself, which is something that she'll have to learn. She sidles the chair right next to the bed and locks the wheels in place, and then stands behind him.

I need to get my arms under here, she says. She pulls his arms up and puts hers underneath them. He's so heavy.

She struggles, pushing him forward, and he turns himself out of the chair and onto the bed. She puts a hand on his back to support him. Pushes him with it, and then she uses her other hand to try and get his legs up. His body turns too much, so she pulls him up the bed. He still gives her nothing.

She tries to manoeuvre him onto his back. She does this by pushing one shoulder and pulling the other, trying to make him do it himself. Now one hand on his shoulder, pulling, and the other on his knee, then his thigh. Incremental stages to get him flipped over. Next, her hand on his shoulder and her other hand looped around his thigh. She heaves and pulls, but doesn't know if she can do it. Heave and pull, and finally his legs start to move, and, almost independently, his torso. He's not flat on his back now, but as near as, and he starts to make a noise from deep inside him. She tries to yank him up the bed again, because he's a foot clear of his pillows, and his legs dangle off the end of the metal frame. Small movements, but movement all the same: an inch at a time. Maybe less. Over and over, tiny repeated movements.

She remembers meeting him for the first time. They're at school, their last year. Everybody says it's perfect. That they're perfect.

Pull and release, over and over, until the pillow is underneath his head, the first pillow at least. The pillows are so thin and unsupportive. No pillowcase. Instead gauze, designed to be easily washed, so that the whole pillow can be put straight in the washer. She tries to squeeze it into a shape that's more comfortable.

Lift your head, she says, knowing that it won't do anything. She bunches the pillows up but she can't make him look comfortable. This would be easier with normal pillows, she says. She tries to shift him up the bed more, but he won't budge. This is as much as she can do. She stands back to look at him, and he rolls his eyes and opens and closes his jaw, and his hands twitch and his legs are totally, unbearably still.

I'm sorry, she says. She's not apologizing for her inability to make him comfortable, she knows, but if anybody heard her, that's what it would sound like. All the way home on the train Beth tells herself that this will be easy. That this is the right thing to do.

When she gets home she sits in the spare bedroom and puts the Machine on and listens to audio of Vic talking about her: not the good stuff, the stuff that he wanted to keep, but the bad. The bits that they wanted jettisoned.

10

On Monday, after school, Laura is waiting for Beth by the gates. She's smiling.

I was hoping to catch you, she says. Good day?

It was a day, Beth says. Wouldn't go as far as the good part.

Fancy telling me about it over a glass of wine?

Beth stalls. I was going to do marking, she says. Her bag feels pitifully light for that excuse. I've got a bit to catch up on.

You could do it after the wine and get it done twice as fast, Laura says. The looseness you get from wine really helps with your marking, I've heard. She persists. Go on. I don't know anybody else, and this is getting pretty tiresome, being here like this. It's you and wine, or by myself in the guest house all afternoon, sweating under my dodgy air-conditioner. Her last try. The first round's on me, she says.

Okay, Beth says. Sure, why not?

They walk down the road away from the school, past the kids. They know what they're like: smoking, playing up. Across the way, a group of them pull their hoods over their faces and start walking with an affected limp. Beth can hear music from one of their cars. It sounds like drumming. Nothing but the headache of a beat.

They have cars, even here? Why would a teenage boy need a car on the island? asks Laura.

How else are you going to crash one and write it off? Beth replies. That makes Laura laugh. They don't really talk, because it's so hot, and then they reach a pub that Beth recognizes but has never been into.

This one? Laura asks. The temperature inside is much lower. They open the door and there's almost a thin mist from within, as if they've opened a freezer, and Beth feels goose-bumps thrum up her arms. They pick a table away from the bar, where it's quiet, and Laura leaves her bag there with Beth while she goes and orders. Beth watches her talking to the barman, who seems like he's been asleep – he rubs his face and yawns as she orders, and he fumbles a wine glass as he places it on the bar, nearly smashing it, but Laura catches it before it rolls off the lip – and thinks about how long it's been since she had a drink out like this. She drank at the Christmas party once, a few years ago, but she never goes out. Not to pubs. Not with her workmates.

Laura comes back with the wine. Went with this, she says, waving the bottle around. It sloshes, nearly up the neck and out. Got the bottle, because it worked out cheaper, if we drink it. She sits down. We'll drink it, right? She pours them both a glass, filling each well over the recommended-measurement line, and then drinks from hers. Sorry, she says, should've made a toast.

You don't need to, Beth says.

No, I do. Thanks for this. I was getting lonely. Here's to not being lonely, Laura says. They both raise their glasses and chink them across the table.

How are you getting on? Beth asks.

Fine, Laura says. She tells Beth a story about one of the boys taking his penis out in class, under his desk. She says, You warned me about him as well, and there was I thinking you were insane. Butter wouldn't melt, I thought, and suddenly . . . Well, there it is.

Jesus! Beth says.

The rest of the class died laughing. Even the girls.

They try. They're good kids.

He had his penis out. Doesn't matter how good a class is, they're always going to push that one. But I'm enjoying it, the teaching. She smiles. Not the penis. They both laugh. They need something, Laura says. Seems like a lot of them here don't have faith. Not big on churches or family here, are they? Beth doesn't answer. She's not big on either herself, but that isn't something she can say. It's not something she can hold against Laura either. The silence pushes Laura to change the subject. So what about you? she asks. She looks at Beth's hand and points. You're married?

Beth has to stop herself telling the truth. It's there, in her mouth. She's suddenly aware of how much she wants to talk about it. Yes, she says. He's in the army, so I'm sort of alone a lot.

No sort of about it, Laura says. My dad was in the army. I get that, what it's like. Selfish, I used to think. Sorry, I mean. You know.

Beth nods. I know, she says. It can be, a bit. She thinks about how many people she's told the truth to since it happened. Her doctor, the psychiatrist she took herself to when she was having trouble sleeping, after Vic went into the home; a man on the telephone, when she called the helpline for Victims of Vacancy; a man who nagged her insistently once, in the early days, in a bar, practically rubbing himself against her body, taking her to the point of tears and then, from him, remorse. Three people, that's what a tight secret it is. And here, now, she's thinking of telling all to a woman who's nearly a complete stranger.

Kids? Sorry, I shouldn't pry.

No, Beth replies. No kids. Just me.

Right, so that's definitely alone then. There's a hint of something in Laura's accent, something Irish maybe. Something lilting. Makes everything she says sound somehow vague. How often is he back? she asks.

Not often.

Where have they got him?

Iran, Beth says. He's out there as one of the last peacekeepers. It's safest: everybody knows about the chaos that was there, and how many people have died in the last decade. They don't push when they hear Iran, because it could mean anything. It's a delicate subject matter to talk about.

How long have you been married?

73

Eight years, Beth says. She's met people like Laura before. Lots of questions because they like being interested. Not nosy, just stockpiles of information, immediately involved in the lives of their acquaintances. What about you? Beth asks. Married?

Me, no. Laura says it with the smirk of somebody who's had this conversation a lot. No no no. I have a boyfriend; Rob. He's noncommittal and infuriating. No matter how many hints I give him he never picks up on them, or he ignores them and plays dumb. He's like a trained dog who chooses when he'll obey. She leans in conspiratorially. Full of promises when there's a treat in the hand, Laura says. We've been together too long now, as well. I think he's complacent.

You live together?

No. No, I won't. She pulls a necklace out from the neckline of her shirt. A cross, with a miniature Christ figure draped over it. I've told him that we should wait, she says.

Right. And he's . . .

He's stubborn. Laura finishes her glass of wine. She necks the final inch back in one. So is this all there is to do for fun on this bloody island? she asks.

11

Laura says goodbye to Beth. There's no thought of this continuing onwards – Beth remembers when that wouldn't have even been a question, that a pub shutting didn't mean you had to go to bed and tuck yourself in and end the night – but Laura's adamant. She's drunk and swaying, and Beth asks if she can find her way; if she'll be all right. She's insistent that she doesn't need Beth's help.

I can get home, Laura says, I honestly can. She reaches over and grabs Beth's shoulders. Beth, she says. Beth. It's been such fun. We have to do this again.

Laura stumbles off and leaves Beth in the street. She starts home. The walk back takes her ages, as she keeps stopping, leaning against walls. She catches sight of herself in the huge mirrored windows of the porn shop tucked between the kebab house (heaving) and the tiny grocers (which is perpetually empty, and seems to survive only on the occasional sale of a bunch of flowers) and she realizes that she doesn't look anything like the woman she's been for the last five years. She's relaxed, and it's all over her face. Her posture, even; the comfortable slump of her shoulders. It's enough to make her cry, and she does, facing the water on the far side, away from the street. She's never been in one of those shops, but she wonders if they can see out of that mirror: if they're all watching the strange woman sobbing on the other side of the window.

For the rest of her walk home – which she extends by taking side-streets, by passing back along the front, by stopping and watching the people drinking in the streets, grabbing each other's arses, chewing each other's mouths off – she wants to be discovered. She wants everything out in the open. She doesn't think about Vic for at least half an hour, and when she realizes that, she feels incredible. Magical, even. He's everything, but that pause . . . to take it was so freeing. She passes students and parents and colleagues, but they don't notice her, or they aren't looking, or they don't say anything. She doesn't know which. She's drunker than she's been in years, and she can feel it through every inch of her.

Beth opens the front door on her third try. She drops the keys on the mat and bends to pick them up, but her ankle shakes as she does it, so she props herself against the frame with her hands.

Shit, she says. She swats the keys into the flat, and they skirt along the floor, making a noise, scratching the fake wood floorboards as they go, ending by the wall of the living room. She kicks her shoes off after them. Then pulls the door shut as she staggers forward.

I'm home, finally I'm home, she yells, and she puts her bag down, takes her coat off and she marches down the hall, pressing one hand against the wall the entire way. Home is the hunter, she says, which is something that Vic used to say, as a joke.

She opens the door to the bedroom and there it is: the Machine. She kicks the power on and the vibrations start, more acutely than before: she can hear it, feel it coming through the floorboards, the carpets, the walls. She can feel its vibrations through the wallpaper. She says his name, once, quietly, to remind herself of him – of what this is all about – and then walks to the Machine and puts her hands on it, palms out, on either side of the front panel. Its vibration runs all the way through the metal of every panel and part as it readies itself. She paws the screen, which is black, blacker still than the metal body of the thing, and her touch brings it to life.

You're in there, she says.

Through the scrolling list of dates one leaps out, one that took place on the day after his birthday that first year of his treatment. She wonders. She presses play, and the doctor speaks, a prelude to Vic.

What did you do yesterday?

Beth took me out for a meal. We, uh. She booked a Greek restaurant. We both really like Greek food.

You seem distracted.

No. No. Just, it's just coming hard today. Difficult for me. Don't know why.

She pictures him there, struggling to keep it together,

and she takes the Crown down from the docking station and nearly puts it on but doesn't. Instead she rests it on the bed next to her, and she moves her right hand from the screen and down between her legs, pulling up her skirt, and then into her underwear, sliding down. She rubs herself as she sits on the edge of the bed, and then moves her body along the lip of the mattress. She remembers how she used to do this before she knew him, when she was still a girl.

She moves herself to the bed proper, face down, hand back inside her, rubbing, her back arched like a cat caught in a stretch. She gasps, one hand propped against the Machine, the vibrations through every part of her body, through her skeleton, through the other hand as it pushes her forwards.

It's over as fast as it starts. She sits up and listens.

Do you mind if we begin the process? the doctor asks.

No, sure. Start.

Talk to me about Beth. How did she feel when you were away?

I don't know, Vic says. Beth's heard all of these recordings before, back when she was administering the treatments for Vic at home. When – she joked with herself – she went rogue.

Don't you talk about it?

We did, but I can't. I mean, she was sad. She cried a lot, near the end.

Do you remember why you came home?

I was, uh. Vic sounds upset, and he breathes through his teeth. Was I sick?

You were sick, yes. The doctor stands up – the noise of the chair legs scraping against the linoleum floor of the hospital – and there's some tapping in the background. Vic, listen. I'd really like you to lean back and shut your eyes, and listen to something for me.

You don't want to talk? Because I can keep going, I think. He sounds desperate.

No, not for the moment. Just listen to this, and then we'll talk afterwards.

There's a click, and the playback stops. The end of that recording, and the start of the first session where the Machine started filling in the gaps in what it had taken away.

Beth lies back on the bed. The room spins. The light is still on, and the Machine is on, and next to her – she reaches her fingers out – and then in her hand is the Crown. She shuts her eyes. She can't stay in here, she knows. Her bed is in the next room. And she doesn't know what she might do.

12

She doesn't hear her alarm. Or she switches it off without realizing, one or the other. Her telephone rings and she answers it, confused, thinking it's the middle of the night because it's still so dark; and then she realizes that she's not in her room. She's on the spare bed. The blackness is coming from the Machine. It's on, still; the screen dimmed, but still alight.

Hello? she asks.

It's Laura, comes the voice on the other end. I'm in reception at work. Are you ill?

No, Beth says, but even as she says it she feels the sick in the back of her throat, rising. Her head pounds. What time is it?

Just gone eight, Laura says. I'll let them know you'll be late.

Beth gets out of bed and stands still, trying to hold down whatever's threatening to work its way out of her.

She gently strips, trying to move as little as possible, and then pulls on underwear and a skirt and a shirt. She walks to the fridge and grabs a little bottle of water, and then drinks it as she sits on the loo. Everything's moving still: she sits there with her eyes shut, the coldness of the water so sharp on her throat it threatens to be her undoing. Eventually she stands up. She braces herself against the wall. She's just doing too much too quickly, she knows.

She pulls her coat on, slips her feet into her shoes. Flats today, even if they don't go with this outfit. She's about to leave when she realizes that she doesn't have her keys, so she scans the surfaces, panicked. She sees them on the floor, by the back wall, where she kicked them the night before, and when she bends to pick them up she sees the Machine through the spare room doorway. The screen isn't dimmed any more; it's lit brightly, and the Crown (which she now sees is up by her pillow) is lit around its rim, small yellow lights that indicate the stages of use. Like traffic lights: red is off, yellow is primed, green is go. When it's green, the Crown must stay on the head. Those are the rules that they were told. (They were never told what would happen if they broke them, and they didn't ask. It's not been done, that Beth knows. Some rules seem serious enough to never be broken.)

She picks up the Crown and puts it back on the dock, and then looks at the screen. It hasn't been used, she doesn't think – there's no way of telling directly, because such an indication hasn't been needed – but she feels okay. She thinks about the damage that she could do to herself, given the chance. She knows that she has these thoughts,

81

but she's close, now. If she'd had the Machine for longer, just sitting there, then maybe . . .

Her telephone rings again. It will be somebody else from school, checking up on her. She ignores it, and she's out of the front door in seconds, and down the stairwell, along the shops, along the front, through the shortcut of another housing estate and then at the gates. Laura is standing in her place, in her classroom, reading the register. She thanks her and takes over, and with every Here, Miss McAdams that the kids give her, her head throbs just that little bit more.

13

The firmware update is the part that she's been dreading. There are privately linked videos on the internet that show how to do the update, found only through the forums that she uses. The videos have told her what to do, with step-by-step instructions. This is all clandestine, all under the radar. She shouldn't have a Machine, and it's not like the instructions are easy to come by. Illegal firmware updates are even more so. Back before the mass recall, when they thought that there was a problem, the first lot of Machines – the ones that could be tampered with, that could have custom firmware installed – were all recalled, all sucked back into the system and, in theory, disposed of, repurposed and turned into the smaller, safer Machines. The one that she has is not small or safe.

The update isn't something that can be done wirelessly, because of how the reboot process works. Instead Beth needs to get inside the thing. There's a panel that needs unscrewing. There's a USB socket inside there, tucked away. Download the firmware to your USB stick, insert it into the Machine. Reboot it by holding all the buttons down with the flat of your hand. Wait there until you hear the triple beep that heralds the Machine's start-up process. Choose to update firmware, when the screen prompts you. Check the firmware numbers. If it says one thing, you've succeeded. Another, try again. Back to the start.

The panel comes away with relative ease. Four screws, that's it. She looks for the screws to the second panel, underneath the screen. They're tucked away. Beth has to lie on the floor to undo them, at the join of the screen and the black metal case. She looks up at the Machine towering over her. She hadn't realized that the front of it isn't entirely flush, but it's definitely not. It has a slight undulation. From the floor, looking over its surface, there are slight peaks and troughs. Like razor-blade-black sand dunes.

The USB socket is crude in comparison to the rest of the Machine. Whereas it's highly finished elsewhere, smoothed over and made accessible, this is like seeing into the guts of the thing. Behind the socket runs exposed wires, reds and greens and yellows, and one solitary black cable that's thicker than the rest, that coils in and over on itself like an intestine, thick and lumpen. The rest of the Machine is cordoned off with internal panels. Beth reaches up and taps one of these panels and it moves, so she slides it. She's intrigued. She expects fans and processors and a wall of circuitry that she doesn't understand, something totally alien to her.

Instead there's nothing. Past the wires, there's a hollow, she thinks. Past it, a cluster of wires, leading to something in the centre, but she can't see what. It's so dark in there: far darker than the outside. Almost impossible, she thinks. She can't ever remember seeing such an absence of light. She backs out and looks at the Machine itself, to work out which part of the shell this area lies behind, and see that it's the bulk of the main section, where the screen is. Again she peers up into it, but can't see past a few inches, because it's so black in there. She thinks about getting a torch, but it would be too easy to be distracted. She has a job to do: there's only five days left.

She goes to her computer. The files – one for every possible firmware combination – have been on the desktop for over a year now, sitting at the top left so she couldn't accidentally delete them. She's bought a new memory stick especially, still sealed, so she scissors and hacks through the blister pack to get to it. It's so light, she thinks.

She puts it into the computer and then finds the right file, cross-matching the file name with that of the Machine. She copies the file across, then renames it into the protocol that will make it actually work. This is the part she's most worried about: making sure that everything works first time. She's thought about this, late at night. If she messes it up she worries that she'll lose her guts and stop. That she'll eke out the rest of her days with that Machine sitting there in the room, a reminder of her failure. And leaving Vic in that place, like he is. She checks the name of the file three times, making sure it's exactly what the online guides have told her that it should be.

85

When she's positive she takes the memory stick back to the Machine. The guide says to switch the Machine on and then insert the stick, before doing a hard reset. She flicks the power switch and the vibrations start, and the noise. Ding-ding-ding. The screen on, she squats and slides the memory stick in. It clicks neatly into the socket, and the Machine whirrs. Sudden and abrupt, the fans kick in, and the whole thing makes a grinding sound, filthy and enormous, and Beth is almost kicked back onto the bed by the shock. The screen goes blank, replaced with its own blackness – false and printed on, pixels approximating the tone that's so exact and pure on the outside – and then the noise abates, slightly.

Okay, Beth says aloud. She looks at the instructions – her own transcription of the videos she's watched, printed out on paper that she's folded over and over and read a thousand times – and it doesn't say anything about this stage, but that's not her problem. She has to stick with the instructions. She can't expect the people who hacked this all together to write down every little detail.

Put your hand on the screen, her instructions say, and hold it there until you get an option by your index finger to reboot. Press it, keeping your hand there.

She can't be sure, but she thinks that the Machine is somehow colder. The screen as well, not just the metal. That must be an effect of having the fans on as they are, so loud it's like being on an aeroplane: the whir of the engines, readying to take off. That burst of noise and power. But here it's coming from this box in her spare bedroom in her little flat. She presses her hand flat to the

86

screen and makes sure it's all touching, and then stands there as the vibrations run up her arm and into her shoulder, and from there to her collarbone and her teeth. Her back teeth she presses together, and they chatter. It's almost like static: like rubbing a balloon on your head as a child, that same feeling. The instructions don't say how long to hold it there for. Her arm runs with pins and needles after thirty seconds, and it's almost painful after a minute, just as the option appears. INSTALL. She moves her finger across to the picture of a button and taps it, and as soon as she does so the Machine stops whirring and the sound completely drops away. She hadn't realized it, but she had been pressing really hard on the screen, and she almost falls forward, suddenly not having to push against the Machine's shaking. The screen goes black – not display black, completely lightless – and the sound disappears, and she's in the room in silence.

She thinks about when they first saw the Machine, when she and Vic were brought in by Vic's therapist. He told Vic how perfect he would be for the treatment, which was experimental but so perfect, so neat and tidy.

Conventional therapy is usually like sweeping everything away. Under the carpet. The doctor, Robert something, he was the same man who then led Vic through his therapy. She and Vic had thought of it as a sales pitch, and a pretty convincing one. This treatment, Robert said, isn't sweeping. It's cleaning. Hoovering. It's taking a hose to the patio and washing away all the grime and dirt, and leaving it looking good as new. You understand what I'm saying, right? It's taking the bad stuff away. All these conversations we have, the dreams, the shock you're going through: we can simply get rid of it.

So why don't more people do this? Vic had asked.

Because it's still a secret, the doctor told them.

Beth watches the Machine doing nothing, and it hits her that she's done something wrong. She's ruined it: all that money, time, thought, down the drain. She reads the instructions again, which implore her to wait. They say, It will take longer than you think. She pushes herself back onto the bed, up towards the pillows and the headboard, and she folds her legs under herself and watches it. Eventually she lies down and shuts her eyes. She thinks she's asleep when she hears the whirring, and the familiar ding-ding-ding, and when she opens her eyes the screen is already bright with the menus.

Has it worked? she asks. She presses the information button and the screen flicks to the year, the firmware. CUSTOM, it says, instead of a number. Shit, she says. Okay. She opens the instruction sheet again, her hands shaking. Congratulations, she reads. Okay.

She flicks through the Machine's menus again. It's internal structure has been rearranged: where the recordings of Vic from before had been buried in a folder of their own, now they're the only thing accessible from the MEMORY tab. She presses the button marked on, to check that the files have survived the process.

What are we doing here, Vic? asks the doctor.

We're here to get rid of the stuff I can remember about the war, Vic says.

And how do you think it's going.

I think it's going. Is that enough?

At this point, yes. Absolutely.

Beth presses stop. She shuts the Machine down, and then she goes to the computer and looks at the videos of the process again, and she starts to cry. She's so close.

14

The next day is hotter still. The predictions were for it to nudge up in to the high thirties, which is more and more common. Beth dresses the same, coats herself in antiperspirant. She drinks glass after glass of water to keep from dehydrating. She looks at herself in the mirror to smooth over her slightly damp brow, to push the hairs back after they've become sticky from the sweat on her hairline. She doesn't care that her makeup is blotchy and matted. She swims for longer than usual, just to try and let the cold water seep into her, to try and make it somehow a part of her: to lower her temperature and allow herself to deal with the day. In her classroom, with her GCSE class, they're going over *The Tempest* to set them up for the last day of term, a trip to London to see the Barrage and watch the play in the Globe theatre, but she's lost them before they've even begun.

Be not afeared, she reads. The isle is full of noises.

Sounds like the new estates in Cowes, one of the boys says, and you should be well fucking afeared there, I tell you! and that gets a laugh. She tries to continue but it's pointless; they're in their own world for the rest of the class, and so is she. She wishes that they didn't have the trip, but it's routine now. Every year, the last day of term. Keeps the kids occupied, and they use what money is left of the annual budget on it, because otherwise that money is lost. Somehow most of the parents found their token monetary contribution – little more than pocket money, really – for the trip. When they give up on the book – the boys protesting about how hot it is, and how they can't concentrate, and how the words sound invented and like lies – she tells them about the floods, and how it happened. Some of the children, Beth discovers, have never been to London.

What was it like when the floods came? asks a girl, one of the few who seem emotionally attached to what they're doing.

It was awful; everything was ruined, and so many people lost their houses, all their things. And you know, a lot of people lost their lives.

Where were you when it happened, miss? asks one boy, one of the kids she most dislikes. One of the school's branded troublemakers. She humours him: at least he's paying attention to this.

I was at home, Beth says.

Did you watch it on the news?

We all did, yes. It was a really big deal. She loads up the projector (whir, and then the background hum of a machine doing its work, she notices; doing its job), and then plays one of the files from the network. Watch this, she tells them.

The class are almost completely silent as they watch the video: there's a bit where a naked woman, comedic in all other respects (unfit, flabby, unattractive), climbs a fence, to the top of her kitchen extension, and then scrambles, sobbing, to her roof to escape the flood; but, mercifully, none of the class laugh. The bodies of dogs and cats in the streets, floating down. The dead being dredged out onto boats. When the video ends there's only minutes until their first class, and they leave quietly. Beth goes to lunch and sits alone, on a table at the far end. She sees Laura, who makes a beeline for her. Laura doesn't ask to sit next to Beth – and why would she? They're not children – but Beth finds it strange, how relaxed Laura is immediately. She starts talking about her life, how she argued with her boyfriend the previous night.

They've asked me to stay on permanently, she says. Apparently Mr Westlake is retiring. Something to do with his heart. She eats only salad, Beth notices. Hard-boiled eggs and crispy bacon and dressing and lettuce leaves today. She forks the food, a piece of each component in each mouthful. So I said to Rob, this is something we could do. He said that it was impractical, but we could live in Portsmouth. I could commute. He could commute. It's a job.

What does he do? Beth asks.

He's a plumber. Electrician. Whatever he can get his hands on. He's a handyman, that's the thing, but they don't call it that any more. We have three telephone lines for all three parts of his business, can you believe that? When there are no kids nearby she leans closer. What are you doing tonight? she asks.

I shouldn't, Beth says, not even knowing what's coming.

Not like the other night. I've got a bottle of wine in the guesthouse, that's all. You can help persuade me that moving here is a terrible idea. Rob'll thank you for it.

I shouldn't, Beth says. I've got marking to do.

Ah, the perennial excuse. Laura lowers her eyes.

I'd love to, but the work. I have to get it done before we break.

I know, I know. It's fine. We'll do it the last day of term or something instead.

Sure, Beth says. She watches Laura walk away and put the remaining leaves of her salad in the bin, the plate on the side.

She remembers how she used to have friends. She used to be sociable. She and Vic went to socials for the army, the wives-and-partners things, and they would sit at the tables with people that they didn't know and they would make friends, even transitory ones who only stayed their friends for the evening. The people you could talk to and make up details about your lives, or spill secrets to, knowing that you wouldn't have to see them again. It didn't matter who you were for that one night. All that mattered was that, the next day, you could start again: she could wake up with Vic and never think about the people they'd met. They were young, and that was how it was for them. You sit next to somebody you barely know; ten

93

minutes later they're your best friend; ten hours later you struggle to remember their name, past the wine and the dancing.

Beth catches up with Laura in her classroom just before the bell rings, signalling the end of lunch.

Friday, I promise, she says. I just need to get past this stuff.

It's fine, Laura says.

Friday we'll go out and have more drinks.

Will there be a social thing? All the staff, something like that?

Oh God no, Beth says. Nobody does that here. Just you and me, I'd think.

Lovely.

When Beth gets home she strips in the hallway and opens the fridge door and stands there in her underwear, pulling herself close to the brightly lit interior. She runs an ice cube over her head and puts more of them into a glass, gets herself wine from the cupboard – she doesn't keep it refrigerated for some reason – and pours it, hardly gives it a chance to rattle the ice before drinking it almost in one. In the living room she puts the television on, opens the windows to get a draft through the flat, opens all the doors, and she stops and looks at the Machine for a second, thinking about how cold its metal is, and how refreshing and relieving it would be against her skin, but she tries to ignore it, knowing that it's ready for Vic now – she doesn't want to mess that up. She puts each of the fans on. On the television they're all talking about it: on *Blue Peter* they're discussing the multitudes of different ways to keep yourself cool when you're sleeping. They show a young boy, twelve or thirteen, waking up and gasping, then wrapping himself in a cold towel that's been kept in the freezer.

Quick showers really help to lower the body's temperature, the presenter says. The boy shivers and grins, because this is preferable to sweating. Don't run a bath then throw the water away; reuse the water, if you really want one. And more than anything, it's important to drink lots, to keep your fluids up. Your health is more important than your cleanliness, at times like this, the presenter says earnestly. He's got sweat on his hairline. Beth defies his advice, and takes herself to the bathroom. She runs both taps, the cold harder and faster than the hot, and when the bath is nearly full, not bothering to check the temperature, she steps in. It's cold, but that's okay: she slides back and under it, opens her mouth, lets the water cover every part of her. She doesn't even think about the bill: since all household water went metered, she's relied on short, sharp showers. When you live alone, it's the sensible thing. This is the first bath that she's had in forever. It feels incredible.

When she's finished she doesn't dress. She towels herself dry, dabbing at her body but leaving just enough water that it still feels cool, and she lays the slightly damp towel on the sofa before putting herself onto it. On the evening news they show footage of some coastal towns on the news – Eastend, Hastings, Canterbury – and of people bunking off work and school, the country brought to a halt by the heat. They dance in the water, the beaches crowded like she's never seen, the sea a mass of hair and bathing suits. The reporter smiles and puts a brave face on it, but he's dripping with sweat in his suit, desperate to join the throng behind.

This is officially the hottest start to a summer on record, he says, making it sound like that's something that the audience at home should be happy with. You always used to moan about British summers: look what you've wrought. Beth checks her email as they cut to *EastEnders*, to the actors sweating, wearing cut-off shorts and open shirts, even hotter under the camera lights. This was filmed months before but feels strangely appropriate, seeing them struggle as much as the rest of the country.

Four days left. She calls up pictures of Vic and her on her screen and looks at them. Four days.

15

Beth lies in bed and keeps her eyes shut. She can see Vic, and she tries to cling onto him. The image of him back as he was. He's telling her about the treatments. What they entail. She's got a glass of water, and he's got coffee. Her arm is still bruised. She holds it close to her body.

They say that it's natural, he tells her. They take away the bits that are broken and twisted and they leave the pure stuff.

What about the gaps? Beth asks him.

They fill it in. The computer has everything it needs to fill in the gaps. They give it a cover story – like, they might say that I was in a car crash – and the computer does the rest.

The computer lies to you?

No, it's not . . . It's more like the computer helps me lie to myself.

Beth thinks about the rules that they were given, a

laminated handbook that was theirs to keep. The things that she should and shouldn't ask Vic about once the treatments started. The things that might happen that seemed strange but that they had to roll with. She would be told the cover story completely, so that she could play along; but the brain often interpreted things its own way. She was to go along with everything.

Never contradict him if he's sure of something, the handbook told her. And make sure he never finds this handbook. Once the treatments are underway, this should be kept secret, because one day he'll come home and he won't remember why he left the house in the first place.

Now, Beth keeps her eyes shut because she can see him as clear as if he was in the room with her. She thinks about how her alarm hasn't gone off yet, and how there's something else. An intrusion into her sleep, because even as she dreams of Vic talking to her – holding her arms, however sore they might be, and telling her that it will all be all right, that all of this will be over soon – she can hear something else. In the background. A grind; machinery, road works. An engine, like a train. The noise of tank tracks. And then she realizes: it's the Machine.

She opens her eyes and she's in the spare bedroom, on the bed. She's still in the t-shirt she sleeps in (one of Vic's, bearing some obscure reference to a film that he used to love) and she's not under the covers. The Machine is on, and the Crown has been removed from the dock, and is lying next to her on the bed.

No, she says. She sits up but her head swims, and she has to steady herself. She gets to the edge of the bed and taps the screen. She wonders if she deleted something from herself: she's certainly thought about it before. Everything that gets deleted gets recorded, and she wouldn't remember doing it. That's the point. Even as she presses the buttons to take her to the recordings, she realizes that this is the furthest she's been in the process. She doesn't know how you would do it to yourself. Whether you'd just talk yourself through something, after pressing the COMMIT button; and how that would feel, talking yourself through to forgetting.

But there's nothing. In the recordings section, there's nothing. It's blank, Vic's stuff having been moved to the main memory. She's grateful: she knows that, after a treatment, there's no way she could have deleted the recording, so she's clean. She wonders why this happened: how she moved rooms, and if she did this in her sleep. What she was trying to achieve. The Machine's growl sounds like the rumbling of her stomach: morning hunger. She switches it off and pulls the cable from the wall.

In the kitchen she takes ibuprofen, gulps them down with a full glass of water, and stands by the sink, shaking. She splashes water onto her face. It's still so early, an hour before she'd usually wake up. Already it feels hotter than the day before.

She spends the hour back in her own bed, staring at the ceiling. She doesn't want to fall asleep – she's not sure that she even could, with this headache – so she tries to concentrate on Vic again. On what he might be like when he's at home, back with her. When she can work on him.

The headache remains. She telephones the receptionist

and tells her that she won't be in, because her head hurts so much that she can't even see properly.

Migraines are worse in this heat, aren't they? Beth agrees with her, even though she's never had migraines before. This must be what it is. She dresses herself and leaves the house. Sunglasses on to protect from the glare, she walks to Tesco and goes to the pharmacy counter, and she asks them for tablets for a migraine. They make her fill out a form: she notices how much the pen shakes; she can barely hold it steady to sign the paper.

Back in her flat she swallows the broad-bean-shaped tablet dry, and then she sits on the sofa with the fan pointed at her head. Sometime after that she falls asleep.

When she wakes up she's moved herself again, to the spare bedroom. The Machine is still unplugged.

16

She can't call in sick again the following day, she knows, not this close to the end of term; so she leaves the house after making sure it's all unplugged. She shuts the spare bedroom door behind her – the Machine's room, she thinks, as she does it – and checks the locks on her front door twice. She doesn't know why. The Machine's not going anywhere.

The heat hits her like a wall. Lots of the kids have already ducked out of school early. They're on the cliffs, just down from the bit that's become famous for suicides. Only a few a year, but that's all that's needed for fame. More than one and you're suddenly notorious. It's only twenty feet lower, but it ducks inwards at the base. No rocks to land on, just water. And this is the part of the island where the water's at its bluest, and for a second, when you look at it, you can see what the island used to be: the sun glinting off the breaks, the cold blue that runs to you-don't-know-how-deep. She recognizes some of the kids, but there's no point in chastising them, because they'll just jump and hit the water, knowing she will never follow them. They stand on the edge of the rocks, risking falling by just being there, given how chalky and loose the ground is, and then they wind up like toys, before springing off the edge, their limbs splayed, cycling and pounding the air as they fly. There's a smack as they hit the water one by one, before dragging themselves out and starting the climb up the scree slope next to the point, then the climb up the chalky sides, a long steep path back to the top. And then the process begins again, repeated ad infinitum. Beth watches them for a few minutes. She wonders what happens to them after this.

At school, the kids who have turned up are restless. They know what's coming. No chance of getting through to them in the final two days, if anybody ever tries. It's easier to let them do their own thing. Takes the pressure off the teachers, takes the pressure off the kids to learn. Everybody accepts that these are days of failure. Still, Beth knows that she probably won't be back here, even if the kids don't yet. Her plan, when Vic is well again, is to go somewhere that's used to the heat. To take advantage of the low prices, to buy up something on an island somewhere else, where they're built for the heat. Teach in a school there. She's thinking of a particular place – it's the sort of dream people had when she was a kid herself, to pack up and move out to the tropics – but she doesn't want to over-think it. She's barely researched it, in case it's tainted. Tempting fate and all that.

And now there's extra reason: the Machine. She thinks about it in her flat, like some growth. Mould. Cancer. Waiting in the room, and somehow alluring, persuasive, even. She wants to get away from it suddenly, because it's a reminder. There's more to it, maybe. But she doesn't want to think about it. Back of her mind, until she gets home.

Laura approaches her in the corridor. Feeling better? she asks.

Barely, Beth says.

Those last few days are a killer, aren't they? You always feel as if your body's giving up early. She turns and walks with Beth, not breaking step. Are you like me, always getting ill at the end of term? It's like everything in me says, Oh, now you can be ill. She reaches out and holds Beth's arm, like a doctor comforting a patient's loved one. You can be ill on Saturday, she says. You have my permission. She laughs. I can't, Beth thinks. Saturday's when I need to be at my best.

They pass some year-ten boys fighting, and they get in between them, pulling them apart. Used to be that they couldn't physically intervene, but here the rules are different. They have to be. One of the children is clutching a ruler, holding it flat against his palm, using it as some sort of blade. A hard edge on it. The other has thick welts on his back, and his shirt's torn and pulled up over his hips. Beth frogmarches them both down to the Head's office, where there are already children waiting, all in similar states of disrepair. She sits them down in front of the receptionist.

Don't give her any shit, Beth says. They both smirk at her swearing. And don't smirk at me. I'm sick of you both. Beth can't remember either of their names, as she doesn't teach them, but she's sure that they're regular trouble-makers. She's seen them before, always sitting here. Waiting.

By the time she gets back to her classroom there's a note on her desk. It's from Laura.

It's going to be a busy couple of days, it reads. See you outside the gates tomorrow at three?

It's an invitation, not a question. Beth breathes in. She looks at a picture of Vic that she keeps in the drawer of her desk. Two days left.

17

She doesn't know what time it is, because the flat's in complete darkness. Outside, on the walkway, she knows, a light comes on at ten and goes off at four. She looks around to see what room she's in, but it takes her some time to adjust to the light. Total darkness, utterly pitch black. That's enough: she fumbles for the spare-bedroom door, opening it and letting light in, the faded orange-grey light from the living-room window. She moves again and feels a sudden tug on her head: and on it, the Crown. She puts her hands up and feels the pads, each on a pressure point. Two on her temples. One on the top of her head, the lid. Two smaller pads at the back, towards the neck, hidden away.

No, she says. Her own voice sounds strange to her: distant and vague. She suddenly becomes aware of the hum, sly and driven, in the back of the room. She can't take the Crown off because she might have pressed something. It could be just the screen that's asleep, because the Machine – it's the only part of the room that the light doesn't catch – is definitely plugged in. She wonders how she's done this all in her sleep. What's making her do it. She knows that she won't have dreamt of anything else: the Machine is all that she's dreamed of for months now, in one way or another.

She edges towards it. They said, If you take the Crown off and interrupt a procedure, you can cause irreparable damage. (She wonders if that damage is worse than the damage that Vic has already suffered; if they're related, these two kinds of damage, or somehow the same thing.)

She presses the screen and it flicks on, onto the home page again. COMMIT. PURGE. REPLENISH. She looks at the options, almost invitations. No recordings have been made: she hasn't used the Machine yet. COMMIT. PURGE. REPLENISH. She wonders if this is it: this is what her mind has been setting herself up for. Telling her, somehow – and Vic's situation has proven to her that the thing works in a way we can't and will never understand – that she should press one of them.

Press COMMIT, and talk it through the plan. Press PURGE and remove that plan entirely, letting the Machine fill in the gaps for you. Like you never thought it in the first place.

Beth wonders if the plan – the whole thing, the Machine and Vic and the island and saving up and everything she's dreamt up for after this stage – is something that she could get rid of in one go. Like pulling off a plaster, swift and sharp. It was always about the depth of the memory:

106

how deep-set it was. With Vic, the hours and hours of interviews, before they even began taking memories from him, covered every aspect of his life. They took him back to his childhood, where he sat in the gardens of military-housing complexes, playing with his GI Joe, which he cast in scenarios with his friends: establishing zip lines with string, launch pads and aircraft carriers with cardboard boxes, theatres of conflict across perfectly mowed lawns. They asked him why he wanted to be a soldier and he said that he didn't know. That it was just all he had ever wanted to be. So when they rooted for the memory, to pull every stem of it from Vic's brain, that was where they had to go. Deep down, to childhood. Beth asked them what those earliest memories would be replaced with.

What does any childhood memory consist of in the first place? the doctor said. It's all much of a muchness. Doesn't impede his education or his learning. This is a different centre of the brain altogether.

So what does it get replaced with? Beth persisted.

Nothing, the doctor said. It's one of the few times from a patient's life that can be removed without replacement, because they remember so little of it anyway. She remembers worrying about that: that the Machine would be putting its own nothingness inside him. A computer-created void. Not just nothing, but like the screen, emulating black, to approximate a state of sleep. A created depiction of nothing. She tried to think about her own childhood: what she could call up was colours of things, and toys; an outfit, maybe, something that she wore regularly; a story told to her so many times about a trip to the zoo – about her father dropping her in a urinal, such a funny story, and she remembered it happening; but did she? Or did she actually only remember the story itself, recounted at opportune moments for embarrassment? And when she was older she remembered birthday parties and holidays and single events, but nothing that she could say was defining.

(That was a long-standing argument of the anti-Machine protestors: who were the creators of the Machine to dictate life and death? To dictate creation? When they protested with their placards, they decided to bring God into it, with the capital letter. They fought for the right to say that the creator defined the soul. That we were made in his image. This is the next stage, after clones and gene therapy: we are changing what that image is. Picking and choosing what we keep for ourselves. Only this time it's not something physical, something transitory and visible. It's something that defines who we are, as people. As children of God. They argued that the memory was tied to the soul. And if we could tamper with memory, how long before we could tamper with the soul?)

Beth looks at the buttons. Her finger raises, and hovers. If she could do it, what would she say? This stage, the recitation, always took it out of Vic, and he was so strong. She had to pick him up from the sessions. She had to cradle his body, helping him from the car to the living-room sofa after the worst of them. When they took the deepest parts.

She hears her bedroom alarm in the other room. She pulls her finger away from the screen.

108

I could do it, she tells the Machine. Like she's warning it. Like, if she did, it would somehow cease to exist.

18

It's the last day of term. Before the day has even begun
Beth is tired: as she dragged herself to the beach and swam
through the cold, every stroke felt harsh and wearing. She
drags her feet during the walk to work, to the playground
where the big coaches wait to haul them across the water,
hundreds of children all desperate to be set loose for the
next six weeks. All along the walk she dreams of this going
well – of her and Vic, hand in hand, talking like before,
everything like before – and she imagines not having to
be here any more. Not here, specifically. More the feeling.
The sensation of the last few years. The heat is impossible,
and worse when she steps onto the coach she will travel
in, cheaply reliant on its miniature above-seat fans rather
than air conditioning. The children swagger and groan as
they take their seats, pre-arranged to avoid chaos. All along
the motorway the children sing filthy songs, variations on
classics. Replacing the word Love with Fuck. The teachers

can't control them, and there's no point. If they do, they become the focus of the songs. Easier to let them be 14 and 15 year olds.

London has become a very different city from the one Beth grew up in. The Barrage wall casts much of the Thames into shadow, certainly at the bankside. Time was, sun like this would have rendered the walk alongside the river heaving with people, queuing for the London Eye or sitting on the grass at the front of Tate Modern. Now the South Bank's nearly empty. The stark concrete of the Barrage doesn't help matters.

Ugly fucking mound, that, says one of the boys in Beth's group.

Pubic mound, more like, another says. They all laugh. The first boy isn't wrong. It looms over them like a dyke of thick mottled cream, tarnished in the last few years from things that have been thrown at it. There are parts where it's been patched, in case; but the biggest issue is what it does to the view.

Used to be that you'd be able to see the ships, one of the male teachers says, as if the boys will be interested in that, young enough to be fascinated by boats and trains and fire engines still. Ships and boats, up and down. The bridge – he indicates Tower Bridge in the distance – would open and close to let them in and out.

Now it stays up, to accommodate the Barrage's height. They didn't expect to have to build the Barrage in the first place, let alone as fast as they did. Beth remembers plans for how beautiful it was going to be, how it was going to complement – their word – the rest of the South

Bank, all the way down to Docklands. It was going to be the most practical kind of tourist attraction, that had been the plan. Then they had to rush it or risk losing more of the coast, and that wasn't an option.

The teachers – seven of them, practically the entire English department – take the children to the Barrage Exhibition Centre, built in what used to be an art museum above a McDonald's. The children cackle about wanting Big Macs, but they're corralled through to the different stages of the exhibition. The teachers work efficiently, and soon the kids are watching videos of waves crashing across houses: starting with the hurricanes in New Orleans, in Japan, showing the destruction that they caused. They all go silent when they see these, and when they see the films of the east coast of England, of New York.

In one room, the children line up and stare at a wall of video screens, a wall that curves around them to the sides and above them, across the ceiling. The room falls into blackness and hardly any of the children snigger; and then the sound of water, of screaming. The video begins slowly, blinking in, as if the people in the room are actually standing at the scene, as if this is their eyes; and then they're suddenly standing on a rooftop, looking down across London as it could be, water troughing the streets. People are screaming through the speakers, begging to be saved; babies are crying, women howling that they cannot reach, a man sobbing that he's hurt, that he's trapped. The camera doesn't move; it just looks around, watching as water starts to fill the city, as a wave brings cars down the streets, hammering through porches, smashing through windows and dredging out belongings. The camera swings around to see the Shard falling in the far distance, the glass smashing, the iron buckling. It looks impossible, and it probably is, but the kids almost uniformly gasp. This is so vivid, Beth thinks. The camera swings back once more, towards the first shot, where the screaming people are now silenced, the streets now empty. There, in the distance, comes a swell of water towards the camera, and the audio starts swelling as well, becoming a cacophony as the water crashes down on the crowd in the room. As it hits, as the camera eye falls backwards, real water, actual water, sprays from some hidden place, and all the teenage girls scream, absolutely caught in the moment. The lights come up, the door opens, and they all laugh and gasp and filter out.

Outside, in the sun, it almost feels like a lie. They all sit on the lawn outside the art museum there and eat the packed lunches that they were given on the coaches, now-warm sandwiches and miniature bags of slightly molten Maltesers. They pose in front of the Barrage wall, all of them, for a photograph which some of the nicer girls print out on their sticker-printers and give to Beth, placing it delicately onto her bag. They run around, playing bulldog on the lawn, boys and girls alike, tearing each other down, tackling each other to the floor. When they're all finished – and a group of boys who had snuck off and bought burgers instead have been rounded up – they walk down the river towards the Globe theatre. They file inside and are immediately less interested, lost by the presenta-tion that they're given by the actor who plays Caliban, even though he's got his makeup on and looks suitably hideous. There's no air conditioning in the theatre, and the ground seems to be giving off just as much heat as the sun. They sweat and swat gnats as Caliban talks to them.

Sit still and hear the last of our sea-sorrow! he starts. Who feels separated and alone, like they're not actually a part of society? he asks, skewing his questions for the teenage audience. Some of their hands slowly creep up. Right, he says, and you should. And that's because we all do, no matter how old we are, or what we do.

Bloody right we do, Laura says.

It's a natural feeling, a human feeling. It's hard, this life thing, the actor says, and we all get through it in any way we can. Caliban – you've all read the play, right? Murmurs. Caliban spent his life there on the island, alone and scared. And in many ways, that's a lot like our lives, isn't it? We spend this chunk of our life alone – or, just feeling alone – and then this ship comes along and our lives are turned upside down. Canst thou remember a time before we came unto this cell?

I'm going to need that drink tonight, Laura whispers again. Tell me we're still on.

Beth had almost forgotten. She nods. The kids traipse over the set, which is only really boxes fastened together to represent a shipwreck, and some more of the cast appear, still wiping their lunches from their mouths, and act out a scene for the kids. Afterwards, they're shepherded through the exhibit on Shakespeare and then back out onto the street, which is cooler and has something resembling a breeze running across it. They gasp for the air.

Stay together, the teachers all say, over and over again, because they know that this is the time the boys are most likely to disappear and try to find shops or trouble. They get to the coaches and file them on alphabetically, class by class, checking them off and making sure that they're all on board, and when they are the doors are shut. On Beth's coach, some of them say that they need the loo.

You can hold it, Beth says, until we get to the services. She sits by herself at the front, the kids putting a few rows between her and them so that she can't hear them talking about their day, or frantically making out on the back rows. She can hear, of course: the slurping, the laughter. They stop at Chichester and let the kids out, and when they're back on the bus the driver puts the radio on and they sing along to songs that Beth doesn't even come close to recognizing. At school, their parents are waiting to pick them up; the ones whose parents aren't there, Beth and Laura offer to wait with (Beth offering first, Laura stubbornly refusing to let her new friend out of her sight). There's six of them, and after an hour – that the kids spend protesting that there's no way their parents will turn up, because they never do, and they know it all too well – Beth lets them go.

Go straight home, and have a good summer, she says. When they're gone, Laura gives an exaggerated sigh.

Thank God, she says. She walks to the gate. Come on.

19

The pub is heaving with under-age drinkers, many of them sixth-formers from Beth's classes.

We can go somewhere else, Laura says when she sees them.

It'll all be like this, Beth says. She walks in and straight past the kids, towards the back of the room where the real locals have gathered. Some of them are smoking: nobody's telling them to stop. She thinks that she can use the kids' presence as an excuse to call it an early night. She thinks about what she has to do tomorrow.

Long day, Laura says. What are you drinking?

Whatever you are.

Pinot?

Fine, Beth says. She forms a plan: to drink a few glasses quickly, not too much, but enough for it to become an excuse. She doesn't know why she doesn't just say that she wants to go home. Laura isn't somebody whose feelings she has to worry about hurting. By the time Laura returns with the bottle, Beth's decided to get this over with. They're poured and hers is at her lips, cold against them, before Laura has even set the bottle down.

Okay, Laura says. You needed that, apparently.

Apparently so.

They're not bad kids, you know.

I said that to you, I think.

I think you did.

They absorb the slight unease of not knowing each other, of being colleagues without the subject of work to discuss any more. Laura brings up the job offer, which is now firm and lettered. There's a contract if she wants it.

Do you want it? Beth asks. She's halfway through a glass. Another sip. Question, then drink through the answer.

I think so. It'll be hard with Rob. Really long-distance all of a sudden.

Won't he move?

We can't live together until there's a ring on this finger, and he's too scared for that. No, that sounds terrible. But really. It would be good though, I think, being here. I don't know how you live here, but there are worse places to work. She notices how quickly Beth's drinking, and she tops her glass up when there's still an inch left. You must have a really nice flat, that's all I'm saying.

It's okay.

Any word when . . . I'm sorry, I've totally forgotten his name. Your husband.

Beth doesn't know if she told her his name in the first place. She's so worried about somebody snooping, Googling him and seeing what actually happened to him. Still, she thinks: now it's too late to affect anything. Vic, she says. Victor.

Vic! Gosh. Proper man's-man of a name, Vic.

He is, Beth says. Goes with the soldier territory.

So when's he home next?

Beth thinks about lying. But she can't, because there are tears in her eyes, and hiding them from Laura – sitting this close – would be impossible without making a scene. Tomorrow, she says.

What?

Tomorrow. He's back tomorrow.

How long for?

For good, Beth says.

She stands in the ladies and wipes her face with dry, flaky tissue paper, and then watches from behind the crowd at the bar, as Laura fills their glasses again – she's one ahead of Laura, she thinks. She thinks about those holiday friends and wedding-guest confidantes. She thinks about the wine inside her. How she won't see Laura again, not after today. She's disposable and transitory, and so is anything that Beth tells her: details forgotten in the blur of the wine and the night and the rush. She orders another bottle at the bar and goes back to the table.

You all right? Laura asks.

Fine, Beth says. She takes her purse from her bag and pulls the photograph from it: Vic in full dress, hat and coat, medals pinned to his lapel. The only part of that life that she kept for herself, even though she was told to destroy it, for both their sakes. Every other photo is generic. No uniform: just a face with no telling details.

Forget who he ever was, they told her. Burn all the photographs, all the evidence. Sell him the story that he's been told.

This is Vic, she says. She slides it over.

Very army, Laura says. He looks nice.

He's sick.

Oh? Laura doesn't realize. She thinks that Beth means the flu, or a stomach bug. Something not worth worrying about.

He's not in Iran. He's in a home. A care centre.

What? She looks at Beth as if this lie has been going on for years: burned, rather than just annoyed by some-body else's secrecy What happened?

Not just now. For years. He's been in one for years. He came back and he was having dreams, and he became violent. She says it in her flattest tone: able somehow to make it sound like something unimportant, this story that she told so many times when he was first taken away from her. When, almost overnight, the situation became intoler-able for her, as everything about him collapsed and devolved.

So he had treatments for it, and . . .

She doesn't have to finish the story, because everybody knows how it ends. A tiny percentage that still rolls into the thousands, men and women taken away from their families, set up in places where fixing them isn't an option – and in return no more than an apology. No compensation, no legal recourse: they signed a document because they were so eager to be fixed in the first place, and they were told the risks. Spelled out to them in numbered bullet points spanning pages and pages, all with their signatures at the foot. So instead they paraded and marched in protest, husbands and wives and children standing next to their loved ones in their wheelchairs. But that got them nowhere, because of those thousands of signatures.

Laura drinks because she doesn't know what to say. Beth fills her glass for her, and her own. She's past her own limit, when she had been planning on making her escape. But it feels good, she thinks, to talk about this. Laura's the first person she's told since she left London. She came here for anonymity and a new start, and to stop people asking her how he was doing. When Laura speaks next, it's the first time she's heard the question in years. It almost sounds fresh from Laura's mouth.

How is he? she asks. She doesn't know how to phrase it. There's no way to ask the question, not really, because the answer is always so clear-cut.

He's destroyed. He's hardly my husband any more, Beth says.

But he's coming home?

Beth nods.

You're taking him out of the hospital? Beth notices something: Laura's hand up at her neckline, fiddling with the necklace underneath her collar. Are you sure that's wise? Laura asks.

I think I can help him, Beth says. I think I might be able to start making him better.

Do you pray for him? Laura asks.

What?

Do you pray for him? Because it might help. It might . . . I don't know, Beth. She's nearly in tears, Beth notices. She drinks more as Laura sobs. Some of the kids are noticing, looking over from the bar where they're dropping shot glasses filled with some liquid the same colour as the Machine into their pints, the mixtures mingling and coalescing. They laugh at the two teachers, and one of them raises his fingers in a V to his lips, pokes his tongue through. Laura wipes her face. How can you help him now? she asks. She seems almost desperate.

There are some people – on the internet – who think you can rebuild somebody. Recreate them, almost.

Oh, no, Laura says. No, no. That's why you got into this trouble in the first place.

Trouble?

It's not our place to meddle, Beth. There's an earnest look in her eyes that Beth's seen before: in the protestors who stood outside the clinics, telling them that it was their own fault when the patients began to collapse. The malice of their self-righteousness.

Look, I shouldn't have told you this, Beth says. She tries to wheel the conversation backwards. Laura used to be logical and easy. Not any more, now that this is out. This is a burden. It's mine, not yours.

No, Laura says. Almost shouts. I think this has happened for a reason. It's good that you told me. You shouldn't go through something like this alone.

121

I should go, Beth says. She stands up. She necks the wine left in the glass. It's already gone to her head: she can feel it, swimming around.

Beth, I could pray for you both. I'll show you how, Laura says. Beth sees the cross front and centre, suddenly brought forward to the front of the shirt, hanging down. Not a simple cross: a crucifix, a miniature figure hanging from his nails. A miniature crown of thorns on his head. That's the best way to deal with this, you know.

Beth forces her way through the crowd of students, ignoring their comments, and out into the air. She expected it to be cool, for some reason, where the pub had been so hot: she'd forgotten. Instead it's dense and cloying. She rushes off. Laura doesn't follow her.

She passes the point where the children leap off into the sea, and they're still there, or a different group of children are. Leaping from the outcrop of grass-tufted rock into the pitch blackness, only knowing that they're jumping out far enough when they smack the water. And when their friends hear that smack they all laugh, as if each plunge is a belly-flop, and each dive a bomb. She stands back by the railing – set twenty feet away for safety, because the authorities didn't know if or when more of the cliff might slump down further – and listens to them, trying to pick out anything other than shouts and giggles. They're only teenagers, somewhere between thirteen and sixteen, she reckons, boys and girls, and she thinks she can see that they're all naked. But there's nothing really sexual about this: just the leap and the darkness.

Down the path, only thirty metres away, she ignores the sign that implores her to call the telephone number on it and discuss her situation with the friendly-looking man on the other end, the sign that tells her that it's never as bad as she thinks it is. She stands on the lip of the cliff and she can feel the alcohol inside her, making her sway. A bottle of wine, that's all it takes these days. She thinks about when she and Vic got together, and how they were. How they would go out and drink with their friends, and how that led to their wedding, where they flooded the guests with booze. A good party, that's all they wanted.

She looks out at the darkness, and she thinks about the nothingness that replaced all of who Vic was, like a virus. Deleting cells, replicating itself. The Machine, filling in the gaps with things that didn't stick, stories of its own creation to cover up the cracks. And what makes her think that it will be so different this time? Because the stories are Vic? From his own mouth, 100 per cent pure and unfiltered, every part of his life spilled onto digital tape? She doubts herself. She doubts the Machine.

This isn't me, she says aloud, to reassure herself. The kids down the way somehow hear her – and she wonders if she shouted it, even a little, or if it was just the wind – and they stop being children and become animals all of a sudden.

Go on! one of them yells. His friends laugh. She's sure that she recognizes the voice: the same cracked broken deepness of the bike boy who lives on her estate, who calls out to her, sexually threatening even for somebody so young. Go on, you cunt! Give the world a fucking break!

He doesn't know who she is. He can't see her from here, and he wouldn't recognize her voice – although, she recognized his, didn't she? – and this is all for show. If she did it, he would never forgive himself, she thinks. That's what she hopes. To teach him a lesson would be the worst reason.

She backs away from the edge. She can't see the boy in the darkness, and they've all fallen silent. There are no lights here, only the moon. She waits, suddenly scared; and then the laughs start again, and she hears the boy jump. She hears his laugh arc through the air, and the splash, and a second – maybe two – where there's no noise. She wonders if he made it.

His laugh cuts through the air from the water below. Beth turns and heads up the path. The estate is quiet. She unlocks the door to her flat. She can hear it, already.

20

Beth sits in the living room on the sofa. Her last night alone. She thinks about the night before her wedding, and the forced trip to the pub.

This is your last chance, her maid of honour told her. You should relish this. Your last night alone!

Last night alone! they all chanted at her in the pink minibus that passed for a limousine.

I hope you make a few decent mistakes, her maid of honour said. She barely drank what wasn't forced into her hand, and when she got home – not quite blind-drunk, but blurred and slurring – she telephoned Vic. He answered her, asking how she was. She told him.

No mistakes, she said.

Okay, he told her. She knew that he could never sleep once he'd woken up, and there he was the next day, at the altar with aubergine eyes. He hadn't slept, and she had.

She opens the bottle of whisky that she's kept

underneath the sink with the cleaning products, out of sight. Vic's favourite, a Scottish one that he got a taste for. Not the best stuff, but certainly not the cheapest. She was saving it.

I need this more than you, she says. She pours a glass and it splashes as it hits, but she doesn't care. The smell on the carpet means nothing. The vibrations through the flat, through the sofa and into her: they're all that she can feel. She swallows it all in one go. This can't be real, she says. You're trying to scare me. She puts the television on, doesn't matter what channel, and she turns on the fans and pours another glass. She can feel it going straight to her. And Laura betrayed her, she thinks: she suggested she was something, but she was something else. How dare she judge me? Beth asks.

She lies back on the sofa, to block out the noise of the turbine in the Machine's room, and the vibrations, and the sudden pain in her head.

What would I like to forget? Vic asks. His voice fills the flat, loud and clear. Like he's actually there, played back by the Machine on the highest volume it can muster. This is from later on in his treatments. When it started, it took forever: like it was massaging his memories to find the knot. One by one, they came. I'd like to forget what I did after I got back. How I treated Beth.

Didn't they medicate you? the doctor asks.

They gave me opioids. Do you know what they do to a person? How much they rob of you? I couldn't take them after the first few.

Maybe they could have helped.

126

No. No. I was responsible for what I did. His voice degrades into tears, and that's the sound that comes over the Machine's thrum: her husband sobbing. I want to tell her that I'm sorry, he says through the tears.

Beth stands up and walks to the doorway of the Machine's room. She doesn't go in: she stands against the connecting wall instead. She leans against it. She cradles a full glass of whisky, raising to her lips every so often and sipping. Letting it sting her lips where the heat of the days has made them crack very slightly.

So what would you like to forget? the doctor asks.

That. I'd forget that I hurt her. I'd forget that I did this, and that I was – that I am – the man I am now. I don't recognize myself when I'm like that. I'd get rid of that.

Don't, Beth says.

I would get rid of everything that made me that man.

Don't.

Do you know what we're doing here, Victor?

You're helping to make me better. That's what I know.

Why you're wearing that Crown? Why we're talking like this?

Something. He pauses, unsure of himself. Beth can hear it in his voice. She knows every nuance. You're taking away memories, is that right?

That's right, the doctor says. Beth can see him now, pressing the PURGE button on the Machine's hulking screen: flushing everything that had been said before away. She rounds the corner and goes into the room, and there's the Machine. She doesn't know how it's playing this for itself. (There was a part of her that expected to see Vic

127

and the doctor, sitting here, playing this out for real: that's how fake this all feels to her, like an accident or a lie, or a dream.)

How dare you? she asks. She puts her hands on the metal, which is so cold, and the shaking, which roars along her bones. Into every part of her. Come on, she says. The screen isn't showing anything. That same painted blackness. Come on. She hits it, a punch with the flat of her fist. Play me more of him. Tell me more about what he felt.

It obliges.

What are we doing? Vic asks, another file starting. Must be the next one, chronologically. I'm so sorry, what are we doing?

Not the doctor's voice, next. Beth's. We're trying something, she says.

It's not time for a treatment, he tells her. I didn't mean it, please don't punish me.

I won't. This isn't punishment.

There are rules, Vic's voice says. I remember that they told us.

No, Beth now says, listening to it. Not this one.

The Beth in the recording is persuasive. She sounds so strong and confident. The rules are for your safety, she says, and we won't break them. But they told me to help you with your treatments, didn't they?

Yes. He's so docile.

Don't play this, now-Beth pleads. She presses the Machine's screen but she can't get it to wake from its sleep. Please, she begs.

What happened earlier today? then-Beth asks. She's wiping something. Erasing something beyond his normal treatments. Do you remember?

I didn't mean to, Vic says.

I didn't ask that. I asked what happened.

We had a fight, he says. Oh my God, I'm so sorry, I'm so sorry.

That's okay. You're not yourself. I have to press this, then-Beth says. Now-Beth sees it happening: COMMIT depressed. Ready. Primed. What did we fight about? then-Beth asks.

I had a dream.

What about?

I was fighting. Some sort of fight. I had a gun. I was, uh. Something exploded. I was there, and then . . . I don't know, I don't know.

Shh. Tell me everything you can remember.

There was an explosion and my head was on fire, like burning, with the pain. And I had to shoot somebody or I would have been dead. I remember that.

Where were you?

Somewhere hot. Not here, though. Hot like the desert, somewhere like that. It was so hot. Went right through my helmet. I had a helmet on. Then I woke up, and you were there, and I didn't mean it, but I was so confused.

What did you do then?

Now-Beth can hear it in then-Beth's voice: the slight tweak of her jaw, which would soon start to swell, although she wasn't even aware that it had been fractured. I don't need to hear this again, now-Beth says. Turn it off. Vic's voice speaks through her, above her. She hits the screen again, so hard that it should break, she thinks, but it doesn't, and then she scrabbles to the floor and to the plug. She pulls it from the wall but the Machine continues to whir. The turbines keep spinning. The voices are gone, but the screen is still on. Backup batteries, in case of power cut. The only way to shut it down now would be to destroy it, to open it up and cut its cords. She doesn't.

She takes the Crown down from the dock and puts it onto her head. Perfect fit, always is.

Is this what you want? she asks it. Do you want more of me?

She doesn't press the buttons. She lies down with the Crown on, and she thinks, as the room spins and she feels herself sleeping, so quickly, so exhausted and shocked and terrified, that it will do what it will to her. And it can't do anything that will change her mind about this.

Tomorrow, she will get Vic from the clinic. Tomorrow she'll bring Vic home.

PART TWO

The problem with memory was that it told us whatever we wanted to hear. It had no shape of its own.

David Vann, *Dirt*

21

In through the front door he falls, because Beth can't prop him up and work the key and keep herself steady, and when she feels herself going she drops him. Better that he take the soft landing than she fall with him, and she bear the brunt, break something. That would ruin everything. He's taken worse in his time. And, she reminds herself, this him is just a form. A shell.

He lands softly, his skin making the only noise on the flooring. Nothing from his mouth. The lift was broken – the lift is always broken – so his wheelchair is still down at the bollards, waiting to be folded and lugged upstairs. She won't need it. Vic's not so gone that he can't be coerced into walking when he needs to, or into supporting some weight on feet which almost seem to drag their toes along the floor with each step. Still, in case. Maybe, she thinks, the muscles will have atrophied a little, and maybe he couldn't sustain this over any great distance. You read about that; it would drive him mad. She would hate to have him back and then have to do years of physiotherapy. Still, she reasons, that would be better than nothing. She pulls him inside the flat, manoeuvring him onto his back. She leaves him there while she runs to the stairs, down, to where she left the chair. It's already gone. Some of the residents are like magpies. Finders keepers, if anything is left for more than a minute. She stands there and looks around, to see if any curtains twitch. She would go to the door and hammer on it and demand her property back, if she could work out where it had gone – but she's completely alone. Not a peep.

Back in the flat Vic is exactly where she had left him. He's gone limp now, all the use of his muscles seemingly gone. She can tell as soon as she looks at him, and it almost makes the getting him up here – how easily he responded to her – like a dream.

Come on, she says. She puts her hands under his armpits and she tries to heave him along the floor towards the section of the open-plan room designated as a living room. It's easy on the laminate floorboards, but the sofas sit across a large rug. It's no longer its original colour. She can't remember what the colour was, or even if it's hers. Maybe it was always here, a part of the flat. She leaves Vic where he lies and pulls the sofas away from the rug, and then moves the things from the coffee table and carries that to the edge of the room.

Only a second, she says to Vic. As if he cares. She rolls the rug up, not doing the best job of it. When it's in a flabby cone she pushes it against the far wall, towards the

133

kitchen door. She pushes the sofas and table back, and then resumes her dragging of Vic. She thinks, he's heavier than he used to be, and then she laughs at this: because when did she ever drag him?

She thinks about the man in his regiment who saved him, who dragged him away from the IED. He was a hero, taking the brunt. Trying to save the rest of them. Managing to save most of them. He dragged Vic away, to get him to medical help. Beth thinks about contacting him: they could compare notes. She keeps laughing at the idea as she pulls Vic's body along. At the sofa she tries to heave him up, but she can barely do it. She climbs up onto the sofa and pulls. It's a strain, and the sofa threatens to tip onto its back, but she manages it: his shoulders first, then his back – his head lolling the whole time, as if it were unable to support itself – and then his hips. From the floor she picks up his legs and swings them around, and it takes effort, but then he's lying prone on the length of the sofa.

That fucking wheelchair, she says. She stands over him and looks down at his face, which has nothing to it. No expression, not even enough to call it expressionless. It's like he's dead, but the blood still pumps. In coma patients it's said that the eyes can still be seen moving under the lids, proof that they're dreaming. Vic's got nothing. What do I do with you now? she asks.

22

Beth lays out everything she'll need for him on the floor nearest the sofas. She's decided that she needs to impose some order. She's going to try scheduled and strictly adhered-to toilet trips, to prevent accidents. Apparently his bowel and bladder have kept their muscle memory: they're relatively stable.

(He can hold it a few hours, was how the people in the home sold it to her. A few hours, and most of the time he'll make it through the night.)

Still, she's got adult diapers in case she needs them – better that, than clean the sofas and the floors, and she intends to make him sleep in them – and baby wipes. She's got a changing mat, which has blue ducks printed along it. Again, the ignominy will be better than the alternative. She's got rubber gloves and bleach and cleaning products, and she's got the materials for a bed bath, in case she can't get him in and out of the real thing: sponges, bucket-deep troughs for water, flannels and a scrubbing brush that's marked SKINKIND but looks more like something she would use on the floors. She's got pamphlets and leaflets that they gave her at the clinic, containing advice that seems like common sense – preventing bed sores, fungal infections – and telephone numbers to call if she needs help. One of the pamphlets is called YOU, YOUR PARTNER AND THE MACHINE. She flicks through it, and it's full of pictures of loving couples where she cannot tell which one of them is vacant and which one is just doting. She's got most of the food out as well, cans of spaghetti and beans and keep-fresh bread, and bundles of snacks, crisps and nuts and dried fruit. When Vic has a bad day, she doesn't want to starve herself, or him. She doesn't even know what he'll eat, so she's got Ready Brek as well. It's too hot for porridge, she knows – it's winter food, tradition-ally – but she's seen them feed it to people who otherwise have trouble with eating solids in the movies. Food and bottles of water – lots of small ones, that she can keep close. The fridge is full of them. She's got changes of clothes for him, already out and sorted: underwear in one pile, tracksuit bottoms in another, t-shirts in a third. She assumes that she won't need anything else: there's no chance of it getting cold in here. It takes her the rest of the day to make sure everything is in its own pile and accessible, and that she's got enough of everything. She doesn't know how Vic will react when she starts the process, so now, while he's not a danger to anybody, she's taking the chance to prepare herself.

Tablets. She notices that she needs to buy tablets: pain-killers. Nothing insane, just ibuprofen, something like that. In case she needs them, in case Vic needs them. She checks on him, and he looks like he's asleep. She can see his chest rise and fall. She doesn't want to touch him. He might wake up. She gathers her purse and her keys, tucks them into her pockets, and then pulls the front door shut quietly behind her. With any luck she can be gone and back without him noticing.

(There's a second when she imagines him waking up and having some sort of fit. They do that, she's been told. She's only seen one once, and it was terrifying: flailing and howling. She wonders what the neighbours will think: fat woman with all the daughters, holding a glass to the wall to better hear what manner of howling, exactly, and how to define it so that she can whinge about it loudly.)

She goes down the stairs and along the front, almost running, past the restaurants to the little Tesco. She can see that there's a queue for the pharmacy, but it isn't until she gets closer that she realizes it's the boy in front of her, talking to the pharmacist. She can see the back of his shaven head: in thick puckered pink skin is the line of a tattoo running right across. It covers the width of his head: and the hair doesn't grow on it, not even slightly. Not even fluff. She's never noticed it before. She's never been behind him before. She can hear his conversation with the man behind the counter.

What the fuck? he asks. That's fucking real. The man behind the counter has got an ID between his fingers, and he's examining it closely, but he doesn't have to. Even from behind them Beth can see that the plastic is peeling, that it's been tampered with. He can't be older than fourteen. Maybe younger.

Sorry, says the shop assistant. You know the rules, I need to see ID.

This is ID. What the fuck else would you call this? The boy rubs his hands over his head, and then turns around. He glances at Beth. He nods, like he knows her. She knows who I am, she'll tell you I'm not a fucking addict.

Beth's gut lurches. She doesn't know what she'll say.

It's not about somebody vouching for you, the assistant says. It's about the ID. I'm sorry, but please move aside. He lays the ID flat on the table: Beth can see that the picture's grainy, not even a sanctioned photo. Shoehorned in. There are customers waiting.

Fuck right off, the boy says. He picks up the card and waves it in the assistant's face. Fucking real, you cunt. Suddenly, he sweeps his arm across the counter, and the stand of cough sweets, the charity collection box, the contraception/STD leaflets, all go flying across the floor in front of them. I don't need this shit, the boy says. He looks at Beth again, and he kisses his teeth at her. From the front, this close up, he's younger still. Twelve, maybe. Maybe younger. His hair is blond and his eyes are an almost yellow shade of green, and his teeth are ragged enough to need braces, but his skin hasn't yet met acne, and there's not even a hint of stubble across his top lip. There's a threat in the way that he looks at her, but she can't take it seriously. He's still a child.

He marches off towards the door, past the security guard – the boy turns, faces the guard, holds his arms outstretched as he walks past, all pomp that he's seen in some television show about worse places than this – and then out of the shop. The assistant comes round to the front. He falls to his knees in the weariest, most protracted way, which says, I've done this too many times.

This place, he says. He doesn't know Beth, or who she is. He's assuming she'll agree. She squats down and helps him with the leaflets. She scoops them up and puts them on the side.

I've seen him around, she says.

Yeah, he tries it every few weeks.

What's he trying to buy?

Diazepam. He says it's for his dad.

They don't need a prescription for it?

Not since last year. Just ID. He tilts his head back and breathes in. Right. What can I get you?

Ibuprofen, Beth says. A few packets.

He takes the own-brand down from the shelf and lines them up. Three?

Yeah, that should do.

Anything else?

You say I can buy diazepam now?

He sighs. One pack per customer, and you have to have ID. It gets logged.

Okay, Beth says, pulling the ID card from her purse. It's just in case.

Yeah, useful to keep them in the cupboard, he says. She isn't sure if he's joking or not. She waits as he runs it

139

through, then pays for it with cash – she's got a lot in her wallet, to pay for takeaways or whatever when she's knee-deep in rebuilding Vic – and the assistant acts like she's not there, suddenly. She's not sure that she cares.

Back along the path, and she reads the instructions as she walks. Where most medicines are vague and loose, this is insistent. NO MORE THAN FOUR PER DAY. The instructions carry provisos and warnings that the makers of the product are not responsible, etc., etc. TAKE WITH WATER AND FOOD. Beth wonders how good Vic is at eating. She wonders if he'll recognize his surroundings, and if that will have an effect. Maybe he'll reject all this: the flat, Beth, the food and the Machine. Maybe he'll rally against it. She stands at the top of the steps. She didn't need the pills, not really. She looks at the door, her front door, and she puts her hands on the wall of the stairwell.

Come on, she says. The woman with all the children is looking at her from her window. Beth wonders if she saw Vic. She's perpetually spying on everything. What would she think he was? She'd make assumptions. Have they ever even said a word to each other? Beth can't remember. She stands and stares at the building: anything to keep her from having to go back into the flat straight away. When she's in there she has to start, and once she's started she can't leave until this is done. However long it takes, marathon or sprint, she tells herself.

Come on. She walks to her front door – the curtains of the neighbour twitch back to their resting place – and she stands there, as if she's forgotten her keys. She listens for any sound he might be making inside. There's nothing. She puts her hands on the lock, turns the key, opens the door and goes in – just as warm as outside, even with the fans. She shuts the door. She locks it behind her. She might as well.

23

She sleeps the last night she'll sleep before she starts working on him properly: the last night when the flat is quiet, when she's not worried about the implications, or whether he'll make noise or choke on his tongue. She's read, on her forums, that this can be harrowing. She's read reports from husbands, mainly, desperate to get their wives back. How demeaning this is to everybody, how degrading.

The things I've seen, one person wrote. I never thought I'd see them like this.

But it was worth it? another nameless forum-user asked.

Oh g yes. Absolutely. Smiley face.

Beth lies in bed and stares upwards. She can see the flaws in the ceiling, where the upstairs neighbours walk heavily. They have an achingly heavy old pram and they keep their baby in it all the time, pushing her around the flat. The creak of their wheels as they do it is maddening,

142

but it keeps the baby quiet. She barely cries. Beth assumes it's a she. The paint in the ceiling easily cracks, and Beth's sure it's got worse. She would repaint it, if it weren't for Vic, and for the fact that she'll soon be leaving the flat. When they're gone she'll sell the place. Then there'll be no rush, and it won't matter how long it actually takes.

She sits on the lip of the bed. It's just past five, and it's starting to get light outside. Beth remembers when you used to have to change the clocks, and when some mornings it would be dark. Dressing for school in the pitch black, and walking to the bus as the sky turned pink. Now it goes from blue to yellow in gradient shades. Her bedroom door is already open, so that she can hear Vic if he stirs, and to allow a breeze – the thought makes her laugh – to pass through the flat. She pulls on clothes. She stretches in the doorway. No point in dragging this out.

She makes herself a cup of coffee in the percolator, one of the stronger blends, and the noise wakes Vic's body up. Its eyes peel apart.

We're going to get on with this, Beth says. She doesn't care if the body understands: people talk to pets and babies to stop themselves going mad. To reassure themselves that, in some little way or other, a level of understanding will be reached one day. Whether that's returning a thrown ball, or a complex understanding of language. Something.

She has a terrifying thought as she pulls tracksuit bottoms from the pile to dress him in: what if she misses a step? What if there's something intrinsic missing from the Machine? Say, language, or the ability to move. Those

143

parts of the brain. What if she makes Vic again and he's left without anything, trapped inside that shell. She stands and worries about it. The urge to prevaricate passes.

She pulls Vic's hospital-issue trousers to his ankles. The smell hits her. She didn't take him to the loo, her first rule. The one she wasn't going to break. He's been sitting here . . . The nappy he's wearing is soiled yellow and brown, and his thighs – thick, dark hair, coiled up like springs – are slathered. She starts to cry, and she catches herself, raises her hand to her mouth. She goes to the kitchen for the wipes and the nappies, and then decides against them. It's too big a job. Instead she stands at his head and puts both her arms under his, trying to heave him to his feet. He's remarkably compliant today, his muscles helping her slightly on the way. He steps, it seems, or maybe just supports his weight a little, and together they stagger towards the bathroom. Beth doesn't have the strength to help him in, so she coaxes him to sit on the edge of the bath, and then swings his legs over. From there she pushes him to kneeling. She gets a plastic bag and pulls the nappy away, and all the shit tumbles out and into the pink bathtub. She folds the nappy – the mess all over her hands, and the smell rank and stale in the small windowless room – and puts it in the bag, which then sits in the corner of the room. Beth pulls the showerhead down, covering it in the shit from her hands, and puts the taps on, and then she sprays the showerhead at the end of the bath where Vic isn't, washing her own hands off, and the taps, and then cupping the water around the showerhead to clean it down. She imagines herself under it, trying to get herself clean.

144

She doesn't know what temperature to use, so she finds a level where it's hot but not scalding. She sprays it onto the nape of Vic's back and his body doesn't flinch. She doesn't know if it even can. If there's any sort of self-preservation instinct. She read once that we are human because we can't drown ourselves in shallow bodies of water: because something kicks in. If our faces meet water, adrenaline courses through our bodies, making our bodies thrash out, trying to wake us up if we're asleep or passed out. Beth pulls the showerhead around Vic's body and sprays it once, just quickly, onto his face. There's no movement there, and he doesn't flinch. She brings it back to the face, and holds it there. She can't even see him breathing through it. She imagines the water eking its way into his mouth and nose, flooding his lungs. And he wouldn't even try to stop it.

Back to the mess, and she washes it as best she can. She doesn't touch it, and she moves the showerhead underneath him as much as she can. She doesn't want to touch the dirty water that's flowing out, the bigger parts of debris getting worn down in the thick hot mire of the plughole, the smaller particles flushing upwards, creating a ring around the tub. She holds the showerhead right underneath him, pointing upwards. No movement from him still, even like this, even with the water splashing around him. Fighting against him, almost. Beth wants to stop this, but he's not even close to clean. She moves the shower around to his thighs and sprays them down, but it's in the hair, so she has to use her hand. The flat of her palm, the fingers lifted away from the leg. She rubs. And his

145

penis: this shrivelled beetle of a thing, years of being used for nothing but pissing rending it sad and weak. She rubs it with her palm. There was time when that would have been enough, and this would have gone differently. There was a time, she reminds herself, when she wouldn't be cleaning shit off it.

She moves the showerhead to his arse again, and between the fleshy cheeks, trying to get it all. She keeps having to shower down the bath. Clean then rinse. Repeat. Clean then rinse, and he's finally done. She washes down the bath with him in it, to make sure she gets it all – all the dirty water that's somehow found its way between his toes, and into the hair of his shins, and on his fingers. She cleans both the bath and Vic's body, scrubbing away with a sponge that she knows she's throwing away as soon as this is done. She looks at him as she puts the sponge into the same bag as the filthy nappy: he's slumped, penitential on his knees.

From here she knows that she's moving him to the spare bedroom, to the bed next to the Machine. She knows that the treatments will hurt at first. It's a pain that he'll get used to, like having a tooth drilled, once he's got over the shock. She wonders how long it'll take to see the first parts of Vic back inside him. How long before he's recognizable again. She wonders if it will be harder or easier to cause pain to her husband when he's nothing but a void. A shell, like the Machine itself.

She pulls back the duvet cover and smoothes the sheet down, and she moves anything from the bedside table that could cause a problem. That he could lash out at and accidentally connect with. She leans over and presses the Machine's power button, but it's still unplugged: the noise is just the low-level one, the power-saving noise. So she plugs it into the wall and presses the screen again. That initial snarl. The internal fans begin. She can almost see them. Flickering, spinning, covered in dust. The dust flying around inside the Machine. She wonders why so much of it is hollow: when they were designing it, what the space was for. Why they needed so much that had nothing in it.

She remembers something about the brain that she read once, or that she was told: that we only use 20 per cent, something like that. A fraction. So much is untapped. Maybe that's a myth, she thinks. It seems obtuse to have so much waste, when evolution has pushed us to our limits everywhere else. Maybe, she thinks, it's just that we don't understand exactly how it is used. It's vital, that 80 per cent. It has to be.

In the bathroom she tries to work out how to get Vic's body out. He's too slippery so she tries to dry him there and then, rubbing the towel over his back and chest. Then down to his thighs, to get them dry, and his feet, as much as she can. She pictures him slipping in the bath and hitting his head, and then blood everywhere. Imagine cleaning that up, she thinks. She tries to get him to his feet but she can't get traction, so she ends up in the bath behind him, pulling him to his feet again, and then easing him over the edge to the floor, one leg at a time. Something in him wants to preserve himself: he tries to balance when he can. He hasn't completely abandoned that. She gets both his feet to the bath mat and then sets about drying the rest of him. Soon she's on her knees, in front of him, drying his shins. She hasn't been this close to him in years.

She sits him on the toilet.

Go on, she says. Go now. Nothing comes out so she runs the tap. She knows that's enough to set most people off. Go on, she says. Then it happens, a slim trickle of piss out of the end of the penis, just enough to say that he's been. Nothing from the other end. She sets an alarm to go off every four hours, reminding her to take him. She doesn't want any more accidents. The clock lets her know that the whole process took the best part of an hour. She can't do that several times a day.

She dresses him, making him step into the pants and the tracksuit bottoms one leg at a time, then pulling them up for him. And a t-shirt, which is a hassle, getting him to hold his arms up as she slips it on. She thinks that a shirt would have been easier to get him into. Stupid, really, never even crossed her mind. A short-sleeved shirt, easy to get on and off, and to regulate heat. Just open it. She kicks herself. Next time, she thinks, and that makes her laugh. As if.

She walks him to the bedroom. The Machine is whirring, and the sound drowns anything else that might be there. It's like a force field, when you walk through the door. Outside the door there's nothing, the ambient noise of the cats on the Grasslands and the birds that they're desperately hunting, and the crying of the fat woman's daughters and the squeak of the pram wheels from above. In the spare bedroom, with the Machine running, none of that registers. Just that fan, or that power supply, or whatever it is. A buzz, a whirr, a hum. A grinding, almost, if you listen to it for too long; or like anything at all. You can make it into anything. She leads Vic's body in, moving him foot by foot, and he stops in the doorway. He isn't looking at the Machine, but his feet plant themselves. Beth has to bend down and shuffle them forward one by one. She's sure that he's resisting.

Come on, she says. It's not that hard. He seems to be leaning backwards, not enough to fall, but enough to change the balance of his body. And there's a noise, Beth's sure, coming from his throat. She leans in close: a whine. It might have been there all along, she can't be sure, but she can hear it now, now that he's this close to the Machine. He's reacting to it. Please, she says to Vic. She keeps moving him forward. Onto the bed, sitting first, then she gets behind him and pulls him up the bed. The easiest way to move him. Soon he's lying down and in the right place. His body seems tense at first, and then she turns his head, so that he can't see the Machine.

She looks at the clock. She angles it to face them. She's broken this down into sessions in her mind, an hour at a time to start with. Pick a file, work through it chronologically to keep track of it all – they're all about thirty minutes long, and the chronology is a structure she'll need to remember what she's done. Put it back in the order in which it was taken. She'll let it talk him through whatever it says, and she'll let it fill in the gaps. She doesn't have a choice about that part.

149

It was always unnerving, wondering where the memories came from when they hadn't existed before. She thinks about the first time that he remembered something that she didn't: when he spoke about what he had done for his twenty-first birthday. In reality he had been training, at some camp or other. He had called her up, drunk, and told her how much he liked her. He was so drunk, he said, that he wouldn't remember it. He slurred it to her down the phone, and she knew that he was lying. He wasn't as drunk as he claimed. And then, that one day, deep into his treatments, he remembered something completely different. An invented scenario in which they had been on a weekend away together. He asked her if she remembered what they had for breakfast, because he did. Something complicated. So much detail, more than you would normally recall. And none of the connections. And she had to smile and agree, and play along, because those were the rules.

Do we have any photos of that weekend? he asked her, and she said no. She reported it to the company, and they sent her a doctored picture, computer generated.

To help establish the fiction, they said in the attached email. She showed the photograph to Vic and he smiled.

That's the place, he had said. Yeah, wow.

Beth wondered if there was a bank of such material inside the Machine, to help establish these memories. Pictures of places that the creators had visited; or yanked from brochures, pages torn out to feed into the thing. And maybe whole stories, created by a team of writers. In some ways, she thought, this is the newest form of drama: the creation of something from nothing, a play that's made to be performed by couples, where one of them is oblivious to the fact that the other is acting. She wonders how that stuff gets inside the patient's head. If it's just zeros and ones, binary burned in.

She tries not to think about it too much.

Beth pulls the Crown down from the dock. This won't hurt, she says to Vic's body, and she pulls the umbilicus towards him, making it uncoil from where it's withdrawn inside the Machine. She manoeuvres herself to the other side of the Crown – nearer to the Machine's control panel, because this is where she'll need to be – and she leans down to put the Crown onto the head. The panels slide on; a perfect fit. She wonders what the chances are that she and Vic have the same size head. She wonders if she has a large head, or he has a small one. Must be her hair, makes her head seem bigger.

The pads sit exactly on the burned-in scars on his temples, like they'd never left. She's got some lubricant at the side of the bed, because she's read that it can make it easier, so she puts some onto her finger and lifts the pads one by one, smoothing the jelly down onto his skin.

Right, she says. I think we're ready.

Beth presses the Machine's screen and it lights up. She can see the options. REPLENISH had always been intended to help those with dementia. To prompt them back into life: a secondary effect of the Machine's powers, and one that the company behind it saw as a lucrative revenue source. There was a huge untapped market there, and the tech was already available at every hospital around the country. Soon it would be in every home that needed it, that was the plan. Fool-proof tech, software, hardware, and those who had loved ones afflicted by too few memories, or too many, could take care of the situation themselves. That was the pitch they gave to shareholders. Beth watched the conference on the internet, back when she was helping Vic herself. She remembers the applause that the announcement got.

REPLENISH. The Machine's fans kick in at double, maybe triple time, and the thing sounds like it's growling. The whole screen vibrates beneath her fingers, and she's barely able to keep her hand there. Each touch is like pins and needles. The file menu appears and she picks the first.

We're ready? Can you say your name for us? The doctor's voice fills the room. She wonders how the Machine knows to not take that information, to not turn Vic into the doctor. There's a lot she doesn't know. She knows that it works, that's enough.

Victor McAdams.

And could you state your rank and ID number, for the record?

Captain. Two-five-two-three-two-three-oh-two.

Great. Don't be nervous, the voice says to him. He laughs. You know why you're here?

Yes sir.

Don't call me sir. My name's Robert. First name terms here, Victor.

Vic.

Vic.

She's putting him back exactly as he once was. She

reasons that this is going to be easier if there are no more lies: if he's back to being Captain Vic McAdams, scarred in the war, leaving the army by choice. No manufactured photographs. She wants him to be exactly the man he was, and they can go through the process – the healing, the therapists, the PTSD counselling – together, as they should have done in the first place. Can't pretend that something didn't happen. Can't just brush it under the carpet.

On the bed, Vic's body moves ever so slightly, twitches left and right. His face spasms slightly, and his eyes – Beth didn't see them close – dart around underneath his eyelids, as if he's dreaming. There's no sound from him, only the rustling of his arms on the sheet.

So, tell me why we're here, Vic.

Because I've been having trouble sleeping. There was an explosion, an IED, when we were on a mission. Went off when we were doing a sweep on a hospital which looked abandoned, and we were sloppy. I took the brunt, here and here. Beth can picture Vic pointing. He always pointed the same way: to his skull and then to his arm, as if the hole in his head and the tear through his bicep were the same thing, the same level of damage. I returned home, Vic continues, and was sent to recuperate, and then given leave. I was rewarded for saving my squad, they said.

You're a hero.

So they say.

And now you're here?

Because I've been having trouble sleeping. I, ah, replay the event. Dreams and such, and lucid dreaming, you called it.

Don't worry about what I called it.

Fine. Sometimes I'll be sitting with Beth and—

Beth?

My wife. We'll be sitting together watching TV or whatever and I'll zone out, and I'll be somewhere else. And I could swear it. If she tries to wake me up . . . She tried to wake me up a few weeks ago and I hit her. And I knew it was her, but still, I hit her. Not because it was her, but I couldn't stop it. I was somewhere else.

By the end of the hour, Beth's worse than Vic. She had pictured him convulsing, worst-case scenario, and yet Vic's body is relatively still. She's the one who's been affected. Hearing him talk about her like this, and knowing that this is what she's putting back into him. That, when he wakes up, he might be back as he was. Her memories of what happened are different from his, though: because she remembers being there, and how he screamed at night, and sweated, and would cling to her when he woke up; and how he worked out all the time, until his skin was glossy and the lines of his scars throbbed; and how he stood in the bathroom for hours, no exaggeration, and used his finger to trace the lines of the scars, up and down, not even realizing that he was doing it, rubbing the already puckered and tender flesh sore; and how she would serve dinner, putting it onto the table at the same time every day, one square meal a day, and he would pick at it, pushing it away, growing ever thinner, while the lines on his face deepened. It never went so far as to be something you could call a disorder, but it was serious enough that she knew there was something really wrong. And she remembered how they could never watch the television shows that they used to, the series about the anti-terrorist group sidelined in favour of cooking shows and renovation shows and soaps, which he used to hate, but which posed no danger of sparking an episode, as he called them. And how, that first year he came home, fireworks night made him like a scared cat, the first bangs prompting him to turn up the volume of the television, and the second round making him put in headphones, and then the way that he shook slightly on the sofa. And how, at his worst, he drank a lot, becoming a cliché, but he hid it from Beth because, he said – when she finally caught him – he was ashamed, and that he thought he had a problem, and when Beth said that it was because of the war, he shrugged and thought about the next drink. And how he said to Beth that they should try again for a child, and she said no, because this was no environment to bring a child into. And how he saw things and remembered things that never happened, long before the Machine got involved, when they argued or reminisced (which was all they ever seemed to do), and Beth would at first contradict him and tell him that he was insane, but then soon, because it was easier, began to placidly agree, and let him have his way. And how he didn't hit her just once, lashing out in confusion about who she was, but how he hit her a few times. He didn't do it like an abuser, though: no trying to avoid visible bruises. He got angry and he struck whatever was closest. Four times, before he hit her, it had been the walls of their house. His fists left indents and cracked thick paint. She had been next, the first time because she was

155

close, and she was asking him to get help because of how little he'd been sleeping. The marks underneath his eyes were like bruises on his cheekbones, or warpaint in some action movie. The second and third times were when they were in bed, and he woke up, and then he swung his fists. The fourth time was when Beth gave him the leaflet that the doctor had left them about the Machine, and begged him to consider it seriously. After that, she told him that there wouldn't be a fifth time.

You hurt me again and this is over, so you have to think about that. What's most important to you? Pride, or whatever's left of this?

Beth takes the Crown off his head and puts it back in the dock, and presses stop on the Machine. It winds down: the sound of an oven cooling, the clicks of an engine in the cold. New noises that she's never heard before and can't explain. Looking at Vic's body, Beth sees that it needs water. She hadn't seen the sweat during the process, but it's suddenly there, seeping out underneath him, sinking into the mattress.

You need a towel as well, she says. She goes to the kitchen and gets a little bottle from the fridge and a towel from the pile she's got there, all cheap, bought from the pound shop and designed to be thrown away if need be. Not made for washing; she suspects that they wouldn't last a proper spin cycle. She uses the towel first, wiping down his chest and then pulling him up, her arm behind his shoulders, rubbing his back down. She props her body behind him and unfolds the towel, laying it flat on top of the sheet. Then she pushes him back down. Relax, she says. She catches herself, talking to it like it's a sentient being. Like it's a him, and can understand her. It can't, not yet.

She stands in the kitchen and opens one bottle of water and drinks it straight down, gulping it. She gasps in between gulps. She wonders at what point he'll be recognizable again: when Vic will start to seep back into his body. The Machine contains all that is left of who he once was. Already it's processed his story, the speech-to-text system inside it turning his spoken, quivering memories into data and patching them. Filling in the cracks in his story. Somewhere, inside the Machine, are the exact constituents of what – who – Vic will be. Like a version of him, somewhere, only maybe not arranged in the proper order, and therefore not conscious, and not alive. The God-botherers argue that the soul is a solid thing, a distinct entity, and that when you tamper with it, you destroy it entirely. A soul that's broken is no soul at all. By that logic, Vic's soul is simply waiting to be reassembled. What is it, before it becomes whole? Before it works again?

With one bottle done and crushed in her hand, and thrown into the recycling bag, she opens another. She hadn't noticed how hot she was. And listening to him, being in that room, has given her the start of a headache – are there fumes, from the Machine? Or is it just the heat of the fans, the hard drives, the memory inside the thing burning its way out? Not serious enough to pop the ibuprofen open – she worries that she won't have enough. They weren't even meant for her, but for Vic.

For when it starts to hurt him. She eyes the diazepam and hopes that she won't have to use them. Maybe this will go easier than she's been fearing.

He still hasn't moved when she gets back into the bedroom. She goes to the Crown, and feels that the pads are still wet with the lubricant, so she puts it straight back onto his head. She knows that listening to the playback of the voices aloud is an indulgence, totally unnecessary. It's something to make it easier for her. What's important is the code that's being buzzed into him by the Machine. But it makes her happier, to hear his voice. To picture that this is how he's being rebuilt, piece by piece, slotting together like Lego.

We're ready, Beth says. She presses play.

Captain Victor McAdams.

Okay, Vic. Want to tell me about your last exercise? As many details as you can remember.

No. Not especially, Vic says. Beth can hear the smirk in his voice. He could be such a shit when he wanted to be. Fine, he says, breathing out. A huff, almost. We were somewhere I'm not allowed to say—

You're allowed to say here.

I'm not.

This is between us.

So it can be between us and I won't say the name of the place.

Do you think that this is all a trick?

You're not army. Whatever you're cleared for, I don't know. So. You want the rest?

The doctor acquiesces. Please.

We were there, checking out a hospital, and there were only three days left before we moved to the next area. So it's routine, place has been cleared out. Should be easy. And there's a school that we checked, right next to this hospital. Hospital used to be a block of flats, but they converted it into whatever. School was empty, and we did it, routine. So we got slack. Beth hears him grit his jaw. His voice tightened when he did it: a level of audible stress. The recording continues: When we got to the hospital – and you have to remember, these things take like half a day to do a sweep, so it's not something we breeze in and out – we were sloppy. No contact in a week. No shots fired in even longer, maybe three or four weeks. So that meant we were sloppy.

Okay.

On the bed, Vic's body quivers and shakes. His hands pull themselves closed, making balled fists. His fingernails, which need cutting, dig into his palms. His toes curl over, the way they used to when he came during sex, his feet forming exaggerated arches, his legs twitching.

We went through and I was taking point, and I didn't see it until too late. Something I triggered that was going to go off, and we were piling through the doorways because we were complacent. I suppose. So when I saw the flash – they do this little flash first, like the ignition on a boiler, the pilot light, you know – and I saw it and I thought, Well, fuck, this is my fault. I take this one.

That's it?

Made sense. I was sloppy. I triggered it, so it was mine to take. And that means I got like this. There's the noise of him moving, in the room. I got like this, and it blew shrapnel here and here.

Beth can see him, slightly re-enacting his movements in twitches and gestures. Remembering it exactly. He was so exact, such a creature of habit. Of repetition.

And that's all I remember, until they dragged me off. I woke up in the helicopter but I don't remember that part. Apparently I was awake, I don't know. And then I was home. I remember seeing Beth when I got back, because she was waiting for me to wake up. That was about two weeks later, when I woke up properly. They'd operated already and everything. Taken the shrapnel out. And there was Beth, waiting for me.

Beth remembers it as well, but she can also remember those two weeks in the hospital, weeks that he has no recollection of, when she stood by this enormous incubator-like device that was keeping him alive, as they pulled the shrapnel from him over the course of two operations. They told her that he was lucky to be alive. She prayed that he would make it awake intact.

Vic's voice tells the rest of the story to the doctor, and to Beth, and they both listen. Here, Beth finds herself sitting on the end of the bed, near to Vic's feet. They twitch and curl up seemingly with every punctuation point of Vic's speech. After a while, Beth puts her hand onto his right shin. She does it to steady them – to let him know that there's somebody there, as if that might help – but she finds that she sort of likes it.

She imagines her husband trickling back into this body. She fantasizes that he is filling up, from the bottom of his

body first, like water into a jug, and she's touching the
only part that might now be him.

24

Vic's cough is what wakes her. She's asleep in her bedroom, amongst the chaos of the vacuum-packed clothing bags that she's pulled out of the Machine's room to make it hospitable, and she's dreaming of something that she can no longer remember when she wakes up, but it's there, insistent, almost itching for her to find it. Then the cough, and it hacks through the mugginess of the flat. It's the first noise that she's heard Vic make since she brought him back, beyond the mild whimpers and whines that she thinks were involuntary; but here his body is responding to something. She gets out of bed. Half past four. She gets a bottle of water, even as the cough continues, and she swigs from it first. It isn't until she gets into the Machine's room that she notices the cough properly. She doesn't know how much these things are or can be personal, but she recognizes it. It's Vic's cough: not just the hacking reaction of a dry throat in a random body.

She helps him sit up slightly more, and lifts the bottle to his mouth. He reaches for it, tongue out, desperate, and she pours it faster than she should, drizzling the water down his chest and into the sweat of his chest hair.

Come on, she says. That's it. He drinks most of the bottle, gulping it down.

Thank you, he says.

What? Beth stands up. She stands back. What did you say? He doesn't move, doesn't look at her. His eyes are open, focused on the ceiling, on the veins in the paint. Say that again. Vic? Vic. She says his name repeatedly, as if one of the versions of it might make sense to him: one with a particular tone in her voice, or a particular lilt. She draws closer again, kneels on the bed and looks into his eyes. They don't search around or try to avoid hers, but they're not with her either. Somehow vague. She looks at his lips. Thank you, she says. Say thank you. But he doesn't say anything.

Okay, she says. She stands again. She runs her hands over her head, and she looks at the Machine. It's plugged in and switched on already, but she could swear that she unplugged it. It's possible that she got it wrong, just as it's possible that she didn't hear Vic thanking her, in his voice, with his polite tone. Nothing casual there. She presses the screen. It's as it was yesterday, as she left it. Five recordings down, one after the other, and then repeated. Blocks of five, at an hour each. Five-minute break between each, for toilet and drink, then an hour's break for lunch, then the whole thing repeated. She doesn't know if the information presented to Vic through the

Crown is the same, though. She doesn't understand the technology at all, even though she's read everything she can about the Machine.

They started with slugs, she knows: removing the part of a slug's memory that told it where food was. Slugs rely on experience to drive them towards whatever it is that they're looking for. They remember. Scientists took that out and made them forget, and the slugs were lost. It wasn't lobotomizing them: it was a targeted jolt. Proper science. An injection, and electricity, like a lightning bolt that only damaged the part you wanted it to. And after that they moved on to other animal trials, nothing cruel about it, because you're making something forget the inane. Nothing important. Brain memory is different from muscle memory: even down to the actual filing system of how we remember. And then on to humans, and the introduction of the Machine, because the power needed to process it all was tremendous. In the earliest trials, the Machine occupied an aircraft hangar. There are pictures of it on the internet, this hulking thing that went back and back, filling the space like the first computers, a room full of wires and chipsets. They took memories away from people, and they discovered that they could also jolt those memories back: that the Machine burned bridges, but could also repair them, in a way. That's what Beth understands: where it came from. They made the technology useable, put it out there before it should have been – when there were no limits to the havoc it could wreak – then tried to backtrack by imposing guidelines, dressing the Machines up as handy household appliances. But it was already over.

164

Beth worries that she's pushing him too hard. That was how she got into this: rushing. She was in charge of his treatments in the latter days, because they wanted to remove the doctor from the equation. It was important that Vic ultimately forgot that he'd even had treatments in the first place. The last day of any patient's experience was to have that part erased, wiping down the surfaces and locking the door on your way out. So Beth was in charge, and she was meant to take her time with the last few stages; ten stages, that was all. But she rushed it, and then . . . That's been hanging over her for years: not knowing if Vic would have been left broken without her help, or if she was the catalyst. One treatment a week, she was told: and she condensed them into a fortnight.

Now, the instructions on the internet forums tell her that it doesn't matter. That the pace at which memories are put back in is at the user's discretion. She wonders who these people are, on the forums. What they actually know. The creators of the Machine are taking so long to work this through themselves, to reach an actual solution and make it public, only promising things in press conferences with their performing test cases. And the guerrilla underground has taken control instead. She laughs, to think of herself as that: part of a movement defying logic, and science, and time. At the forefront of something. She laughs because of how she got here.

It's nearly morning, she says. You need to use the toilet. He's made it through the second night dry, apart from the sweat. Tomorrow night she'll give him a sheet instead of the duvet. She didn't even think, because the duvet was what they had in their old house, and the decoration, the furniture. All of it imported to make this bedroom feel as much like their old room as possible, with the exception of the Machine, filling that wall, in case that helps to nudge his memory even slightly. She helps him up and leads him through. His walking seems better. More focused, somehow. She sits him on the toilet and stands outside the room.

The day I watch you take a shit is the day I know this marriage is over, Vic joked once. But it wasn't really a joke, she didn't think.

Back to the bedroom, she says, and she would swear that he leads slightly: that he's the one who instigates that first assisted step, and that he knows the direction, that she doesn't have to twist his body to meet it. He kneels onto the bed as well, she thinks, and when she goes to turn his body to lie down he doesn't feel as heavy as he did the day before. Maybe just a night's sleep, and Beth is less tired herself. She takes the Crown down and puts it on him, and the black marks are back, she notices. Not that they ever left, but they faded, like the way that bruises fade, only they never completely abandoned his scalp; and now they seem brighter. Which makes sense, because they're always going to be tender, Beth supposes. She notices that the Crown has pushed up some of his hair into a tuft; she smoothes it down.

She presses the button and gets the next recording playing. REPLENISH, like a shampoo, like an energy drink. Vic's voice is all she hears. She almost entirely blocks the doctor out now, as if he's not important. She thinks that that must be what makes him good at his job: his ability to fade into the background. Vic talks about what made him want to get into the army, and how his father pushed him. Background experiences that made him who he was. Who he will be.

With the first shift over, Beth gives him food. This morning it's soggy cereal, corn flakes left to melt in milk. Beth has to lift the spoon and open his mouth with her finger and slide the food off and onto his tongue, and then close his mouth, and he swallows of his own accord, an exaggerated motion in which he seems to tense every muscle in his jaw and neck in order to make it all go down. Then they repeat the process, so eating the bowl of cereal takes nearly half an hour. It's the longest break he'll get before lunch.

The second session begins, and the playback follows on from the last. Beth sits and listens and looks around the room, and suddenly the hour is gone. She finds herself staring at the photographs that she's put in cheap frames on top of the chest of drawers; or at Vic's body; or at the bowl of potpourri. She can't remember how long ago she put it in the room, but it still smells. The sort of thing her mother would have done. She's looking at the Crown on his head, listening to nothing, it seems, thinking about her own headache – how these sessions take it out of her as well, and that's important, that the partner understands and feels it – when the doorbell interrupts.

Who's that? Beth asks, a jerk reflex. Asking Vic that question. Something she hasn't had the chance to do in years; he always used to be the one who opened the door to people. She would always tell him to go and do it, and assume he would know who it was before he even looked. As if he was always expecting somebody.

The bell rings again, and it's followed by a knock. Three knocks, rapid and harsh. Beth stays where she is, staying quiet. Nobody ever comes to see her. Might be that it's the neighbour with the girls. Another series of raps on the door, and Beth moves to the doorway of the bedroom to get a better look – to hopefully see a shape through the pebbled glass at the top, and somehow recognize the person from that vagueness.

The letterbox flaps. Beth? It's me. Laura's voice. I know you're in there, Beth. Please answer the door, she says. You don't have to do this alone.

Beth stands and holds her breath, and she completely forgets that Vic is behind her with the Crown still resting there on his head.

Beth, Laura says again, but she lets the letterbox snap back into place, and her shadow – just a shape – moves away, and down towards the window that looks into the living room. The curtains are closed so she can't see anything, but her shape lingers as she tries to peer in.

Beth's phone rings: the house line, because that's the only one that Laura's got.

Come on, she hears Laura saying through the window, which is cracked slightly open at the top to let the air in. Answer, answer. She paces and lets it ring, and Beth stands completely still and there's no noise apart from the roar of the Machine, but that must be too quiet for Laura to hear, even though inside the bedroom it sounds like a gale, when you really focus on it.

The phone rings for a minute and then stops, and there's a few seconds where Beth wonders if she's gone – Laura's silhouette is nowhere to be seen – before a note is pushed through the letterbox, and then she walks past the window.

Beth goes and picks up the note, which is a single folded piece of paper, but pre-written, prepared, as if this – her not answering or being out, one or the other – was an eventuality Laura had anticipated.

Beth, I came to offer you my shoulder and my advice. I can help you through this. You shouldn't make these decisions on your own. Call me. Laura.

I'm not on my own, Beth says aloud.

25

Beth carries the note around with her as if it has a special meaning, but keeps it either in her hand (where it scrunches in on itself) or in the back pocket of her shorts (where it attempts to smooth itself out again). She thinks about it as she feeds Vic his lunch of apples and pineapple and tinned peaches, mixed down in the processor, like this is some fad diet, and when they resume their sessions in the afternoon she sits and reads it over as Vic listens to himself talking about his training. These sessions are the worst: the ones that have only to do with his army background, that she listens to because they're there.

Am I being selfish? she asks him in their fourth session of the afternoon, pausing the playback for a second. Would you even want this, if it was offered to you?

The Machine's noise is something that should be ruinous. It should destroy her, to hear it, because it's so pervasive and so intense. There's no escaping it when the

Machine is working, or even when it's idle. And she's felt it shaking a few times before, but now, as she sits at the foot of the bed, she could swear that the vibrations from it are coming through the carpet. She climbs off as Vic talks about the speed with which he can strip and clean and rebuild a rifle, and she lies on the floor with her head on its side to see if the carpet is actually trembling, as she suspects. She feels it in her face: that slight tickle, like pins and needles.

When the fifth session is over she takes the Crown off and puts it back in the dock. She doesn't unplug the Machine, because the hum when it's on standby is almost comforting, she thinks. She wonders if Vic likes it. If it's reassuring. She hauls him to the bathroom again, and makes him a dinner of spaghetti hoops on two slices of mushed-up bread, and puts him to bed, making sure that the bed is dry (which it is, as the heat pretty much ensures that anything left for half an hour bakes itself dry). She gives him water, but not too much.

Shower in the morning, she says. He shuts his eyes without her having to tell him to, but that might just always be the way he's done it. When he's tired, he knows.

She sits on the sofa with Laura's note in her hand and pulls the laptop out and starts to flick through her usual forums. She searches to see if there's anything about Machines vibrating, and if that's a side effect of the custom firmware. She's become an expert on these things, she thinks. Ten years ago, firmware wouldn't have even been a word to her. When that search throws up nothing she searches for threads on The Positives, the name they use for those carers who've successfully brought people back from vacancy. There are six on her main forum, the one where she actually has a username and a login, and they were the only six people people she knew of who had managed to get hold of Machines. She was lucky number seven. The firmware was all programmed by the first one, and he shared the wealth. Swedish, lost his wife in the same war as Vic fought in, and he was desperate, because he didn't have money. And their government banned the Machines; his chance of anything happening of its own accord was slim to none. She sends him a question.

How long did it take for your wife to become herself again? (Recognizably.)

Beth presses SEND and waits for a reply.

The users of the forum are dedicated and passionate, and they're all willing to help. The users say that you don't know what families of the vacant are going through until you go through it yourself; the only people who can help are those who feel your pain. It's a motto of the forum-goers. Beth sits and rubs the sides of her head, where the headache has set in – like spending too much time near a photocopier, and so intense, concentrating on this, putting all the tension into her head and her jaw, making her bite down on nothing, making her tense her entire face over and over, every muscle in it – and she's thinking about the ibuprofen when the reply comes.

Hi there! It was exactly two weeks after we started. We took it easy because I was sacred.

Beth thinks that he means scared, but she could be wrong.

I did not want to hurt her. So it was two weeks before she said something that was exactly her. But she made noise that she was getting better before that, and so I persevered. Are you going to be hopefully joining the club of the rest of us? Because we can give you any more help, if you need it. Just say the ask. Smiley face.

Beth doesn't reply. She thinks about it – she types a reply, which she deletes twice – and then shuts the laptop. She still has the note, and she reads it again: Laura's handwriting, which now looks over-rehearsed to her, as if she wrote this once on another sheet and copied it out, like writing letters to relatives when she was a child. And the words: suggesting that she needed help or advice. That she wasn't entirely sure of what she was doing. It's an intrusion by somebody on the outside, someone who was barging in where she wasn't wanted. She hasn't been through this pain, and she can't understand it, so she can't expect to help.

Beth puts the TV on and then mutes the sound and leans back. She shuts her eyes. That's all it takes.

173

26

The sky crackles.

It wakes Beth up because it's so noisy, like firecrackers snapping away. The television is halfway through a Japanese cartoon, but that doesn't give her a time to use as reference. The clock says that it's just gone midnight, which means she's barely been asleep any time at all. It's so dark in the flat, only the TV is giving off any light at all.

Snap, snap, snap.

She stands up and stretches, and her head feels clear enough, but the air in the flat is horrible. Hot, not just warm, and nearly wet. On the rare occasions that they have storms, they're perfect for clearing out everything. Like a reset button, and they leave the ground smelling – what was it that Laura called it? Petrichor? Petrichlor? – and the sky clear. And everything's cooler for a few days. Not long enough to get used to it, but in the same way

174

that people used to celebrate the British summer. They get out and enjoy it while it lasts. It's no longer something that everybody has to fight against.

Beth walks to the window and pulls back the curtain. The rain hasn't started yet, and she knows what she expects to see, but it's different. The sky isn't just black: intermittently a filthy grey shade, lit by the lightning. There are other people outside, and in the distance she can see the sun buried underneath the clouds. It's 11 a.m. The sky crackles again, and the lightning rushes across it, smacking into itself. It's bad special effects from a science-fiction movie. It's one of those gadgets where the electricity is attracted to somebody's palm resting on the glass. It rolls through the clouds – like horses through waves, Beth thinks, which she remembers from somewhere, but she's not sure where – and it seems to leap before it dissipates. She forgets about everything else: Vic, the Machine, her own life. She opens the front door and breathes it in, the damp, the sense that it's about to happen. Everybody senses it.

And then it rains. It thuds in single drops first, thwap, down onto the concrete, and they're almost big enough to make their own puddles. They're as warm as everything else. Thwap, thwap. More of them. Each of the residents of the estate stays under cover, even her next-door neighbour, who hides indoors as her daughters run out, well past when they should be asleep. After the drops comes the flood, a gush of water coming down on them. Heavier than Beth's ever seen before, she thinks. Nobody talks: down in the courtyard people stand huddled. It seems almost reverential. The rain pours and then the lightning comes, and all across the sky it can be seen, ripping down from the sky, smacking onto buildings. The lights are on in all the flats one minute, and the next they're gone. The power tears out through the entire estate, and as far into the distance as Beth can see from the balcony: no lights down at the shops, no lights on the estate past that, or the houses that run around the edge of the island further down. Total blackness, apart from the lightning.

Snap.

Beth rushes back inside to Vic and the Machine, and she doesn't know what she expected, but it's still making that low-level hum, and it's still going. It's still plugged in and she doesn't know what she expected, because that battery keeps on going, and now she wonders why everybody else doesn't hear it: when the rest of the ambient noise is gone and all that's left is the Machine and the light from it and that noise, which comes from somewhere at its back, in the dark, somewhere that she knows doesn't have a speaker and shouldn't be able to make noise. And what if Laura is right? With her protesting and her crying and her berating and praying to God? What if this is as unnatural as she's suggesting? She reaches out slowly, tentatively, and she presses the screen – Vic doesn't stir, completely knocked out by the day – and it lights up, and the light fills the room.

How are you still working? she asks it. That rumble, like the thunder itself. Roll of noise; pause; flash of light. She's terrified, but this is what she wanted. She wanted Vic back. Somehow she's getting him.

176

There's time to do another, she thinks. She's awake, and she's got power. One more couldn't hurt. She pulls the Crown down and rests it on Vic's head. She wonders if it works when he's asleep; if anybody's ever tried it. She could be the first, a pioneer.

She presses play. Outside, the lightning fizzes.

27

He's totally compliant when she takes him to the bathroom and he uses the toilet and then she puts him into the shower. Again, Beth thinks that he's making this easier on her, although she can't tell whether it's an effect of the Machine and he's becoming more himself, this quickly, this efficiently; or whether it's just that the body is helping more, as if it's getting to know her. But he works with her, and he lifts his feet more, and in the shower he isn't as curled up. When she lifts his arms to wash underneath them, to soap up his armpits – the sweat has settled into his skin – he holds them aloft briefly. She finds the process much more appealing: this is nearly her husband again, and it's nearly her husband's body that she's touching.

The flat is cooler than it was, because it's happened: the sky has cleared. It's instantly less muggy. Beth looks outside and it's bright but clean. Something fresh in the air: that smell.

She puts a new sheet on the bed as Vic sits crouched in the bath. The breeze – there's a breeze! – that comes through the flat is wonderful, even though it's still warm. Beth leaves Vic almost naked as she lays him down on the bed, only underwear protecting his modesty. She pulls the Crown down and presses the screen, and it's ready and waiting, exactly where she left off. The Machine's start is like a yawn, a stretch, preparing itself for what it has to do. She lubes the pads and presses them onto his head, and she pushes the button. He flings himself upwards suddenly, arching his back. He swipes with his arms at his head.

No, Beth says. Don't. Vic stops swiping at her and knocks the Crown off his head instead. He opens his mouth and noise comes out, a blast of something atonal, barely recognizable. It's not something she's heard before, and it doesn't stop, even as his body bucks and his jaw moves between open and closed with a jarring sharpness, and his tongue pokes out, the muscle seeming to push itself to breaking point in an attempt to get out of his mouth. Please stop the noise, she says, and she rubs his head – the lubricant smearing under her touch on his temples – and that seems to calm him a little. Even then the convulsions (because that's what Beth thinks that they are) continue, and she rubs more and makes a 'Shush' noise, over and over. He's shaking, so she moves closer and puts her arms around him. She leans in. Please, she says. He resists but she gets close enough to properly hold him, hooking her arms behind him and closing her hands together to keep purchase.

179

She notices that the Crown is dangling down from the Machine, is tilting onto the floor. And then she notices that his voice, Vic's voice, is playing.

You want to know what I wore at our wedding? he asks. Why does that matter?

Just tell me, the doctor says. You know how this works.

Fine. I wore full regimental dress. Everybody did, all the wedding party. My ushers all did, because they were all from my unit.

What are their names?

The ushers?

He reels them off. That part had to be taken. It devastated Beth at the time. The photographs that got doctored: of Vic in a normal suit, like any other wedding. Who is he, and what did he do? Nothing to indicate that, because he's in a suit. No ushers, because they were all in uniform. People taken away from him, just like that. A click of a mouse. Beth wonders, as she clings to him, why they ever thought that it was a good idea, or that it was even fair.

That's what this is like, the forum-user wrote. It's like, we made a decision and it was a bad one, so now we're putting things back the way that they were, through magic or whatever.

Beth thinks about that: about how she's only undoing five years of hell, and innumerable hours of pain. She holds Vic and wonders if he'll thank her for this: and if she'll tell him the absolute truth about how he ended up here. That it was her decisions, not his, not theirs, and her eagerness to push him. Because she thought that he was so strong.

180

After a while the noise ends, and Vic's body's mouth closes.

Okay, Beth says. She stands and lets him lie down. When she lifts the Crown from the floor she's sure that his body flinches, even though he's not looking towards her and the Machine. I won't, she says. We can have a break.

She goes to the living room and turns the television on, and puts the volume up. She finds it hard to hear what's being said, people arguing, getting up from their chairs and threatening violence, waving their fists. She realizes that she's left the Machine on. Vic is still speaking. How did she not notice? It's so loud, and the noise of the Machine itself. She goes back to the Machine and is about to press stop when the recording ends. It's been an hour since it started, and the time's passed so quickly. All spent cradling him.

Beth runs the taps and wets her face, and then moves a kitchen chair into the widest path of the breeze. She leans back and lets it brush over her wet cheeks and lips. In the corner of her eye she sees the tablets stacked on the work surface: the ibuprofen first, but then the diazepam.

Not yet, she says. She's shocked at how weary she sounds. How much this is taking out of her, as well as him. She doesn't move. She sleeps.

When she wakes up she finds him waiting for her, where he was. The Crown slides straight on again. She tightens the straps, and fastens the jaw-strap, because she doesn't want it being knocked off. The Machine leaps at her palm's touch, and that vibration starts up again. She remembers

181

the way that the ground shook during the flooding, and this is like that, after it finished: feeling uneasy on your feet, the trembling that runs through your legs and for a second you don't know if it's nerves or actually something physically happening to the ground, or if the two are even any different. She chooses the same passage as the morning's attempt, and she doesn't look at Vic's body as she presses play. She gets close to the Machine, hands on either side of the screen. And she leans in, so that her head is almost resting on the black metal above the screen, propping her up, because the tremors run right through her. Everything in her body shakes, and she can, for a second, feel all of her bones: big and little, teetering against their connections, rattling in their sockets. She can't hear anything past the noise of the Machine, and past the clatter that's now inside her own head. As if this pain – because that's what it's heading towards, clinging to this thing – might be some sort of penance for pretending that, behind her, there isn't her husband's body, writhing and bucking on the bed, making a noise that sounds like something almost digital, unnatural and blunt. And this is just the tip of it: if it hurts now, it will only hurt her more as he becomes more himself. And especially as he becomes more able to vocalize. Will she have the strength to continue when he's able to ask her to stop? When it's his voice, his personality, half-formed?

She shuts her eyes, and that's nearly enough to make this bearable: when all that she can hear is the Machine and that's all that she can feel, even as her eyes vibrate behind her eyelids, this seems less real.

The first audio cycle ends, and the Machine quietens. Vic's body doesn't, so Beth presses play on the next file. No break; no time to reconsider.

28

She thinks that it could be a dream, but it's so vague that she can't tell. Vic says her name, over and over again. Muted and not quite right. The sounds are there but the mouth isn't forming them quite properly. It wakes her and she rushes through, and there's Vic, sitting on the edge of the bed.

Beth, Beth, Beth, he says. He rubs his face with his hands.

Oh my God, Beth says, and she puts her arms around him. She doesn't know how much of him this will be, and she could pull away and that noise might start again. He says her name seven times and then stops, and starts crying. She tries to soothe him, and in a second he's asleep. She lies him down and watches him. She lies next to him, in the nook made by the curve of his sleeping body, and she sleeps herself.

This could all be a dream, she thinks as she drifts off.

When she wakes up she's in the room with him, but the Machine is on, and it's playing; Vic's speaking from another time entirely. Something from much later on in his treatments. She keeps her eyes shut, because she's asleep, she tells herself. She doesn't need to wake up yet. She doesn't need to know what's happening.

Word association, the doctor says.

Okay. Then they do it, a series of words that are connected and trite when Beth hears them back. All so obvious.

Morning, the doctor says.

Sun. The sun, Vic replies.

Bullet.

Pain.

Beth opens her eyes and sees the Machine's screen lit up, playing back. It's been activated: REPLENISH is illuminated. She's on the bed. The Crown is on the pillow above her head; she looks up, peers up, and there it is, blinking. She sits up – Vic doesn't seem to notice – and she pushes the pillow away.

I didn't do this, she says. I didn't take this down. She looks at Vic and grabs his arm and shakes him. Was this you? she asks. Did you get up? Did you do this? He doesn't make a noise, but the Machine does.

It changes pitch. It shifts upwards, less industrial turbine, more washing machine or dishwasher, something normal and practical and household. Only louder. So much louder. Beth picks up the Crown, holding it between two fingers. The Crown itself shakes. She hadn't realized that. Maybe that's what hurts Vic: maybe it's too tight on his head.

She slides it back onto the dock, and the voice persists.

Stop it, she says. She presses the screen but it keeps playing, so she doesn't even fight it. She pulls the plug. It keeps playing. Fuck off, she says. She hits the screen.

Death.

Parents.

She shouts at the Machine, which wakes Vic up – his eyes peeling open, that's it – and then hits the screen again.

I'll fucking break you, she says. Stop playing that.

It stops. The screen goes black. Vic shuts his eyes.

Beth paces the flat in the darkness and then goes to her room. She shuts the door almost all the way, and then she lies on her bed. In the darkness she counts to fifty. Something that she learned from Vic, an army trick.

When stress descends, count back down, he had told her.

From ten? she had asked.

God no. If counting from ten solves it, it wasn't proper stress in the first place. Fifty. A hundred. A thousand.

That's what you do?

Yeah.

How long does it take?

If I make it to zero it means I'm going to sleep, he had said.

She counts. Somehow she sleeps.

29

When Beth wakes up, the mugginess is back. The storm did its job clearing everything up for a day, but it was just an aberration, and she's got a headache that suggests tension in her jaw, grinding of her teeth, a bad night's sleep. She stands up but the flat's swimming, and she steadies herself on the dresser and then the doorway. The door is open; she only dreamed she closed it. That's what it was. Unless he says her name, it was a dream.

In the Machine's room, peering through the pain and the blurriness of being awake, she sees Vic on the bed, the Machine back on standby, its noise back to low-level ambient, like a normal computer left on overnight. The Crown is on the dock, and there's no evidence she was ever even in here.

She wakes up Vic and helps him to his feet.

Say my name, she says, but he doesn't. He looks at her, though: and he makes eye contact for a second. He turns

187

his head away then and he flaps his jaw open and shut. He's more animated than she's seen him in the last five years. It feels like we're getting somewhere, doesn't it? she asks.

She takes him to the bathroom and pulls his trousers down before making him sit, only he's got an erection. She hasn't seen him like this in years, and she knows it's nothing – blood and muscle, involuntary, nothing to do with her – but she doesn't want to be faced with it now, and she doesn't know how to make it go away.

We'll have to wait, she says. She knows that if he pisses now it'll go everywhere – he used to apologize for it when he would wake up like this before, saying that he couldn't control it, that it wasn't his fault, that she should blame whoever came up with such a shitty design in the first place – so they stand there as nature does its thing. Minutes, and she doesn't look. He's not Vic again yet. She waits.

Afterwards, she puts him onto the bed. The writhing starts before she's even turned the Machine on: as soon as the Crown goes onto his head he kicks out his legs and struggles. She thinks about binding his arms. This needs to be easier. She takes the branded, boxed pestle and mortar from the cupboard – a wedding gift, never used until now, something that they never understood when herbs and spices were so easy to buy pre-ground – and she tips a couple of the diazepam tablets and a couple of ibuprofen into the mortar. She crushes them together, round and round. She's left with a thin white dust, so thin that it could almost just spill into the air. Like talc. She takes a small bottle of water from the fridge and unscrews the lid and tips the contents of the mortar bowl into it, then puts the lid on and shakes it. She stands by the fridge, shaking it.

She hopes that she's doing the right thing. Would he be happy with her for this? Vic didn't like tablets. Didn't like painkillers, or anything that dulled him.

I like knowing exactly what's wrong with me, he would say. Then, after the war, he no longer had a choice. Would he thank her for this?

Beth holds the bottle to his lips and helps tilt his head back. He drinks in gulps, no finesse. She's the one who stops it from dribbling down his face, manoeuvring the bottle to almost make a seal.

There, she says. She crushes the bottle and puts it into the recycling bin and then stands in the kitchen, to wait. She doesn't want to wait in there, because the Machine is waiting as well. The power is all back on – must be back on across the whole estate – so she opens the fridge and smells the milk, to check it's okay. It smells fine. She puts the coffee machine on and makes herself breakfast: yoghurt in a bowl, a few spoonfuls of sugary jam on top. It's not exactly appealing, but her stomach growls in acceptance. She's eating the last few mouthfuls, one eye on Vic's body, which has slumped down again of its own accord, when there's a knocking on the door.

Beth, comes Laura's voice through the letterbox. Beth, I know you're in there. I can hear you, and the lights are on. Beth, come on. Answer the door.

Beth stays completely still. She puts the spoon down

as softly as she can manage, in the bowl of yoghurt rather than on the side, to minimize noise, and she shuts herself down: breathing as quietly as possible.

Beth. Come on. The only words that have been spoken to her in four days, by a woman on the other side of the door, and they are the same words that Beth has been saying to herself. Beth, come on. What are you doing? Have you got him in there with you?

Beth watches the shape of Laura moving from frame to frame, from the frosted glass of the door to the clarity of the curtained window, as if she's nothing more than a shadow. She raps on the doorframe and the window. She flaps the letterbox and her eye peers through. She says the same things over and over again.

I'll wait, she says. I've got all day. It's my summer as well.

You have to go home, Beth thinks. You're not even from the island.

I'll sit here and wait for you to open the door, because you have to, sooner or later. She's not joking. The sound of her slumping down against the door comes in, and the sound of her opening something, chocolate or something, and of her humming a song that Beth almost recognizes. Something that the kids in the school sing, or have as their ringtones. Laura sings along after a while. Don't, she sings, cos here it comes, here it comes. When you keep them down, when they pressin' you down, you better save your own blood, because here it comes: here comes the flood. Her singing voice is reedy and half-uttered, but the words are clear as day through the opened windows. Beth

190

thinks about the diazepam, which is probably set into the body's system now. She looks into the bedroom as much as she can without moving her chair, and Vic's body is asleep. The eyes are shut at least. She thinks about how it can just wear off. She's probably got, what, four hours? Five? Before he's back to wide awake, not dulled by the painkillers. That's a window of opportunity she'll lose if Laura really doesn't leave.

Go away, she says.

What? The scuffle of Laura standing up, leaning her head close to the opened window.

I said go away. Please go away. I'm fine.

You're not fine. You're going to do something that you shouldn't.

Don't tell me what I shouldn't do. Go away.

I'm waiting here until you let me in.

You can't come in.

Don't do this, Laura says.

Beth goes to the window and shuts it, slamming it so quickly that Laura doesn't have a say in the matter. Laura presses the doorbell, so Beth goes to the box and turns the volume off. Laura hammers on the door, so Beth hammers back.

I'm not coming out, and you're not coming in, Beth shouts. Leave us alone.

Us? Laura's voice cracks. You've got him in there with you?

Just go away, Beth says. She sounds defeated, on purpose: hoping that Laura hears the sadness in her voice. She walks to the Machine's room and shuts the door

191

behind her. Slams it. She doesn't know if Laura leaves or stays, but here she is with Vic. She turns the volume on the playback down, which means it's going to be hard to hear over the grind when the Machine gets going. But regardless, she doesn't want Laura to hear this.

The diazepam has done its job, and he's pliable. She slips the Crown onto his head and he hardly murmurs, and then she presses play on the first file she's got lined up for the day. The Machine's noise, she wonders where it's gone. She can still hear it, but it's like it's hardly there, or it's part of the background. She remembers being a child, when they – her whole family – moved to a house in west London that was next to the underground. The first few nights the trains kept her awake: bedtime meant the sound of the brakes and the engines as they came in and out of the station at the foot of her garden; and then there was the sound of the planes from overhead, the flight path directly intersecting with where she lived, coming and going at all times. They made more noise on the way up, she thought, as she watched the lights through the darkness. But she got used to it. Three nights of watching the planes, and waiting for the last train to pass through, and that was it. No more. As a child she told her parents that she had done it herself.

I wished that they would stop, she told them. So I wouldn't be able to hear them any more.

Now, the Machine is there, but somehow it's lower, inside her. Like the noise is synchronous with herself: with her headache, which throbs incessantly as she stands near the Machine, and the rumble in her gut, which she takes to be hunger but which edges towards nausea. But then she looks at Vic as the playback occurs and he seems more whole. He's getting there, she tells herself; a construction site, with signs up and barricades, but he's getting there.

He rolls slightly, from side to side, as if he's lying on waves. Somehow suddenly tidal. He makes a noise, like before, but much quieter. A digital murmur, nothing more, really. The Crown blinks. Over the now-quiet speakers, Beth can make out words.

I always wanted to be a soldier, he says. I always wanted . . .

As the voice on the recording drops, she stops listening. Instead, she watches him: the muscles on his arms. Where they had dropped and sagged as he stayed in the clinic, and the flesh had taken back his army physique to nature's settling point, all of a sudden it looks as if it's becoming stronger. She touches his bicep and it's firm. She squeezes it and it's not what it once was – she pictures him as he was, taut, pinched flesh, a body destined to cause envy in his friends and hers, built from training rather than pride or conceit – but somehow it's getting back to how he was. She tells herself to read about muscle memory: about whether this is something others have experienced, as a by-product. His body resetting itself to the way that it once was. She peels up the t-shirt he's wearing, and there: the fainting trace lines of his stomach muscles. The iliac crest she used to stroke.

So they told me that if it was what I wanted . . .

She stands and looks at herself in the mirror on the dresser: at how she's faded away over the past five years.

Living by herself, and the toll. And the time. She's sure that, as she looks at Vic, he hasn't aged. What she thought was salt-and-pepper hair starting to creep in looks different in this light. She thinks about giving him a haircut, back to how it used to be, so short that it was barely there at all.

Like this never happened, she says.

She wonders what he'll see when he's awake and himself again: when he looks into the mirror; what he'll expect. Will he want himself as he was, or will he know? She's not getting rid of the last five years, because the lies are something that she needs to extinguish completely. So will he want them? Will he want to see himself and know what he's been through? Will he want to see the time he's lost in his eyes and on his face, and running through every vein in his body? And when he looks at Beth, what will he see? The woman who destroyed him, or the one who recreated him, returned him to what he was?

She opens the door to the bedroom as soon as the playback ends, before the next one starts. Laura's still there: the shadow of her head, leaning back against the window. Beth goes to the fridge for water, and she drinks it herself though it is meant for Vic. With the window shut, the heat in the flat is nearly intolerable. She takes another bottle into the room and shuts the door behind her, and presses play.

30

Another day. She gives him the diazepam in his drink, without food inside him. It sets in faster and heavier without the food, and she's wasting time. DO NOT OPERATE HEAVY MACHINERY. He drinks it without saying a word, the whole drink down in one, and then lies back.

Thank you, he says. I was so thirsty.

She sees herself as if in a film: where the actor has been told to stumble backwards, shocked. Display an extreme reaction to this. Emotionally push yourself. Imagine that it's real.

What did you say? she asks. Her voice is so shaky, so barely there. She sounds as if she might be sick, as she listens to her words: the filter of it in her throat, the words catching on rising bile.

Thank you. He turns and looks at her, only not quite at her, his eyes off somewhere else. It's so hot. He smacks his lips together. Can I have more? Still no real eye contact. Beth steps forward and lifts the bottle to his lips, and he sucks on it, almost, like a baby at a teat, and she tilts it more.

Go on, she says. Her voice: her head. The pain in it, because she's so tired, and she's been doing this for so long, and now this, so suddenly? He can't be back, not yet. What do you remember? she asks him.

I, uh, he says. He searches. His eyes flit around the room. They look for reference points. They look for something to latch onto.

Do you remember my name? she asks.

He looks at her, but not at her eyes. The rest of her face, her body. Up and down.

Beth?

Beth. Do you remember your name?

I'm Victor McAdams, he says.

What else? Where are we? She sits on the edge of the bed. She's not touching him. She worries that, if she touches him, he might disappear; like he might not be entirely real, not yet.

I don't know, he says.

How did you get here?

No, he says.

What's the last thing you remember?

No, he says. No, I can't get this, I can't. Oh my God, I don't, ah, ah. He panics, and he moves more. He tries to push himself up to sitting, but the drugs that he's been given are settling in, and it's tough. He's pushing against them. You have to let me up, he says.

I can't, Beth tells him, not yet. Lie down. Shush. She rubs at his temples as he gives in, because the drugs are so much stronger than he is, and he lies back. This will hurt, she says. But I've never been so convinced that I'm doing the right thing. She pulls the Crown down and puts it on. No lubricant, because he doesn't seem to need it any more, as if the Crown has grown, somehow, to fit around him more comfortably. He murmurs and rocks again, but she starts the Machine nonetheless. She knows her way around the screens without looking: she can sit with him and stroke his brow, fingers running all the way to the pads of the Crown as she presses play, and then his voice amidst the sound of the engine as it roars at both of them, and amidst the tingle from the pads and the screen. With one hand on his head, and the vibrations there, and the other on the screen, taking in the vibrations from the Machine, she feels like the central part of a circuit, the part that completes it. Vic is incomplete, and she will help.

No, he says now, as the Vic on the recording describes who he used to be.

Are you Vic now? she asks him as he lies there, the sweat dripping from his body. Like a fever.

At the end of the session she walks out of the room and makes breakfast for herself, and downs bottles of water at the sink. She pops ibuprofen from the packet and swallows them, three, then adds a fourth minutes later, even though she knows that they're not an instant relief, that they take time to work. She stands in front of the fridge and lets the air from inside it steam up around her, and soon the flat is full of something like smoke but it's only condensation. She loses track of how long she's been standing there. She drinks another bottle. In the reflection of the oven door she looks at herself: her hair, her face. One of the first things that she'll do when she's fixed Vic and brought him back to her is sort this out. A haircut, a trip to a department store, if there's one wherever it is that they end up. She makes a note on a Post-it stuck to the fridge to do more house research when Vic's sleeping tonight, so that she's prepared. Somehow this is all going faster than she dreamed. She gave herself six weeks, and yet now, after only one – not even one, not really – he's showing signs.

She peers at the window. Laura's gone. Beth wonders when she left. If she stayed until the night, or gave up long before. She knows that she'll be back, because Laura has that sort of insistence. The sort that doesn't just slip away.

31

She wakes him for lunch, the session complete, and an extra hour and a half of sleep for both of them, to get over it. He opens his eyes at her. She's put her face close to his, so that he can't avoid looking. Her eyes at his.

Come on, she says. It's time for lunch. Are you hungry?

I think so. She smoothes his hair where the warmth of the Crown has made tufts, like horns.

Come on, she says. We should eat. I've made lunch. She helps him to a sitting position, and his head lolls, and he moans. I know it hurts, she says, but it'll get better. She moves his feet out of the bed and tells him to stand up, and he shuffles forward. Then he puts his feet onto the floor itself, and tests his toes. I'll help you, she says. She tries to take his weight, but he shifts so much of it back to himself, more than he has before during this process. He treads gently, toe to heel, like a series of pictures of somebody walking, rather than somebody actually doing it. He stumbles, and the weight on his ankles isn't there. He shakes. Okay, Beth says.

Toilet, he says. So they go there first, and she helps him sit down. He pisses and shits, and then cries when she has to help him clean himself afterwards. He hardly speaks, not really, he doesn't say that he's ashamed that she's doing this, but she can tell. It's something ingrained and deep inside him. Shame and self-pity and self-hatred and a humiliating desire to do this himself. He knows that there's something wrong. She wipes him and he rests his face on her arm, her chest, and shoulder, and he sobs. Beth doesn't mention it afterwards, taking him to the table and sitting him down. There's an omelette in front of him, softly fried, more scrambled egg than solid.

Can you manage it? Beth asks. He shakes his head, so she feeds him first. He opens his mouth and she slides the egg into it, onto his tongue. He swallows of his own accord. He cries as she feeds him, and tries to manage words.

My head, he says.

I know, she says. Finish lunch. You still remember who I am?

Beth, he tells her.

Okay, she says. You'll be okay, I promise. Do you know what we're doing here?

I don't know, I don't know. He still resists eye contact. She puts the egg into his mouth: the diazepam she's crushed up buried somewhere in the butter and cheese that binds the thing together. He swallows and then refuses the next mouthful – turns his head – so Beth tells him that he has to have a drink to wash it all down. He takes it.

She helps him back to the bed before he starts to get drowsier. His increased responsiveness is certainly making this easier, and with each step he takes it feels like he's taking more and more of his weight. He lies down of his own accord, and he shuts his eyes and smacks his lips.

Do you know what that noise is? Beth asks him. She's referring to the Machine.

I don't know, he says through the fug.

It's okay. Don't worry. She takes down the Crown and presses the screen.

32

Laura hammers on the door with the balls of her fists.

This is wrong, she shouts. Beth, you have to listen to me! The neighbours have come out of their flats to watch, because they assume it's a domestic – and that's one of the pleasures, for them, of this block's forecourt, the sheer number of arguments that spill out of the flats and onto the concrete, complete with whatever's thrown out after the offending party, and usually a crying brood, begging for whichever parent has the greater potential for violence to calm down. They stay standing as Laura continues her tirade. What you're doing is wrong, Beth. What you're doing is against everything that we are!

Beth sits on a chair at the dining table as Vic rests. She watches the shadows of Laura's fists raise and fall on the glass.

Beth, answer the door. Answer the door.

Or what? Beth asks. She doesn't shout it, but she knows

that Laura will hear.

Or I'll tell people what you're doing.

It's not illegal to stay inside your flat. This is a game in which neither of them is going to say it first: Laura in accusing Beth of something that's barely common knowledge, something that barely exists as a possiblity; and Beth won't admit any more than she already has. And Vic isn't here against his will. He was checked out of the clinic, taken by his wife for the summer, a break from the monotony of his care, and he won't be returned because he's being changed.

You know what I'm saying, Beth. She hushes her voice to a spat whisper. Let me in and we can talk about this.

This isn't your business, Beth says. She drinks water and rubs her head where it's sore – she's so tired still, and when she closes her eyes all she can see is the Machine, that wave of ever-deep black metal – and takes more ibuprofen. She counts her pills: half the diazepam gone, half the ibuprofen. She's been using more of them than she anticipated. She'll have to do another run: late at night, she thinks, when there won't be people outside, when she can rely on Vic to stay asleep. He's excellent at that. Sleeping through the night, never waking, never making a peep. That's something he was good at before he went to war, being able to drop off anywhere, any time. Cars, trains, the hard benches of an airport: he could sleep on them.

You need help, Laura says.

I can handle him.

Beth, you need friends and you need help to see you

through times like this.

I'm sorry, Laura.

I don't know what you're doing in there, Beth. I don't know what you think you're doing, but it's not your husband inside there—

Stop it.

—because he was destroyed, and he cannot now be reconstructed, not from nothing. That isn't your right. She pauses. Genesis 2:7: the Lord God formed the man of dust from the ground, and he breathed life into the man's nostrils; and the man became alive.

You seemed so normal when we first met. Beth says it to hurt her, and there's silence for a while, as the slump comes: Laura's clothes dragging themselves down the door.

I'm not leaving, Laura says. I can help save you, don't you see?

There's nothing to save, Beth says. She shuts the door to the Machine's room again and puts the Crown on Vic's head. She presses play, and Vic's voice emerges: so instantly reassuring.

I'm having trouble remembering things, he says.

That's natural, the doctor says. You had a nasty accident.

Yes. That's what I'm told.

You don't remember?

No.

The recording is from after it was all settled: after the majority of the work had been done. From here, they told Beth, it was just cleaning up. From this point onwards, anybody could talk him through it.

And then shouting, coming through the flat.

What's that voice? Beth, who's in there with you? Laura beats the front door again, and Beth remembers that the playback is still at full volume, so that she could hear it over the Machine. She wonders why Laura hasn't heard the Machine itself: supposes that she's assumed it to be a normal household appliance. She wonders if the neighbours have noticed the vibrations coming through their floors or their ceilings. If the shudders carry through the foundations and supports and make their light fixtures rattle and their carpets hum. Beth, I can hear voices, who's in there?

Beth opens the door. The voices fill out into the rest of the flat.

I remember being somewhere. The desert? Is that where I had the crash?

What crash is that?

The, ah, the car crash. That's why I'm here. Speaking to you.

Who are those voices, Beth? Laura sounds desperate. And then Beth unlocks the front door and opens it. The sunlight from outside is brighter than she thought: it's been a few days – how many? – since she left the flat. Laura's there, fingering her necklace. Oh my Lord, you're seeing sense. You're seeing sense. Beth looks around. Fat neighbour is there, pretending to be hanging out washing across the balcony rail (which they're banned from doing). The kids stare. Across the way, some of the other families stand on their balconies and watch, because Laura's voice is shrill and loose and echoes across the courtyard. Below them, a group of youths in the courtyard, standing on the benches and the flower-beds, look up at Beth and Laura. The boy is there: the one with the scar and the bike and the naked leaps into water that he can't judge the depth of; and he spits onto the floor and stares, and doesn't stop staring at Beth as she scans the complex.

Go away, Laura. I won't ask you again.

You need me, Beth. You need comfort and advice.

Just go away. She picks up Laura's bag from the floor, which is open, spilling with her wallet, a bottle of water, a bag of crisps and a book, and Beth knows what the book is without even having to look. She hurls the bag over the railing towards the youths, who laugh and act like it's a bomb. Apart from the one with the scar, who doesn't move.

What? Laura asks, and she turns and starts to run to the stairs as the gang look at the bag's spilled guts.

Beth slams the door shut behind her. She walks into the bedroom and the recording is still playing, but she speaks over it. She talks to Vic about Laura, and how irritating she is. How she won't leave them alone. How she – Beth – needs to get out of this place, because it's all becoming too much. She wonders if he's becoming more receptive. If, somehow, he can hear her through all the other noise.

33

Beth watches Vic sleep. It's dark outside now, and she's put him through more than she planned: the pills were still having an effect, so she drove on for another hour, risking accidents and fits that didn't happen. When he's finished he wakes up for food. He doesn't say anything until he's at the table, until his meal is all but done.

What happened to me? he asks.

What do you mean? Beth replies.

I had an accident. I can't remember things.

Like what? she asks him.

I don't know. Victor McAdams. I'm a soldier. You're my wife. Your name is Beth.

Yes.

And there was an accident, I remember that.

You were shot, Beth says.

Shot. I was a soldier.

Yes.

Shot. He raises his hand to his head and rubs the scar on the side, above the burned-in one from the Machine. I was in hospital. He starts to cry. I can't remember some of this, and I don't know where I am. I don't know where I am.

Beth can see how close she is. She comforts him, holds him, and he says that he's tired. She's got two diazepam left, and they were meant to be for tomorrow, but he starts heaving tears and air, so she pops them from the blister pack and offers them to him.

This is medicine, she says. You should swallow them. She holds the water for him, and it's a struggle but the tablets settle in and down, and he gulps the rest of the water. They'll help you sleep, she tells him. She sits with him and they do nothing – no talking, no moving, just her holding him to her – and then she starts to feel his head nod forward. So she tells him that they should go to the bedroom, because he'll sleep better there.

She gets him to his feet and leads him towards the Machine's room, but something stops her. The noise: it's deeper and more present, and something's wrong in the room. Like the Machine knows that she's prepared him for the next session, and resents it. Which is insane, she tells herself, because it's a machine, a thing, and there's nothing inside it but wires and microchips and hard drives and space for the fans and the dust. But still: the noise sounds worse. Desperate, almost. She tells him to wait for her, and he stands independent in the doorway, leaning against the frame. She unplugs the Machine from the wall. Still there in the background. No respite.

Not tonight, she says. She doesn't know why she's talking to it. Why it deserves that from her. She looks back at Vic and pulls the door shut. Not the spare room, she says, come and sleep with me in here.

In bed, he takes his side like it's ingrained in him to do so, and he slumps into a mattress that has seemingly remembered his shape and his form and the way that he sleeps, and into the pillows that nest around his head. His eyes are shut instantly, and Beth pulls the door shut, leaving the room in darkness and silence. She closes the front door behind her and she's suddenly out in the wild of the estate. It feels different to her now, as she sees her reflection in the mirrors of people's windows on the way to the stairwell, and sees her hair unkempt and greasy – has she showered while she's been making sure that Vic's body is as clean as it can be? – and her clothes thrown on. This is how she looks, and how Vic will see her. She tells herself that she has to make more of an effort in the future, as he wakes up more. She takes the stairs two at a time, almost jumping downstairs. She hates the blind corner here. She hates that there's no way of seeing what's waiting for her at the bottom. And yet she's never met anybody or been threatened there. It's just the potential for harm, or surprise. Sometimes that's more worrying than the harm itself.

The rest of the estate is quiet, so she's out and onto the road before anybody sees or hears her, and down towards the strip. She has to walk past the takeaways – the smell of the curry place makes her hungry for something that isn't eggs and tinned spaghetti and frozen slices of bread

– and that means joining the crowd outside the kebab shop. She knows that the boy is there before she's even close enough to make them out as individuals, past their white t-shirts and their football-kit-material shorts and their white trainers and their shaven heads, and she knows that he'll be the one who comes over to her. She sees them turn as a mass and look at her, and this is when she's outside the Indian restaurant, and she thinks about walking in and acting like this was her intention all along. But she needs more pills, because she's so close, and Vic is so close. Another few days of keeping him down and she'll have him.

The boy – now he's there, an individual, not like the others, somehow, there's something worse about him – steps forward and spits at his feet and his head lolls. Left to right, lolling and rolling. He doesn't make eye contact with her: he fixes his gaze on her chin, or her neck, she can't tell.

Fuck you looking at, he says. I seen you around, right? His voice is slurred. Again, she can't work out how old he is. Somewhere between twelve and seventeen. Some vague age that can't be pinned down.

Beth doesn't say anything.

No, don't fucking ignore me. He's not pushy, physically, staying a few feet back from her. He walks as she does, matching her path, crossing his feet with an almost-grace. Don't fucking do that, now, missus. His friends laugh. They pick at their teeth and watch her with their heads tilted forward, staring out from under their brows. They open their mouths and smack their lips and rub at their fresh tattoos. Don't you be fucking doing that, now, because I am not to be ignored. I am not a man you just walk past, eh? You see that?

You're not a man, Beth says. She regrets it as soon as it's out there, but there's something about how long this has been going on. She has to stand up for herself and stop this. He's only a child, she tells herself.

The fuck you say? They all shift position, falling into a line and arcing around her. Cutting her off. You stand near me and fucking say that again, okay? Okay? Okay? Okay? He repeats the word over and over again, sounding more threatening with each spit of it. His friends smile each time. Beth looks at his hands, and he doesn't have a weapon, and she hates herself for saying what she did. She thinks about running. She looks for an exit. Okay? he says again. They get closer. Still not looking at her face: instead he stares only at her neck, definitely her neck, she can see, now that he's closer. She wonders what he's looking at. If he can see her pulse through her skin, or her throat as she gulps back the warm air that she's breathing in too quickly. There's something more predatory about it.

Step the fuck back, all of you, comes a voice from behind. It's the waiter from the restaurant. No trouble, just step back from her and get your kebabs or whatever, and I won't have to call the police, will I. Beth sees that he's holding a cricket bat out in front of him, waving it around. It's heavier than he expected, clearly, and it's loose in his grip. One of them could knock it away at any moment; but they don't. They back up.

211

You're looking to have your place busted up, one of the boys from the back says.

No, I'm not. I'm looking to stop you boys getting in trouble with the police. You know that, right? He looks at Beth. Go, he mouths. She turns and runs off, and none of them apart from the boy look at her go, because they're fixated on the waistcoated restaurateur. She stops around the corner and thinks she's going to be sick but she isn't, and instead stands on the spot with her hands on her knees and coughs at the ground. She breathes these heaves, and then leans back and sniffs in the air, and tries to hold it in. She counts down from fifty. It's not quite enough.

Tesco is bright and painful, and she walks to the pharmacy counter in a slight detour, down past the meat fridges and the cold front that occupies the air alongside them. It isn't until she's past them that she sees the railings up at the pharmacy, and the man behind them packing things away.

Please, she says, I didn't know you were shut.

Nothing I can do, he says.

Please. I'm desperate. He shakes his head. I need to get some painkillers.

Diazepam lady, he says. I remember. You gone through them already?

Yes, Beth says.

For an emergency, you said. To keep them in the cupboard in case of something, right? So there's been a few emergencies the last week, yeah?

I've come out for this, she thinks, and she can feel herself shaking as she grips the counter. She doesn't know if it's shock, or nerves, or something residual from the Machine, because it definitely feels the same, vibrations rather than tremors, something inside rather than something muscular.

I know what you're like, he says. Sort of person you are, I know you.

You don't, Beth says.

Listen, right, we got a register, and you're on it now. Because it's people like you give us nothing but problems – in here, middle of the night, trying to buy this stuff. He glares at her through the railings. Go find a normal dealer, plenty round the estates.

Please, Beth begs.

Said we're shut. The shutters darken and everything disappears: the background bottles of pills, the cough sweets, the man, everything. Beth's nails dig into her palms. She turns and heads to the aisle where they sell these things without a prescription, and she finds the fastest-acting pain-relief tablets and scoops up a handful of boxes. At the front counters the security guard wanders along and keeps an eye on her, and the clerks all look at each other and smirk with their eyes. One of them looks down because she can't stop laughing. It's a quiet night, and this – probably telephoned through by the pharmacist, to tell them to watch out for her, because this one could be trouble – this is entertainment for them. Like a soap opera.

Twenty-six eighty, the cashier tells Beth. You want a bag? The adjacent cashier smiles and laughs into the hood of her top.

Yes please, Beth says. She can't do anything, and the cashier flaps the thin bag on top of the piled painkillers. She pays by card and packs them up, and as she leaves, the security guard walks slowly behind her. She thinks that he's looking for bulges in her pockets.

Outside, she breaks down. She walks around the side of the shop and it overwhelms her: the feeling that this – providing the diazepam – was one small thing that she could have done to help him. She's carrying on, that's not even a question. But the diazepam was to have been a gift to him: the ability to make it not hurt, and she's failed. She sobs in the alley that intersects the supermarket's delivery road, and she tries to keep it as quiet as possible. The wall is gravelled, pebble-dashed, and she smacks her hand against it. Only once, but it's hard enough that each stone seems to break the skin, and when she looks at her palm she can see tiny red marks where it's not quite bleeding. Her headache comes back and courses through her, and she opens one of the packets and takes two of the pills, dry swallowing them. They stick, and she can feel them sitting in her throat. She doesn't know how to move them, until she gets water.

She walks back to the strip, hoping that the boy and his friends will have gone: but they're still there, outside the kebab shop. They're laughing harder than she's ever heard them laugh. So instead she walks the other way, further down the strip, towards where it becomes the seafront. She finds the sole taxi rank servicing this part of the island. There's a queue, and she joins it: behind the swaying man who clings to the woman with the smeared mascara. Beth waits, and they shuffle forward as cars drive up and take them away, and finally it's her turn.

Where to? asks the woman behind the counter.

Beth tells her the address.

That's no distance. You can walk that.

I'll pay double, Beth says.

Your money, the woman says, and she shrugs, and she says the address into the radio and the man on the other end sighs. She's paying double, the woman says.

The car pulls up two minutes later and Beth slumps down in the back seat. They drive back the way that she's walked – past the pharmacist standing outside Tesco talking to his workmates as they drag on cigarettes, no doubt telling them about the addict who tried to scam him for tranquilizers – and then past the boy, and the youths all duck down to look into the cab but they can't really see Beth because she turns away from them, so they look at the driver, make noises and shout abuse at him. The one boy isn't looking where the rest are. His eyes are down, still, Beth's sure, pointed right at her neck. They all laugh and one throws a half-empty bag of chips at the back of the car, and they laugh again, apart from, Beth is sure, the boy.

Fucking monsters, the driver says. Pardon my language.

No, it's fine, Beth tells him.

Animals. Don't know how we're going to survive, if it's them lot representing where we're fucking heading. I'm trying to make a living, and now I probably got to clean chilli sauce off my car before I start tomorrow as well, and what the hell are they doing? Standing there, being wankers.

He pulls over and Beth gives him a ten, and he thanks her when she tells him to keep the change.

Have a safe night, he says. She walks through the estate and runs up the stairwell, and it isn't until she's on the tier outside her flat that she sees him: across the way, directly opposite.

The boy.

Is that where he lives? Has he always lived there? He isn't looking at her. He isn't looking at anything, she sees: his head slumped over, his eyes shut. He's waiting for something. Beth fumbles with her keys and jams them into the door, and she can't get inside and shut it fast enough.

Vic is still asleep. Beth sits by the side of his bed, taking the pills from their packets and crushing them up into a powder, and then trying to work out how much is too much.

34

Beth lies herself down next to him on his bed at some point and she turns her body towards him and tries to sleep. She knows that it will come eventually, but it's the getting there. She watches his face, and she shuts her eyes when she gets sad from staring at it.

She wakes up with his hands on her: his fingers on her back, and his other hand at her crotch, pushing apart her legs. His fingers, once heavily calloused from the guns and the weights and the sand, are still slightly rough, and she remembers this perfectly: how it felt to have them in here. They cling to the inside of her thigh and knead it, and they brush up against her, and she's ready almost instantly. She doesn't know how much of this is Vic, but this must be because he's nearly real. His finger slips across her. The same moves he always used to use, and she kisses him. She pushes: he used to like that, when she was the aggressor. He could start things, and she wouldn't touch him, but she would push back with her mouth.

So she kisses him harder. She keeps her eyes closed, because she doesn't want to know if he'll be looking at her. He always used to look at her, his eyes open. He said that it made it feel better. More real. This feels real enough, Beth thinks. She pushes him back, his fingers still moving around her, and she slides on top of him. She manoeuvres, and then he's inside her.

And the Machine is there all the time: that low-level noise that lets them know it's still there, and that it's still waiting to be used again. Beth pushes her whole body down to grind herself against him, and it doesn't take long. She falls off him: in the heat, so sweaty so quickly. She thinks that she'll have to change the sheets. She doesn't say anything, and neither does he.

She lies next to him, trying to hear his breathing over the Machine; or maybe the Machine's noise is his breathing, she can't be sure. The heat becomes stronger somehow: as if it's coming up through her body, and she's making the heat herself, not the burning sun or the holes in the ozone layer that they warned them about for so long. She makes the heat. She feels her head with the back of her hand and can't tell if it's a temperature. So she gets out of bed and dresses herself lightly, her swimming costume and some shorts, that's all. She walks back through the estate – it feels like days ago she was last here, not just earlier this evening – and she finds the beach opposite the stretch of shops where everything is dead and everybody else asleep, and she slides into the water. She swims out as far as she can, until the island is hidden by the darkness: only the blip of lights run across the view. She looks at the water as she treads to stay still: and the ripples on the surface that tell her that the vibrations have followed her even here. She stops and bobs, then sinks. Down. She shuts her eyes. Down. Cold all around her, and she can't feel the warmth of the outside air, not even slightly.

She thinks that she could stay under: but even as she is thinking it something kicks in and her body writhes and forces her upwards, and she gasps for air when the surface breaks. She's drifted closer to shore: she can see the estate from here again.

She swims back.

35

As soon as he wakes up she gives him the powder, worrying about the amount, stirred into orange juice to mask the taste. It turns the juice cloudy and grainy, and he pulls a face as he drinks.

No, he says. Oh, no.

It's only orange juice, Beth says. To reassure him.

Beth, that's not orange juice. That's like chalk. Yuck.

Beth sits and stares at him. Suddenly nearly himself. Everything: the way that his face moves, that his tongue spits the words, that his hands ball when he doesn't like something. His shoulders. And that leads her to his face, which is looking cleaner and healthier, and his arms, which are definitely trimmer. More toned. She wonders if he could press what he could when he was still at war, because this – Captain Vic McAdams – is the man she's getting back. Not the shell that came back from war, or the shell that she helped make with the Machine's treatments.

And then he tries to stand. He moves to the edge of the bed and swings his legs down, and it's like he never stopped being himself. Feet go onto the floor, and he pushes himself to standing, and then rocks backwards.

Woah, he says. Unsteady. I'm a bit dizzy.

How's your head? Beth asks.

Swimmy. I need . . .

Lie down, Beth says. How many pills were in the orange juice, she wonders. Five? Ten? All six packets made a pile of dust that filled half a mug, and this was a few teaspoons siphoned off and stirred in. But he's weak anyway, she knows that. It's been a long time.

Where are we? he asks.

In my flat.

What about our house?

I can explain it, but—

He doubles over and clutches his temples.

Jesus, this headache, he says. Jesus.

Come and lie down, Beth says. She has to support him, but it's still easier than it was. On the bed in the Machine's room he lies down, and in the darkness she soothes his head. She rubs her fingernail over the skin where his hairline sits, and he falls asleep. She takes the Crown and slips it onto his head. She tightens the bracing straps. I'm sorry, she says.

She presses the Machine's screen. The vibrations and the noise, seemingly more intense again. She feels sick, and she has to hold onto the Machine as it makes her rock. She queues up the file and presses play, and on the bed Vic screams and bucks.

221

Oh God, he says, through the cries. Oh please. Please. Beth turns and holds him. She presses him to the bed, to try and stop him moving. Oh fuck, he says. This hurts oh my God it hurts so much.

I'm sorry, Beth says.

Oh my God. He passes out suddenly, and there's no movement, not even a twitch. It's sudden enough to make Beth feel for his pulse.

Do you know what makes it feel worse? the Vic on the recordings asks, his voice suddenly filling the room.

No, the Beth on the recordings says. What makes it worse?

That I can't remember how we first met, he says. I don't know why. It's just a mist.

We met at a dance, the recorded Beth says.

That's right. Okay. I think I remember now.

Beth now moves her hand to her mouth, because she doesn't want to make any other noise. This was the part she didn't want to hear, that she tried to pretend didn't happen. This was her taking over the treatments, and changing the schedule to fit her timetable, not Vic's, because she wanted a husband who was at home and normal and didn't have gaps and patches that needed filling. This was a Beth who did three treatments a day when she should have spaced them out: three a week, they told her; a Beth who watched the bruise-burns appear on his temples each day with more speed, and then stay there; a Beth who was convinced that this was the solution.

Who sat in the clinic with Vic, in a room where they couldn't see the Machine, and plugged him in and let it run and run.

They trusted the patients to do this at their own pace – there's no right or wrong, the doctors told them, and that was their failing right there, that's when they sealed their fate and condemned all these people: in not locking it down – and Beth was well aware that she was abusing it. How many of these recordings are there? Of her gently leading Vic down corridors to find patches, and then letting the Machine make of those patches what it did? Trusting in it – behind a wall, not even just a curtain, but something that they couldn't see but could definitely hear, the continual churning behind and above them – and letting it do what she should have done herself?

She wants to turn the volume down, but here they are: herself and the man that she first created, as they go through the process. As she hears herself pushing him.

I don't know, the Vic on the recording says, by way of an answer to a question.

Yes you do, the Beth says. Try and remember. You do know.

Okay, he says. Jesus, my head hurts.

Don't stop now, the Beth says.

On the bed, Vic starts his bucking again, awake, his mouth suddenly frothing. Beth pins him down as much as she can.

I'm sorry, Beth says.

36

On the forums, the person who built the Machine's new firmware used a construction analogy.

Before, the post said, it was like you were building extra floors to a building, like a block of flats, when there wasn't the structure for it. You weren't supporting it with pillars and scaffolding, just putting it on the top and hoping for the best. And then, at the same time, you're pulling out the bottom floors in big chunks. You're taking out the basement and the lower levels, taking out the foundations, and you're leaving the whole thing unbalanced. They – the doctors – didn't think about that. So, what happened next? I apologize, because maybe the analogy is crude, but the whole thing collapsed, and the building that you were adding to was destroyed. Not just the new parts, but all the parts, the older parts as well. Might as well have been flattened. Now what you're going to do is build something new on the ground. The building-up part, that's not what made it collapse. It was the removing of the foundations. That's why this is safe, perfectly safe, for them. No danger for them, and no danger for you.

Beth tells herself to remember that post as she clings to Vic, who she's not given a break, because they're into this now. Soon he'll be strong enough to refuse the treatments, to maybe even run away – and that's a real worry for Beth – so her window has grown smaller. She gave him chalky water this morning, far chalkier than the orange juice even, and not long after drinking it his eyes rolled, but he's still awake, so she has to hold his arms to his side as much as she can. She can't be sure but she thinks that he's pissed himself, because he's so damp, but his whole body is glistening with sweat, so it could just be that. And the Machine is making this so much worse: the noise is incredible, inside her head, intensifying her headache. Every part of them, every part of the room seems to shake, and when there's respite – in the pause between audio files, and as the Machine rests briefly in between sending whatever it's sending down the Crown's umbilicus to Vic's head – Beth feels sick, and clutches at her head, and even takes the tablet powder herself, poured into a bottle of water and necked back.

This is torture, she thinks to herself. She doesn't know how long she can keep it up. The day moves by and the night comes, and she wants to sleep but that's pointless now, because she's so close. In his gasps of consciousness he begs, and he's her Vic again.

Tell me how you feel? she asks on the recording.

I feel incomplete, he says.

How do you feel, she asks him now, as his eyes snap open, and he vomits and definitely pisses himself this time, so she forces more water into his mouth to wash the taste away and keep up his fluids. It might be chalky but that's better than nothing.

He tries to answer her but nothing comes out. Still, she can see it in his eyes: who he really is now. How much of him is Vic again.

I love you, she hears him say, but then it's gone, swallowed by the noise of the Machine and the noise of his thrashing as a new session is firmly underway, and she doesn't know if that was the voice of him now, or from the recordings made long ago when she destroyed him.

PART THREE

Memory is the space in which a thing happens for the second time.

Paul Auster, *The Invention Of Solitude*

37

I told you about that boy, didn't I? Beth asks Vic as he sits down next to her at the table.

I'm still aching, he says.

But I told you? What he was like?

You told me. You used the c-word.

Well, he is.

I don't know what you want me to do about it, he says.

I don't either, she says. I'm just saying, before we go.

He's a kid. I'm not going to hit him.

Okay. I don't know how old he is. She pushes her fried breakfast around the plate. She isn't really hungry. It's been three days since she had him back, and she's barely slept, and hardly eaten. She tries to act as if this is normal, because she's sure that it will be. Any second now. Vic has eaten his. He used his fork only, and he cut the egg and sausage up with its edge, and scraped them along the plate as he did it: and then, when he was done, pushed the plate away from him. Only an inch, but.

The Machine sits switched off, but still that means nothing to it. The noise has dropped to low-level, admittedly, but it's still there. Even though it's unplugged, and declared on its screen in big bold letters, COMPLETE. On the forums it says that when that message appears, you're to stop. After that you're pushing your luck. Beth doesn't want to do that again.

But now this is a fine line, because Vic remembers everything. He saw the Machine and opened his eyes and asked Beth if she had gone through with it, then.

We decided that I wasn't well enough, he said.

We did. Together.

Beth watches him in the bedroom as he dresses. He poses in front of the mirrors in the way that he always used to. Putting underwear on first and then standing and breathing in, like it was the most natural thing in the world to constantly watch the way that your body rose and fell. He dresses and tells Beth that he wants to go for a run.

Too much energy in me, he says. I'll be back soon. Everything about his body is taut and lean. His shoulders, through his t-shirt. And the clothes that he wore five, ten years ago, exactly as they were back then. The films and bands that he liked then, which of course he still likes now, because he knows nothing else. But then, Beth thinks, she's not exactly experimented herself: here, trapped with her possessions and her life.

Vic stops at the mirror by the front door. Will these ever disappear? he asks, rubbing at the temple bruises.

229

I don't know, Beth says. On some people they do.

How long have I had them?

Years, Beth says.

Then I should grow my hair. Cover them up. People will know if I don't, won't they.

Maybe.

I'll grow my hair. He walks back over to her and bends down and kisses her on the lips, his lips parting, the dart of his tongue that way he used to, wetting her. A prelude. I forgive you, he says to her as he pulls back. For everything you've done. And then he turns and he's out the door. Beth follows him slowly. She watches him: down the stairwell, through the courtyard, each of his steps the same size as maybe two of hers, almost bounding, and then he hits the road running and then he's a flash in the distance. White and grey of his tracksuit. Beth draws her gaze back to the flats, and to the ones across the way. Where she had seen the boy. She doesn't know which flat might be his, because she rarely sees anybody coming or going from them. And he belongs to parents, surely, because he can't be old enough to be living alone.

She waits, in case he appears. Now that Vic's back, he's the perfect deterrent. See how large and imposing and army my husband is? And everything that you said to me, the threats, how scared you left me. Would you fuck with him? He doesn't appear, but there's a breeze which makes the waiting better. She shuts her eyes for a second. She still needs to catch up on her sleep, because it's so hard to drift off with this new body next to her: all of his weight and warmth, and the sound that he makes as he sleeps.

He's so silent that you think he's stopped breathing, and then there'll be occasional gasps of air into his lungs, and his entire body seems to convulse with the action of taking it in. When she opens her eyes she expects the boy to be there – the villain of a horror movie, sneaking up on her while her eyes are shut, weapon in hand – but there's nothing: only the cats below, wandering from the Grasslands at the back, mewling for Beth to drop them some food.

She takes a can of tuna and peels the lid back before emptying the contents down onto the courtyard. The cats smell the fish and pounce, all of them, and there's two at the front, eating most of the tuna, before one of them just seems to know when to back off, and leaves the other to a feast. It stays there, long after the tuna is done: nearly out of view, close to the side of the building. Beth watches it standing there until Vic returns, dripping with sweat.

How can you run in this heat? she asks.

It's good. I've run in hotter, he says. You know what it's like, running in Iran, sack on your back, in full gear? Boots and everything? You get used to heat.

I know, Beth says.

What can I eat?

We've already had breakfast, Beth says. She thinks about the remains of hers lying in the bin. Maybe the cats would eat that?

Right, but I'm still hungry.

I'll make you something in a minute.

I'm going to shower. Can you turn it on for me while I get undressed?

Beth flicks the switch and checks that the water is cold enough, and then stands back. Vic climbs into the bath, all rippling muscles and memory of youth, and then lets the shower wash over him as Beth watches the steam rise from his flesh.

38

Beth still doesn't sleep, even as he does. She lies next to his body and watches the ebb of it. She tries to match his breathing: to draw her own breaths in as Vic takes his, so that there's some synchronicity, and the noise – which is so alien, more alien even than the distant hum of the Machine from the adjacent room – might somehow fade into a background of her own creation. She counts his breaths, which are naturally slower than hers.

That's the thing about sleep, she thinks: the body slows down. In sleep, it quietens to an energy-saving crawl. In danger, it becomes hyper-energetic, surging with adrenaline. She wonders what her own body is doing: lying in bed, constantly on the verge of consciousness. If the rest she's getting is worth anything at all. She counts his breaths to five hundred, and then starts counting down. She makes it nearly halfway before stopping.

At 4 a.m., according to the clock, she gets up and paces

the kitchen. She opens the fridge – such a simple pleasure, that burst of cold – and drinks water, then uses the toilet before putting the television on and watching the news. The shallow news cycle in the middle of the night, the same fifteen-minute segments repeated with tweaks, as the stories roll in, and the scrolling texts at the foot of the screen giving real-time updates, suggesting that the newsreaders aren't even broadcasting live. Beth wonders if they're asleep as well: tucked under the desks, waiting until a real emergency springs up. She tries sleeping on the sofa but she can't even begin to shut her eyes. The alarm clocks are all off, because she reasons that Vic needs the sleep. He's not used to this, she thinks, and that makes her laugh; because what exactly is he used to? He's used to being nothing, she thinks. He's used to being a void.

It's a bad thought, and one that she banishes. She tells herself that she has to remember that he's here now. She wanted her husband back and here he is. He's mostly-formed and tweaked and as close to perfect as she can reasonably expect. And he'll get better. That's what they say on the forums:

Remember: this is just the start.

The news flicks to a story about the economy, and she realizes all of a sudden how out of touch she is: how little she knows about the state of everything. Outside her flat, everything is carrying on, motoring forward. Inside, it's just her and Vic and the Machine.

She opens the spare-bedroom door. She's told Vic that they don't need it any more. She's been honest about what happened; about why it's here.

I bought it so that we could make you better, she said.

Okay, he told her. He didn't ask anything more than that. He only said, a few hours later, I don't like it here.

What? she asked.

The Machine. In that room.

Okay, she told him.

Don't you trust that I'm better?

Of course, she said.

So why do you still have it?

I'll sell it, she told him. I'll put it on the forums and sell it. Somebody else will want it, you know. Easy sale. And we can use the money. She blabbered excuses to him, to make him feel better. Now she looks at it, growling at her. Or maybe like a purr. Such a fine line between the two.

I should thank you, she tells it. You gave him back to me. She calls up the screen with her touch, a single stroke of her fingers, and it lights up. She's left the room light off, and the screen casts its own colours: blue on the far wall, green on the ceiling, white everywhere else. And some black: black light, which she didn't even know was possible, making parts of the room – corners, nooks – darker than they were even without the screen on. She flicks to the recordings, selects one and presses play. She acts like it's an accidental choice, but it isn't. She knows which one.

I know how this goes, Vic's voice says. What do you want me to talk about, Robert?

I'd like you to tell me your name, like always, the doctor says.

Victor McAdams. He sounds so nervous. Now, in the present day, she can hear the confidence in his voice. That's what the Machine has embedded of itself: the confidence that this is right. That he is who he is.

Tell me some other things about yourself, Victor. Where do you live, for example?

London.

Oh, whereabouts?

Ealing. Beth remembers their house. Their beautiful house, and their brutal mortgage, and their struggling to keep it. Another life entirely.

Okay. Are you married?

Yeah, Beth. He sounds so happy when he says her name. As if she's the thing getting him through this, she thinks. That's what she would like it to be: that she's what got him through the early days. He did this for her, and their marriage. They spoke about kids. About being old. Elizabeth, Beth, Vic repeats, like he's trying the names on. The reassurance of repetition. At this point, he still remembered everything. He knew what the Machine was going to do. He repeated her name, Beth thinks, so that he could cling onto it. This is something he never wants to lose, because they were meant to be together.

Beth stops the recording. Maybe she could sleep here, she thinks. On this bed. She peels back the duvet and heaps it on the floor, and she lies down on the sheet that's been washed countless times since Vic came home to her. Even now it smells of him, of his skin and his sweat. Something about the Machine's noise is comforting to her. And that makes her uneasy, because it scares her

– and she's right to be scared, she tells herself, something so powerful and confusing right there, with the power that it has. It's rumbling. Like those planes overhead, when she was a child, and the trains at the bottom of the garden. She shuts her eyes. The smell of the pillows is stale sweat, but again, that means something. In this heat, it's a smell she's used to. Nothing off-putting about it.

She shuts her eyes and the room moves with her. As her body turns over – always moving from her back onto one side, then onto the other, once before sleep – so too does the room, it seems. And then there is the noise of the Machine, which starts in one place only and then envelopes her. It's in the walls and the floors, and the vibrations come up through the foam in the mattress and through the sheet, and through the pillow where it touches the wall. And she can hear the voices: Vic and the doctor talking in the background, in the far distance, so quiet they're barely there. The pressure on her head, which she's sure is the Crown, but it can't be. Because the Crown is still on the dock when she opens her eyes, and the Machine is silent and sleeping, and the room is dark again. It's getting light outside, which means she's had barely any sleep: and from the living room she can hear the panting of Vic, press-ups in full flow. Trying to drag his body completely back to being what it used to be. His hair already looks longer, a few days of growth having a nearly transformative effect. Where the darkness of the scruff around his temples has grown, the blackened patches look almost like part of the hairline. As if they're almost meant to be there.

Beth walks to the doorway and watches him. He turns and smiles at her.

Sleep well? he asks.

Yes, she says.

39

Vic tells her that he wants some fresh air, and that they should go for a walk, down to the sea.

We should do things together, he says. Beth's scared of seeing Laura, because she's had more answering-machine messages left for her: begging and pleading, and telling her that there are other ways to deal with this; having no idea that it's too late, that Vic is already back. She suggests that they stay inside instead.

We can look for flats, she says.

I don't even think we should move, Vic says. This place: it's got a lot of potential.

The flat?

The island. I've seen it when I've been running. Used to be an amazing place. He doesn't ask what happened to it, or why she's there. No inquisition at all, she thinks. He takes everything at face value.

I want to go, Beth says. I'd like a new start.

Well, while we're here then. He pulls his shoes on, sitting on the chair by the door. Come on. It won't kill you.

Beth's terrified that they'll open the door to Laura, but there's nobody around – it's so early, Vic somehow operating on the rigid wake-times he got used to as a soldier – so she takes his hand and leads him through the estate, even though he's run it a few times now and knows the way out. She takes him down the stairs. It makes a difference, having him with her. She's not threatened by the blind corner.

As they walk down the path, the whole strip is empty. She's grateful: the boy is probably still asleep, sleeping off whatever it was that he did last night. The restaurants and takeaway look like they're dead rather than just closed; and the Tesco – Beth winces as they pass, because she can picture the pharmacist at the front, waving his fist at her as if they're both in some cartoon, and saying, Get out of here, and don't come back! – is quiet inside and out. The shutters are up, which means they're open at least.

I fancy a pastry, Vic says.

Not here, Beth tells him. There's a place along the front. We can sit down there.

They walk down to the bit of beach and tread along the pebbles. Vic picks up a few stones, the flatter ones, and he goes to the edge where the water is almost still and he winds his arm back. He takes on the stance of a professional, if such a thing exists: a posture that looks ideal, to Beth, somehow absolutely perfect, Adonis-like. He is a work of art, a creation carved from marble and memories. She wonders if the models for those ancient

Greek statues would pose, without a break, for the duration of the sculpture's creation, or if it was done in sessions. The seemingly unimportant parts – the flats of their backs, or the flattened plateau of an inner-thigh – carved out when the muse wasn't there any more, when the artist was left to his own devices. Vic's tight arm springs and his fingers splay and the stone fires out at such a flat angle that it's almost imperceptible for a second, and then it hits the water. It bounces, and again, and then carries on, almost gliding.

Still got it, Vic says.

He throws another, and another, and then one followed so quickly by another that the stones almost dance together, the second ricocheting off the ripples that the first creates.

Jesus, he says. Still got it.

They walk further along the beach, picking their way over the most stable areas: the larger stones that aren't likely to slip, avoiding the scree closest to the water. Beth threatens to slip on one rock, but Vic catches her. He rights her. They get to where the sand has been placed – hundreds of tonnes of the stuff, brought here by the council to entice people to the beaches when the tourism started to die, the inspiration for hundreds of costly promotional photographs that only helped to sink the island faster – and that lets them get closer to the water. Vic takes his shoes off – he's not wearing socks – and he paddles.

Freezing.

Should be.

How can people swim in this?

I did. I do.

Really?

Most mornings. It's always this cold.

But the air's so hot.

Doesn't make the water boil. It would be a worry if it did. The cafe is down the way, so Beth tells him she's going.

No, he says. I'll go. You stay here. Sun yourself.

Milky white.

Milky white?

That's what they call a latte, she says.

Milky white it is. She watches him head up the embankment and onto the pavement, and then pulls a lounger – one of those old-style ones, with the different-coloured rubber bands making up the bulk of the bed – and makes sure that the legs are dug in. She sits on the end and watches the water, and she zones out – watching the waves – until she hears the footsteps behind her. Too many for Vic alone. She knows before she turns.

What the fuck is this, the voice of the boy says. She's here looking at the fucking sea. It's not going anywhere, love. Beth turns round to look at them. Four of the boys, and two girls with them this time. Bikini tops, shorts, hair cut so short they are almost bald, like the boys, but with length at the back, pulled into ponytails. They're almost identical, but one is fatter. You going for a swim, love? the boy asks.

Please go away, Beth says.

Fuck's sake, get her? He laughs. I'm being all fucking

nice, and she tells me to go away!

Please, she says.

You can fucking beg for all I care.

My husband is only getting coffees.

They all laugh. So now she's got a husband, has she? Never seen you with him before, love. What's he look like?

Like a vibrating plastic cock, one of the girls says. They all laugh.

Yeah, that's what he looks like. And you sent that to get a coffee did you? What's he going to do, stir it with the tip? They laugh again: from the back of the pack, the laughing is almost incessant.

He's a soldier, Beth says.

Coo! They all coo. Sounds like a threat. What's he going to do? Have my eye out? Beth notices his hands: he's got a stone in one of them, and his fingers are tight around it. His other hand flexes, in and out, as he breathes. Fist, open. Fist, open. Come on, he says. Tell me what he's going to do to me.

Beth cries instead. Please, she says, please leave me alone.

They start to back up, because she's making real noise, huffing breaths in, and spitting them out as sobs. They back up, ten feet, and they start to turn, apart from the boy, who stands firm. He's not budging. He can smell weakness.

And then Vic shouts from the road. Beth looks up and sees him pelting towards them.

Get back, he shouts. They ignore him as he runs, and screams. What are you all doing? He gets to Beth and puts an arm around her, shielding her as she cries, and he looks at the boy. What the fuck did you say to her?

The boy ignores him. He looks at Beth, and he kisses his teeth, and spits onto the sand.

Another time, he says. As he walks away, Beth sees his fingers open and the stone falls to the sand, patting into it. One of the only stones on this part of the beach, a lump of solid black stone in amongst all the gold. As soon as they're all out of earshot – on the street, all laughing, all grabbing at each other and heading back towards the estate – Beth starts crying harder, almost hyperventilating as she tries to breathe.

Oh my God Beth, don't, Vic says. She can't help it. He rubs her back. Shh, he says. He makes soothing noises and tells her that it will be okay. Come on, he says. Come on.

When she's pulled herself together she tells him what happened. She can hardly get the words out, her breath still tight and hard to find.

And then I saw you coming, she says.

Yes.

You didn't get the coffees.

I dropped them when I started running. I can get more.

No, she says. Don't leave me. Let's wait here. They sit on the sun lounger, and then Vic leans back.

Can't even really see the sun under the clouds, and yet this is how hot it gets, he says. He's making observations on phenomena that the rest of the world's lived with for five years. It's crazy.

What would you have done? Beth asks him.

244

With what?

With that boy.

I told him to get off you.

Would you have done more? Would you have hit him?

If I had to. How old is he?

He's done this before.

What?

Lots of times. He's made me so scared. Beth says the words, and thinks how weak she sounds to herself. That's living here, and being alone, and being so nervous all the time. And, she briefly thinks, the Machine. Something about it.

How many times?

I don't know. Five. Maybe.

Threatened you like this? He turns to face her fully, and he puts his hands on her arms. He actually threatened you? Why didn't you tell me?

I thought we would leave, and I would never see him again.

You won't. He does this again, I'll beat the shit out of him.

I don't even know how old he is.

If he's old enough to scare you he's old enough to be scared.

I don't want you getting into trouble.

I won't. I'll just scare the little shit. There's something about the way he says it that suggests he's lying. He stands up. Come on, he says, let's get home. Get you a cup of tea. He looks in the direction that the boy and his friends went. Come on. He helps Beth to her feet and they start to walk. He sets the pace, and they tread faster, and soon he's pulling her along. He wants to see them again, but they don't; and then they get onto the road, and the kids are nowhere.

As they pass the shops and the side roads he looks down all of them, and he almost snarls at strangers who might, from a distance, be the boy. They get past the Tesco – Do we need anything? Vic asks, desperate to go inside and see if the boy is lurking in the booze aisles, but Beth pulls him back and tells him that they've got everything they need – and the takeaways, and then they're on the hill back to the estate when Beth hears the boy. She looks down to the point where they leap into the water, and they're all there. All of them, four boys, two girls, all stripped down to their underwear.

Fucking jump, the boy yells.

That's him, Vic says. That's him, isn't it?

Leave it, please, Beth says. She looks down and sees the boy looking at her.

Cunt, he shouts, and he leaps off the edge backwards, facing them. Cunt, he yells again mid-air, and the word trails down as he plunges, and his friends laugh before following him, one by one. Each one smacks into the water.

Please leave it, Beth says. Vic picks up a rock – two handed, bigger than his fist, something heavy – and he leans back and then hurls it into the water. What are you doing? Beth screams, but they hear it splash, and voices laughing. He missed. Vic breathes deeply, and his shoulders move up and down, regular with his breathing.

I'll fucking kill him, Vic says. He kicks the ground with his trainered foot, and kicks it again and again. Rocks fly, and he starts smacking the wall with his open palm, over and over again, and Beth has to step in to stop him, putting her hands around his hand and holding it, but she's not strong enough, so he crushes her hand into the wall. It doesn't break any bones, but the pain is extraordinary, and she staggers backwards. Vic notices and stops everything, freezes, and it's like his face changes: the rage gone, replaced by total concern. Oh Jesus, he says, oh my God are you all right?

I'm fine, she says.

Let's get back. I'm so sorry. He goes first until the stairwell, and then stands back and almost ushers her up the stairs, and then he offers to open the door but she wants to prove that her hand is okay, so she struggles with the keys and unlocks their front door. He goes in first and stands by the sofa, guiding her to sit down. Ice, he says, and he goes to the fridge and then holds a bag of frozen peas onto her hand. He looks at her hand as if he knows what he's looking for – Beth assumes he's seen a lot of broken bones in war – and reassures her. It'll be fine, he says. That'll heal up nicely. He sits on the other sofa. I don't know what happened, he says. I don't know what came over me.

You got angry.

I got angry before, didn't I? When I got back from war.

Yes, Beth says. Her head murders, the pain actually worse than the pain in her hand. Can you get me headache tablets? And some water?

Oh sure, he says. I hit you, he says as he opens the fridge. On the arm, right? And that's why you threatened to leave me. He pops the tablets from their plastic-foil beds. I remember that.

Yes.

It doesn't mean anything. It's not like it's that bad, not like it was. I'm not the same person.

No. Beth wonders what the gaps were filled with. If they diluted the temper he had before, or maybe added to it. He hands her the tablets, which she throws into her mouth, and then the bottle, cap already unscrewed for her. Thank you, she says. And then she leans back, turns her whole body onto the sofa. I'm tired, she says.

Okay, he tells her. You rest.

Okay.

She shuts her eyes and listens as he walks around the flat. He opens cupboards and closes them, and then rifles through the clothes, taking the rest of his out of the vacuum-packed bags and putting them onto hangers, and then adding them to the rails in the bedroom wardrobe. He talks to her, even though he thinks that she isn't listening.

I'm going to put the rest of the stuff into the spare bedroom, he says. He opens that door, and the noise of the Machine is back. As if it could be forgotten about. You said you'd sell this thing, he says, and even going into the room he sounds nervous. The Machine is the only thing that can do that to him. Maybe he's worried that this can all be undone, Beth thinks. That I could turn around and wipe him, as easily as I made him. He moves the bags anyway.

Beth sleeps. She drifts off, worrying about what will happen. Because he hit her before, but never like that; not with that fury.

40

Beth wakes up to Vic's voice. He's talking about what he did before.

I hit you, he says. I didn't even think about it when I did it, but that's what happened. I used to only think about the stuff in the war, and thinking about it was a perfect way to get it all out. And then I came back and I didn't . . . I had blind spots. That's the only way of putting it. I had these blind spots where I can't even remember what happened now, but I got really angry about little things. And then I hit you that Sunday.

Beth opens her eyes. She's in the Machine's room. Vic's voice is playing over the speakers, and it's like the Vic that's lying next to her is speaking, but he's not. The Crown lies between them on the pillows, an intruder in their bed, their lives, their memories. The voice continues.

We were out for lunch, and I can't remember what you said, but I left and you chased after me and then I did it in the car park, near those woods. And you wanted to leave me, and I didn't blame you. Because that was something I would never have done, not the real me. It was the war that did it to me, you get that, don't you?

I do, her voice says, coming from the Machine's speakers. (And where are those speakers, she wonders.) But you regret it?

Oh God yes. Totally. I've never regretted anything more. That's not me, don't you see that? You know that it's not me. You know that, because you know me, Beth. You know me better than anybody else.

Beth remembers this recording: finding it when she was doing the cleaning-up sessions. He started crying when he was talking to her, and she probed deeper. He remembered this, and now it's back in him, because that's how this works. She sits up and presses the stop button, and the voices hang in the air.

Wake up, she says to Vic. She shakes him and he opens his eyes. Did you use the Machine?

No, he says. I wanted to sleep, so I lay down in here.

How did I get here?

You joined me, he says. Go back to sleep.

The Crown is here. The Machine's been on. It was playing something.

What?

It was playing something.

We were asleep.

She stares at his eyes. This is the biggest change: eye contact. What happened the day you hit me? she asks.

What?

Why did you hit me?

I don't know, he says. I didn't even think about it. It was when I came back from Iran, and I had the – you remember – the blind spots. Couldn't remember things properly. And the dreams. It was a rage, really. I took it out on you.

Where were we?

In the car park of a pub. I told you that I was going back to war, and you said that I couldn't, so I lost it with you.

You told me what? Beth stops and squints at him. That had never happened.

I told you that I was going back to Iran.

That didn't happen.

Of course it did, he says. He looks terrified then, as if he knows it sounds shaky even as it comes out of his mouth.

Tell me more about it? (She has no idea what time it is, but there's no noise from anywhere else, only the Machine stirring away, as always.)

What do you mean?

If you were going back, tell me more about it. Why?

They called me and said that I was important to them. And that I had to go back to Iran, to help with a mission.

You left the army.

They said that they were reinstating me. Look, he says, this is what happened. I can remember it! I can remember everything! Why the fuck don't you believe me? He stands up and starts pacing in that little room, in the space between the bed and the dresser. The door is shut. Jesus fucking Christ, this is exactly the problem. This is why we argued before, and why we're going to argue now.

I put your memories back inside you, she says, in her quietest voice. And I didn't put some story about you going back to war in you. That's from the Machine.

I told it to the doctor then. I told it to him, and that's how it's back.

You didn't. I've heard every recording. I know who you are as well as you do.

Shut up.

I know you as well as you know yourself.

You don't have a fucking clue what I know! he yells. He picks up the potpourri dish and throws it at her, one swift movement; the circular vessel spinning through the air like a clay pigeon, and it collides with her, on the side of her head. It scrapes across her hairline before bouncing away at her ear, and everything in the dark room flashes white suddenly – the light, the walls, the Machine itself, as impossible as that sounds – and she falls backwards. Not from the impact, but the shock. And then Vic's body – which, from that angle, is hulking and malformed, like the twenty-year-old Vic, with his constant intake of vitamin drinks and bench-pressing – disappears into the living room and then out of the flat.

Beth lets it all go black. She lets the whiteness fade and the sleep – because that's what it feels like – washes over her. She's out of control, and alone; and there, on the pillow, the Crown is lying right next to her.

41

Somehow she sleeps most of the day, waking when it's night and dark in the flat, and when she wakes it's to sobbing and clattering from the living room. She sits up and sees that the pillow is damp, and the Crown has somehow been knocked to the floor. She sits up further but she's woozy, and she has to brace herself and focus on the only light in the room – the Machine – to steady herself.

Vic, is that you? she asks. She sees the potpourri tray beside where her head had been. Vic? She stands up, using the chest of drawers to keep steady, and her knees shake, but she's strong enough to move along the line of the furniture and to the doorway. She looks out into the dark flat, and she can hardly see him. His shape in the light from the window and the door.

Don't, he says. I'm so ashamed.

It's okay, she says. She thinks about how she's going to

blame herself, because that's the path of least resistance: to just take the fall, and say that she pushed him. They'll get past this. After all, she thinks, hasn't she already decided that she's going to live with him and his temper and – if they start again – the dreams? That's going to be her lot. Listen, she says to him, things happen. I'm fine.

It's not that, he says. She steps forward into the living room itself, and she can see the trail of darkness that runs around the collar of his t-shirt, and down his arms.

What happened? she asks. She touches him, and he's wet and warm, but not the warmth of the outside, not that dry heat: a pulsing, damp warmth. The smell of cleaning products and something else, something rotten. Oh my God, she says, you're hurt. His tracksuit is soaked through, but it's drying off, mostly; and his hair is wet and the water droplets in it cling to the strands.

I'm fine, he says. He's shaking, like he's the Machine itself, and his flesh the channel for those vibrations.

I'll get a towel, Beth says. She turns on the light in the bathroom and sees the blood that covers her hands, which is now on the light cord and the sides of the sink and the taps as she tries to wash it off, and she looks in the mirror and it's also all over her head: but this isn't the blood from Vic, it's from the gash that runs nearly all the way from her eye to her ear, so sharp and deep it looks to have been made with a knife, not a seemingly harmless ornamental dish. She lifts water to her head and feels the sting, but it's okay. Not as bad as it looks, she thinks. She takes a flannel and soaks it and wrings it out, and then rushes back to Vic, picking up a bucket from the kitchen on the

255

way. She peels his t-shirt off and starts wiping at the blood, to see where it's coming from; and she gets it off his arms and then his neck, or at least makes it more liquid so that it runs clear and down his body and starts to soak into the waistband of his tracksuit bottoms. He notices her blood when she's cleaning him, leaning in close to him.

Your head, he says. Oh my God, Beth. What have I done?

It's okay, she says. I've made my bed, I'll lie in it, she thinks. She nearly says that as well, but stops the words. There are no cuts on Vic's shoulders or neck. What happened? she asks him. She wrings the flannel into the bucket.

I saw that kid, he says.

Oh God, she says. She knows instantly what he's done, because there's no other way that this story can end. She doesn't want to know any more, but she has to. She knows that.

He, uh. He said things.

He always says things.

You said that he threatened you, and he did it again. The things that he said.

Where is he?

On the beach, Vic says. I left him there.

Come on, Beth says. She grabs her keys and opens the door and tells him again to follow, but he's shutting down. You have to show me where! she shouts, and that shouting makes him move. He slopes towards her, dragging every part of himself, and she's sure that he's making a noise – a moan, something from deep inside, and it's a noise

256

that she knows so well, a noise that's been there for so long, sitting in that room and in every part of her flat and her life, and inside her head. She pulls the door shut behind them and rushes down the stairwell, and she almost forgets about the blind corner until she's past it, and she has to tell Vic to keep up. He doesn't seem to be listening: this is all happening at his own pace, Beth thinks. She can't shout at him here, because the whole estate will twitch their curtains and peer out at them. So she whisper-shouts, her voice feeling hoarse in the warm still air. Where is he? she asks him, and Vic points: not to the sandy beach at the end, but to the area of scree before the pebbles begin. Beth rushes to the line of shops and then down the steps that she never goes down, because what's down there, at the water's edge, is rough and hard and unpleasant, and it's never used. It's where the seaweed and rubbish get caught up on the rocks, and that's it, nothing more.

Only now, she sees, there's the boy. His eyes are shut and his body is at such an angle that she just knows, before she's even there, because he's been placed there, rather than having chosen to lie like that; and there's so much blood, and it seems to be coming from every part of his skin. As if every pore decided to bleed at the same time. His clothes are torn and his face is beaten and red and swollen, and Beth swears that she can see fist marks in his cheeks, but that could be swelling from being in the water. She squats next to him and thinks about touching him to check, but there's no need. And there's no doubt that it's the same boy. He's eleven, maybe, twelve, maybe older. She has an urge to check his body for evidence of

257

his age. She tells herself how sick that is: as if knowing might make this better or worse.

He must have ID, she says. She checks his pockets and pulls from one of them a thin white sleeve with a bus ticket and soggy bank notes and there, an ID card. It says his name and his address. And his date of birth. Beth puts her hand to her mouth, and watches it shake as she lifts it, and feels it tremble against her lips. She reads the rest as fast as she can. It says that he's diabetic. It says that the contact number, in case of emergency, is his father's. Should we call him? Let him know? Beth asks, but she knows that they won't. Nobody's seen this: them with the body. This part of the beach is so enclosed, so rarely visited, that nobody will have noticed.

I pushed him from the cliff, Vic says, suddenly. I hit him a couple of times and then I picked him up and held him above my head and threw him over.

Where they jump?

Yes. That spot. He said he was going to find you, and the things that he said he would do, I got so angry. I wanted to teach him a lesson. His face collapses. I think I didn't throw him far enough.

What?

That's how it happened, he hit something else. Rocks, so I dived in after him, and I swear Beth, I saw him as I was falling and I thought I could save him. So I brought him here, because I really thought that he might be all right.

Jesus Vic, she says. He looks like he wants to be held, but she can't touch him yet, because she doesn't know what this means. Which part of him did this: the part that was there before, the soldier and husband; or the part that remembers things that she doesn't.

Can't we leave him? Vic asks. His friends will find him, because I don't know what will happen to me.

Oh Jesus.

I'm sorry, I'm sorry. Vic holds his arms out, a toddler wanting reassurance. Pick me up, it says.

We have to go, Beth tells him. She thinks about the blood on the rocks where he would have landed, and hopes that the water washes it off – it should – and that his friends will find the body and that will be that. They'll assume he fell into the water from the cliff edge; or that he jumped and accidentally hit a rock; or that he did it deliberately, maybe. Suicide rates are high. He was troubled, and they surely all knew that. It's not hard to recognize in him, and everybody will testify to it. If they realize it was no accident they'll just assume it was one of the many other enemies that the boy's no doubt accrued. They walk back up onto the street and she checks herself, that there's no blood on her, and sees that she's clean (apart from her head), and so she takes Vic's arm – her hand wrapped around his forearm, not holding his hand – and she pulls him behind her. It's still dark, and they stay quiet, neither saying a word as they walk through the estate – the quiet, damp squeak of Vic's trainers, and the noise from inside him, his lungs or a moaning, Beth can't tell, those being the only noises that accompany them – and then into the flat.

You need a shower, Beth tells Vic. He strips and stands

in the bathtub and she turns the tap on, and then leaves him to do the rest. His body looks weaker than it did when he left the house: thinner, somehow. Like seeing the boy on the beach took a part of him. Maybe just in the way that he holds himself, in the slump of his shoulders. Scalded, knowing that what he did was wrong.

Beth waits for him in the Machine's room. She looks at it, and she presses the screen. She thinks that she can wipe this: from Vic's mind, from her mind, if need be. She's read stories about criminals who have had things wiped from their memories to give them perfect deniability when taking lie-detector tests. But she won't do that: because she doesn't know what erasing something now might do to him. Might leave him vacant again, and she doesn't think she's got the strength to go through all of this again.

You fucking monster, she says to it. What did you put inside his head?

The Machine seems to start the fans in reply, and the screen gets somehow brighter, and then the thing hums and shakes even though it's not switched on. And even as she blames the Machine, she thinks about her arm, and how troubled Vic has been. Is this better or worse?

In the bathroom, Vic starts singing, a song that Beth's never heard before, that seems to have no tune and no melody, only words, and they make no sense to her.

42

Vic is still asleep when Beth wakes him. He's curled up on his side of the bed, his body presents an implausibly small form; his breathing is constant and sharp. He doesn't move as Beth does, and she makes it out of the bedroom and into the living room without disturbing him.

She turns on her computer and goes to her forums, and she searches for other people who have had issues with the Machine; or with the people that the Machine has built up. One woman reports that her husband has trouble sleeping, not just insomnia but something worse and more deep-seated, and he has to take pills to knock him out, but that's a small price to pay to have him back; a man's boyfriend has been slightly more aggressive, but nothing that can't be handled, just shouting at other drivers; another man's wife has completely lost her sex drive, total lack of interest, and she cries when he tries to instigate it with her. Beth starts a topic, staying casual, not giving anything away. She asks what other people think the memories which the Machine puts inside their loved ones really are. She refreshes the page, but there are no immediate replies.

She washes their clothes in the bath, making sure that the water runs scalding hot and then adds bleach. The blood spirals, whirlpools around the plughole, but it's too thin to leave a ring around the bath itself. Too thin for that.

She checks her phone, and there are messages from Laura.

PLEASE TELL ME YOU'RE OK

I HOPE YOU KNOW WHAT YOU'RE DOING

IT DOESN'T HAVE TO BE THIS WAY. THE LORD FORGIVES.

They're all written in capital letters, shouted at her with the same insistence that Laura had when knocking on the door. Beth wonders why she didn't spot that insistence in everything: the way she drank, the way she fingered her cross. She wonders why she was friends with her in the first place: she doesn't want to tell herself how lonely she actually was.

Go away, Beth says to the text messages. She stands by the window, thinking that they should leave: this is a definite full-stop to their time on the island, even if Vic protests. He'll have no choice now. She imagines him more placid after this. Easily persuaded, in his guilt and shame.

And then out of the window she sees the crowd in the courtyard below: the policemen, knocking on doors, talking to residents. Across the way, two more stand on either side of the door to what must have been the boy's flat. Flowers along the wall. This has all happened so quickly. Beth touches the side of her head: the cut is now scabbing, it still needs a clean and some proper attention. Not stitches, at least, it's healed too fast for that. Her head throbs. She can hear the Machine. Vic's breathing.

She opens the front door. From here she can see down to the street, and there's a cordon and a group of people milling around outside the shops.

I'll be back, she says to the flat, and she takes the keys and walks out. She heads down to the centre of the estate and the police stop and look at her. What happened? she asks one of the officers. She has no idea if she's a good liar or not.

Are you a resident here?

Yes. What happened?

He ignores her question. What number, please? She tells him. He looks up her name on a sheet. We'll be around in the next half an hour or so. We'll let you know everything then.

Beth sets off down the path, and she almost runs to the crowd who are gathered around the steps down to the water's edge. There's an ambulance but the doors are shut, and the crowd aren't saying anything. She sees the waiter from the restaurant, and he smiles at her, like they're old friends.

All right, love. He rocks back onto the heels of his shoes, then to his toes, stretching up to see over the crowd.

What happened? she asks him. She wonders if she is

just establishing an act or genuinely wants to know what they've found. As if maybe last night could have been a dream.

They got a body down there, he says. Washed up or something. Some kid from the estate. Apparently it was the little one, he says. You know the one I mean?

I don't know, Beth says. She pictures him, and his glare and his scar. There were lots of kids there.

Right, right. Fucking hell, though. They found him because of the seagulls, that's what I heard. Because they were all around this morning, pecking away. What a way to go.

Beth feels sick. She clings to herself to keep it in. The smell of the salt and the sea, and the breeze – such a slight breeze, but it's there – coming from the front, and she's glad she can't see it or smell it. And then there's a sudden commotion: and walking backwards up the stairs a para-medic, holding onto one part of a stretcher. Beth wonders, for a second, if the kid's alive, but then she sees the thick black rubber of the body bag that lies on it, and she thinks of a maggot: the loose skin, and inside it something worse, soaked in filth, a developing fly, waiting to emerge and reproduce itself. The paramedics ask the crowd to step back, and wind their way to the ambulance, and they open the door and slide the body into the back.

Where are his parents? asks Beth.

Doesn't have any, that's what I heard. The waiter cranes his neck to see. Apparently lived on his own up there.

What?

Dad's recently been banged up, that's what somebody

said. Mum's gone, or dead. She isn't around. Lives by himself. Always gave me all that shit, always having arguments with me, he was, and now he's dead. There's something conspiratorial about the way that he says it, as if what he really means is, Don't tell the police that I argued with them, and I won't tell them that you did. Fucking hell, he says, and he laughs. This'll do wonders for the tourism, eh?

Beth gets back to her flat just as the policemen are talking to the fat neighbour. She's out on her doorstep, mopping at her eyes – did everybody know the boy? – and the children are all around her, running up and down. She stares at Beth as she passes, and one of the policeman is nodding his head. Beth opens the door to the flat. Vic is awake: sitting on the end of the bed.

They think I live alone, she says. So stay here, stay quiet. Just let me talk to them.

Who's they?

The police. They're doing interviews. She doesn't look at him. She drinks water and takes headache tablets, and then steps outside, pulling the door shut behind her. They're still with the neighbour, so she heads to the railing and looks over it. She tries to make this feel as casual as possible. Nothing to it. To her this is a normal day, only one loaded with intrigue. She thinks she should ask questions. That's probably what somebody who knows nothing would do.

They thank the neighbour – the one who did most of the talking puts his hand on her arm and tells her to call if she thinks of anything – and they turn to Beth. The consoler consults his sheet.

Mrs McAdams?

Beth, please. She holds out her hand to shake theirs: her palm hot, her whole body hot. They shake it, but don't tell her their names.

Mind if we ask you some questions?

No, sure. Sure.

You know what's happened?

I saw the crowd down there, and the flat opposite, obviously. They said that there was an accident?

One of the boys who lives on the estate has died. Did you know him? They bring out his picture and hold it up. Oliver Peacock, the officer says. Went by Olly. The picture has him smiling. It's a few years old, taken when he was still at school. He's so young. Grinning, because he's a kid and he was told to, and it was school-photograph day. He's in a uniform from her school, tie done up, shirt buttoned, not quite posing.

I teach at his school, Beth says.

You know him?

No. I mean, I've seen him around here. Not in school.

He was excluded earlier this year.

Oh.

But you've seen him on the estate.

A few times.

The other officer speaks finally. We've heard some reports about trouble he caused. Ever give you any? he asks.

Beth thinks about lying completely, but plays along. He shouted things sometimes, she says.

What sort of things?

Names. You can imagine, kids' stuff.

Do you know where he used to hang around? The things he used to get up to?

By the shops. They hung around there a lot. And he used to jump off the point with his friends.

The point?

Suicide point. They would jump out and into the water. The police look at each other. They close their notebooks, and one pulls a card from his pocket.

You've been really helpful, he says. He hands her the card: his name, his telephone numbers. Anything else you think will help, give me a bell, okay?

And then they're gone. Vic appears from the bathroom as Beth steps inside the flat again.

Is it okay? he asks.

It's okay, she says. She checks her phone. Another message from Laura.

BETH PLEASE DON'T DO THIS ALONE YOU DON'T KNOW WHAT PEOPLE ARE CAPABLE OF WHEN THEY ARE GODLESS.

I don't know what we do now, she says to Vic.

43

Laura's next text arrives at almost exactly the same time as the banging on the door, and Beth reads the text as she opens the door, thinking that it might be the police. They left the estate the night before, taking the cordon away from his flat and getting the landlord – who owns so many of these flats – to lock the door, but Beth's on edge, convinced that they'll reappear and intrude and make guesses, and want to ask her more questions. So she opens the door without looking, clearing the text message – WE HAVE TO TALK, PLEASE – and it's Laura herself.

I thought this was easier, Laura says. To just come around and see you, because then you would know I was serious, Beth.

Because your last visits didn't give that impression? Beth asks. She sighs. Please go away, she says, and she shuts the door, but Laura puts her hand out, between the door and the frame. She braces but Beth stops it shutting.

Don't do this, Beth says.

You've messed with things that you don't understand, Beth. Don't you see that? Don't you see that it's not yours to play God?

I didn't play God, Beth says.

He's in there with you still, isn't he. It isn't a question.

I'm on my own. Laura pushes the door slightly and peers past Beth. He's in the spare bedroom: waiting there until she gives the all-clear.

Where do you keep him?

I don't keep him anywhere, Beth says.

He isn't right, is he? I know about it, you know. Back when they used it on people with dementia, they weren't right either. That's why they stopped it: people left wrong and vacant, you know that.

You don't know what you're talking about, Beth says, but she can even hear it in herself: that there is something wrong. The Vic she loved would never have done what he did. And it's true: the dementia cases remembered things wrongly sometimes. A hazard of the treatment, they said. Better than the alternative, they said.

Laura shuts her eyes. Lazarus rose from the dead, because he was touched by the son of God, she says. Jesus healed the sick and the lame: Jesus, not the physicians, not the doctors. He could heal mankind, body and soul, Beth. Don't you see?

There's something insistently pleading about this, Beth thinks. Histrionic as it is, her performance is almost convincing.

Can that thing heal the soul, Beth? Or does it replace it with something much weaker? Laura leans in towards the door. Oh Beth, we were friends, we were. I could feel it. You're better than this.

I'm not, Beth says.

He's in there, isn't he?

Please, Laura, Beth says. Go away. Please just leave me alone.

I can tell. He's in there. You've helped to make a monster, Beth. When he was lost in the first place, that was God's will. People cry when their loved ones die, but there's a plan, Beth. He was part of God's plan. That insistent tone again, and she jams her shoe further inside the doorway, and puts her weight behind the door to keep it open. You should have left him well alone. She backs away from the door. Yours is not to meddle, she says. She makes a sign of the cross.

It was God's will that he took a bullet? The dreams, the nightmares, the pain: that was all God's will? Beth feels the bile in her throat: just as when she used to take him to the clinic and they would be there, protesting outside, their heads wrapped in cloths and their arms cradling crucifixes and signs that screamed THE SOUL IS SACRED, telling her to think about what she was doing. And she said, at the time, I am helping my husband: as she led him out after the sessions, drained and weak, ready to sleep it off, and they threw themselves on the ground and begged her to reconsider.

It certainly wasn't God's will that he would be rebuilt in an image other than that of our Lord. An image that was created by man. A false prophet. She backs away more. She's completely different: her eyes crazed. Beth sees her here and doesn't know how they ever became friends. She tells herself that you don't know about a person until they show themselves fully. Here, Laura is exposed. Beth shuts the door. She shouts through the wood.

Leave me alone, Laura.

Laura doesn't leave. She stays standing there, Beth sees, waiting by the railing. She's sure that Laura is praying.

Beth goes into the bedroom. Vic is asleep on the bed: the Machine is powered up. The noise is still there.

What did you put inside him? she asks. What did you do? She touches the metal: the vibrations run all through her skin, and over her and through her. When you filled in the gaps, what did you fill them with? She sits down. Vic's asleep, she can tell from the breathing. What did you make him from? She lowers her voice and touches the screen and looks for something that might be an answer. She asks a question, feeling stupid for even considering it: because this isn't a story or a film or a joke or a song, or anything that isn't her life. Her actual life. Did you put some of yourself in there? she asks.

The Machine seems to shudder in a way that Beth hates.

44

The text message wakes Beth up, but Vic sleeps through it. It nags three times to be read, so Beth does, if only to shut it up. She knows that it will be Laura – nobody else messages her, not these days – and she almost dismisses it without looking at it. But she doesn't, and then she sits on the edge of the bed and reads it again, and again. And she goes to the living room and reads it again, aloud, as if that might, somehow, make it feel more real.

THE BOY WHO DIED. WE BOTH KNOW WHO DID IT.

Beth's reading it again when another text comes through.

SO HOW CAN YOU LIVE WITH YOURSELF?

Beth sits on the sofa and puts the television on. They have to leave the island now, she knows. There isn't much time left.

45

Vic wakes her. She thinks, first thing, that she seems to do nothing but sleep: that this has taken so much out of her that she can hardly stand it. She's on the sofa, curled up, her whole length pressed tightly between the sofa arms, and her body aches and moans as it unfolds itself.

You're asleep, he says.

I know. I slept here.

You need to clean your head still, he says. She reaches up and touches the scab, hard and thick, and her hair is caught in it, knotted. She can feel the skin underneath the scab healing, slightly tender. She needs a shower, and she needs to clean the wound, and the hair. We'll have a scar in the same place, he says. He touches it. He knows exactly how to touch her still. I'm worried about you, he says.

Don't, Beth says.

I am. I do. He sits on the end of the sofa newly vacated

by her feet. I don't know why I did it. I don't know. There's something about him that doesn't look sad, Beth thinks. As if he'd eaten something that he shouldn't have, or fucked another woman: a crime that had a payoff. A result. Something done to appease a hunger. I think maybe the Machine could wipe that I did it, he says. Is that a good idea?

No, Beth says. Don't even think that.

But it won't do any good, knowing it. And you could wipe it as well. Get it taken away, like it never happened.

It did happen.

Yes. But.

We have to leave, Beth says. Laura knows.

Your friend.

She's not my friend.

She knows?

Yes. She knows that you're back. She's . . . Beth's about to say something about the Machine, about what Laura thinks of it, but she catches herself. She doesn't want to make Vic angry. Or the Machine. But she thinks about that boy, and how Vic saw him as a threat. She doesn't want the same for Laura. She's just nosy, Beth says, and she's insistent, and she won't leave anything alone.

He smiles. You used to hate that in people.

I still do, Beth tells him. She smiles at him, but it takes effort. He dresses himself, and she watches his body putting itself into his clothes, and she wonders if she could remove his memories of the murder. She couldn't do it again, no, no chance of her putting him back into the hands of the Machine, because she couldn't bear to see

274

his face contorted that way again; and that noise from his mouth; and she couldn't stand the wrenching away, piece by piece – like a finished jigsaw being picked apart, finger-nails pushed under the pieces to remove them, watching the picture fall apart.

So we leave, he says to her from the bedroom. Right?

As soon as we can.

How soon is that?

Today. Tomorrow at the latest. We pack what we need, that's it. Landlord can throw the rest.

What about that, in the other room? He looks at the bedroom wall, as if he can see through it to the Machine. She knows he can hear it, even though she's never asked him. She just knows.

We disassemble it.

Okay. Vic nods, but Beth's sure there's something else there: a twitch. A tic.

She fetches bags from the bedroom, from underneath the bed: two large holdalls, one that used to be his, in their previous life, and one that used to be hers, and she puts them onto the bed and peels them open. She starts with her casual clothes: the stuff she can wear day to day, regardless of where they end up. She had planned for the UK, but there's a lot to be said for abroad. Heading to France, maybe, where their money might go a bit further; or Spain, if they can cope with the heat there. She thinks about how much she's been sleeping, and laughs at how easily she could adjust to the siesta lifestyle. Maybe Spain, she tells herself. Get the ferry to France, buy a car, drive down. Get the ferry to Spain itself, if Vic's up to it. He used to get seasick. She wonders if that – his seasickness – will have made the transition, because it wasn't mentioned in any of the recordings. Is seasickness part of a person? Or something embedded in a memory?

Vic stands by the front door.

I want to go for a run, he says.

It's best if you don't.

Why?

Because of the police.

They won't ask me who I am.

Just stay here, please, Beth says. She realizes that she sounds desperate: but she doesn't know why he's being so casual about this. He sits on the sofa and stares at the wall, as if that is all that he is: he runs, he argues, he occasionally comforts her and apologizes. Why don't you watch TV? Beth says.

No, he tells her. There's no petulance in the voice, just a declaration that he doesn't want to.

Then help me pack this stuff.

None of it is even mine, he says, which is untrue, because all the male clothes are his, every single item, but how would he remember that? So Beth does it for him: folding his t-shirts and shorts and trousers, which all seem to be white or shades of white, and which take up twice the space of Beth's own clothes. She puts in toiletries, but they're all hers, and then she decides against it: he needs ownership, she thinks. So she puts them back in the bathroom and decides that he should buy his own when they get to wherever they're going, buy real male-scented toiletries that he wants to use. But then she wonders if he'll even know what he wants, or if he'll stare at these things on their shelves in the shop, and she'll ask him what scents he wants, what sort of products, and he'll be blank and clueless because it doesn't matter to him. Because he never cried to a doctor, or to Beth, about the shampoo he preferred, and so it was never logged, and so it was never put back in. She wonders if maybe the gaps that the Machine filled in, if maybe one of them will have taken care of that. She wonders what Vic can smell at this moment. She sits on the bed and wonders these things as time rockets past, and all she can think, as she reaches every empty conclusion, is that she's made a terrible mistake.

She takes one of the painkillers she bought, that she didn't crush up for Vic, and another straight afterwards, deciding that one isn't enough. Two isn't even enough. Vic is asleep again – both of them are constantly exhausted, but after what they've been through maybe that's okay – so she opens her laptop, standing with it at the kitchen worktop. On her forum, she looks at the topic that she created, and the replies. There are a few standard responses, from users who assume that she's having problems – We're so sorry, they say, or It'll get there, give it time – and then there's one from somebody whose username she doesn't recognize. This is their first and only post.

They write that they've been a long-time lurker on the boards, but that they never had the urge to write anything before. They write that their partner – their choice of word, keeping everything ambiguous – had treatments in the earliest days, to get over a terrible event in their life.

When they came out the other side, their faculties were hanging by a thread, and one day that thread snapped. It was, the post says, the worst day of their lives. (Beth thinks about what the writer wouldn't have given to have had the Vic she was presented with: rough and unfinished and crudely drawn, but stable; and how she had destroyed him because she wanted so much more than that.) The writer's partner spent four years, nearly, in a home, and then they were pulled out – not by the writer, but by the company who made the Machines. They needed people to trial their cure on: the writer didn't see how it could make things worse.

There were five trial cases, the post says, and nothing has been said of them in public. They signed non-disclosure agreements and waivers of responsibility, but it was a way to get their loved ones back, in some shape or form. A year, they spent being worked on. (Beth thinks about her time rebuilding Vic, such a condensed period.) And then they were handed back to their loved ones: complete, or so they were told. Beth reads all this with her hands gripping the laptop sides, and biting into the inside of her cheek, worrying the flesh there with her back teeth. But they weren't complete: the author of the piece doesn't go into specifics, but says that there was something wrong.

They had it all back, says the writer, but there was something missing, and it made me think that there was something wrong with the way the Machine glossed over the gaps. But what if that wasn't the problem? What if the problems – my partner had a temper, and said things that they would never have said before, looked at me like

278

I was nothing, dead, filth – what if the problems are something that's part of us already?

What if they're part of humans, and we paste over them; and the gaps that are left after this, what if they're just holes that let the darkness out?

Beth stands back from the work surface. She doesn't write her own reply to the post; not because she doesn't have anything to say, or doesn't think that she can contribute, but because she can't stop shaking, and she clings to the fridge, which is behind her, and she can feel that shaking with her, and she thinks, How did the Machine do this to us?

46

They're not finished packing, so Beth tells Vic that she'll get them a takeaway. She asks him what he would like from the Indian, and he says that he doesn't mind.

You must mind, she says.

I really don't.

Spicy, creamy, what?

For fuck's sake, Beth. Just whatever. Whatever I like. He makes fists and bangs them on the table and doesn't look directly at her. You can go out and I can't? he suddenly asks.

No. It's not like that. But nobody knows you're here, Vic.

What are you so scared of? he asks. Are you ashamed of me?

You killed that boy, she says, her smallest voice. He still doesn't look at her. He doesn't apologize, or explain, or even react. He's just still.

She slams the door as she leaves, and she walks down the balcony and into the stairwell, and she forgets about the blind corner. She's never met anybody here, even though it has always felt like a threat. And then now she turns it, and there's somebody there, waiting, or just getting ready to climb the stairs. Laura. She staggers backwards, and then she smiles: out of pity, or pleasure, somewhere between the two.

I was coming to see you, she says. She reaches out and takes Beth's arm before she's even had a chance to react. I wanted to tell you that it will be okay: that you can tell the police, and I will support you. You had nothing to do with it: it was all that monster of a husband of yours.

Get off me, Beth says. She starts to walk: she has to carry on. Twelve hours and they'll be on a boat to somewhere else entirely. Laura runs behind her, stepping double-fast to keep up.

Beth, she says, you have to listen to me.

I don't.

This is creation, Beth. You don't mess with creation, as it is the purview of our one God, Beth. Don't you see that?

Beth stops and turns. I didn't mess with creation, she says. I put back what had been taken out. Nothing more. This isn't some bullshit that involves your fucking church, Laura: this is my husband, my life.

And what about that boy's life?

Beth turns and walks on again, because she doesn't want to react. Laura shouts after her, not bothering to match pace now, but still walking.

Did he deserve to die? Laura asks. Did he fall at the hands of the monster you call your husband, Beth? She shouts loudly enough that somebody listening could hear, which scares Beth slightly, so she walks even faster. Did you really think that he could get away with this?

Beth steps inside the restaurant and stands in the entryway, in front of the curtain that leads to the tabled area. There's nobody at the bar. She breathes. She can't hear Laura any more, not from in here. She shuts her eyes and counts down from fifty. She's wondering if it will be enough, when the curtain rustles and the waiter appears.

Jesus, he says, you all right?

I'm fine.

Yeah, okay. You want a drink? She doesn't answer, but hears the pouring of something anyway, then the clink of a glass on the side. Go on, he says, and she does, and it's bitter and sharp, but exactly right: enough to wake her up a little, to shock her into remembering where she is and what she's doing. You want food, or you just hiding from somebody?

It takes her a second to realize he's referring to the trouble she had with the the boy, not Laura. She glances through the glass frontage, and can't see her anywhere.

No, I want food, she says. She orders a korma and a makhani and some rice and a naan.

Two of you eating, eh? He says it with an implied nudge. He's smiling.

Yes, she says. My husband.

Good for you, love, good for you. He disappears and she hears talking from the other end of the restaurant, then the slam of the kitchen door. Done, he says when he returns, five minutes at most. He stops and looks around. Quiet night, he says, as if it's ever not. You want a seat?

No, she says. Can I wait here?

Course you can. You want me to leave you alone?

No, she says. It's fine. They stand in silence, and then she glimpses herself in the mirror behind the bottles of alcohol that line the rear of the bar, and she sees what a state she looks. Like one of those women that they used to avoid on the train: her hair is pulled and lank and greasy, and around the scab it's deep, thick red, almost black-red; her clothes are misshapen and malformed around her body, which has been losing weight. Has she been forgetting to eat? Her face is pale and wrongly hued. She looks older than she is, and that scab . . . She touches it with her fingertips. Inside her head she can hear the noise that her fingernails make, the tap-tap-tap on the hard shell.

What did you do? the waiter asks. If you don't mind me asking. Oh my God that was rude of me. Sorry.

No, she says. It's fine. I fell over. Scraped it.

Ouch. It looks well nasty. You been to the doctor? He knows that she hasn't. He wants to drop the hint that she should. They both know it.

No, she says. I need to clean it more.

Scab like that, might need a stitch.

I think it's healing, she says.

Okay, he replies. Okay.

She puts her head down and looks at the floor. At the carpet, which is red and gold, and meant to invoke something, along with the music: the sensation of being somewhere other than a small restaurant on the Isle of Wight, a small place of faded glory; as if, instead, you're in the Taj Mahal, one of the great wonders of the world, a place of regal majesty. The carpet, the cold gold trim around the bar, the cutlery, the nearly erotic imagery on the walls, the piped-in sitar music. It's all effect, nodding to a colonial memory. It never works, nobody is ever impressed by the facade, but it's ingrained now. Part of the culture. She doesn't say anything more, and neither does the waiter, not until the food is ready – the ringing of a bell, calling him to collect it – and then, as he hands it over, he puts one hand on hers.

If you need any help, come back in here, he says. You know what I'm saying. Okay?

Okay, she says. She doesn't look at him, even when he holds the door open for her and she slides past him and into the warm night.

She's past the shops – which are all quiet, the group of kids mourning and silent after the death of their friend, or put under some sort of curfew by their parents, maybe – and has reached the point where it happened, when she sees Laura, standing by the sign that implores people to rethink their decision and to call a number that might help them, because we've all been through feelings like that, and we're all in this together. You and me, the sign says.

This is where he fell from, that's what the paper says. Laura looks at the lip of the cliff edge, as if the ground itself is guilty.

Don't, Beth says. You don't know what you're talking about.

Is this where you did it?

You don't know what you're talking about. Beth tries to walk on, but Laura reaches out and grabs her arm, and she does it with enough force that Beth spins slightly, and she feels her ankle going, and she's suddenly on the ground, and her hands are on the rocks and stones that surround the point. The bag with the curry splits and the cartons seem to bounce up and collide, and they spill, the thick sauces going everywhere: on the ground, on Beth's knees, slapping onto her top. Laura stands back and looks at her, and she opens her mouth as if she's about to say something but nothing comes out; just a gasp that might pass as an apology, over and over again, inhaling breath. She steps backwards, and Beth thinks, You could fall, and she hates herself for thinking it as soon as she has – those are the words that form in her mind, almost spoken, an invocation – and then Beth shuts her eyes. She holds them shut.

She hears him before she sees him: all heavy feet and thudding breaths, and he runs past her and to Laura. He's got something in his hands – a rock? Something heavy, certainly – and it collides with Laura's head.

Vic! Beth screams, and Laura crumples. Beth sees her fall to the grass: hitting the ground as if she came down from a much greater height, loose and free, like she's floating. She lies on the floor and blood comes from her head, and Vic stands over her and gasps.

I had to help you, he says.

Beth doesn't reply. She pushes herself to her feet – he holds out his hand to her but she flinches away from him – and then looks at what he's done. There's nobody else around, and everything is quiet. There's a faint smell – pot, it smells like – on the air, coming from the estate. Laura isn't moving: the wet blood on her head curiously mirroring the dried blood on Beth's. It's thicker, Beth thinks, and she would be more worried if Laura wasn't still breathing, and if the blood didn't seem to have stopped flowing from the wound.

Beth? he asks.

Don't, she says. Go back to the flat.

I can help, he says, but she thinks she knows what he'll suggest, because he's done it before, and how could she forget that? How could she let that slide?

Just go. Quietly. Please, Vic.

He does. He backs up the road, watching her as she stands over her fallen friend, and he only turns when he reaches the top, when he needs to look where he's going, and then he's gone. Beth picks up the takeaway and bundles it into the bag, and she puts the bag into the bin across the way. It's all ruined now, spilled out and wasted. And Laura: she moves slightly, her hand and her arm. Beth bends down.

I'm so sorry, she says. He didn't mean it. You might be right, you should know that. You might be right that there's something wrong with him, but I don't know what to do about it. Laura flinches as Beth says it. I'm sorry. We don't have long together, and we have to get out of here. You were my friend. Laura's eyes open and she looks

286

at Beth. She focuses on her, and one of her eyes has got a bleed in it, running in from the left, running down the veins and flooding the rest of the white. Laura opens her mouth to speak.

Monster, she says, and her eyes roll back.

Please don't, Beth says. She thinks about leaving Laura there, but she knows; and now that is what will be solidified in her mind: that she was attacked because she knew too much. Beth wonders how this works now, because she doesn't know. She knows TV shows and movies, but not real life. If the police will even take Laura seriously.

Then she hears it, and she feels it: this far down the hill, this close to the sea. She feels it through the ground: a tremor, and she looks around, thinking that it could be more of the land falling into the sea, just like the times with the floods; and then she hears it. A groan that comes from the estate, but she can pinpoint it exactly, because she knows what it is.

It says, You can make this better. You can take this away from her. And Beth doesn't even stop to think about it. She bends down and puts her arm underneath Laura's, and she pulls her to her feet. The walk back to the flat isn't too far, and she feels stronger than she did before. The adrenaline that a father feels when his child is trapped under a car, and he tells the newspapers, afterwards, that somehow he found the strength to lift it, to bend his knees and do something superhuman. Laura's limp body needs constant support, which she gets: and Beth practises what she learned with Vic when she brought him to the island. She walks Laura, one step at a time, to the estate and then up the stairwell, propping her body and getting her up the stairs that way – and she suddenly can't remember how she did this with Vic the first time, this leg of the trip. It's like he turned up on her doorstep and that was a new start for them.

She opens the front door, still clutching Laura's body. She lowers her to the floor by the door, so that she's sitting with her head resting against the wall. The lights inside are off, apart from that ghostly glaze coming from the Machine's room; and Vic is sitting on the sofa. She can hear his breathing; and the breathing of the Machine, somehow synchronous.

Why is she here? he asks. He sounds only slightly scared. Everything else in him is passive.

We can take this away from her, Beth says. Vic turns his head to look at her, but it's too dark to see him properly. She knows that it's wrong: his shape; the way that he is; the things that he remembers. It's all wrong. The things that she knows, says Beth. She doesn't have to know them.

Somebody will be looking for her.

Nobody knows she's here.

This seems so cruel, he says, and he sobs. This big man, so big that he seems almost supernatural, and what he's actually made of, Beth doesn't know, because her Vic would never have killed that boy and he would never have attacked Laura like that, and she has to tell herself that, because she knows that this is wrong: but it's something that she worked for.

We have to put it right, she says.

She was going to hurt you.

She wasn't. She grabbed me. It didn't mean anything, she says. She wants to say, This isn't an argument about how inhuman you are. It's about how we deal with Laura.

People are capable of anything, he says. It's inside all of us.

Where did you hear that? she asks. He doesn't answer. She walks past him and to the Machine's room, where the door is open and the light from the screen is casting itself across everything, and that's impossible, unless he's been in here. But she doesn't question that, not now. She tells Vic to bring Laura through.

No, he says.

Don't do this, Beth says. He doesn't react: he sits on the sofa, and is how he is. So she goes back to Laura's body and drags it through the flat and to the Machine's room. She puts her on the bed – and Laura looks wrong there, because it should be Vic, Beth's used to it being Vic – and she takes the Crown from the dock. She uses lubricant, because it's kinder; and it slides onto the temples.

She waits for Laura to wake.

47

Laura's eyes open as her hands go to the top of her head, and she feels her way around – patting them onto the Crown as her eyes realize what's happening. She sucks in high-pitched air.

Where am I? she asks, even though she knows. Beth is sitting at her side.

Please, she says. You have to tell me what you think you know.

What have you done to me?

Nothing, Beth says. Not yet.

You're a monster, Laura says.

No, Beth says.

What have you done to me?

Tell me what you think you know. Beth's finger hovers over the COMMIT button, waiting for that moment.

You'll go to hell for what you've done, Laura says. She spits it at Beth, suddenly more righteous and furious than she has been. No gentle persuasion. Vitriol.

Why were we even friends? Beth asks, and she leaves it there. Laura doesn't answer for the longest time, and then:

Everybody gets lonely, she says.

I'm not lonely any more, Beth says.

No?

No. Tell me about what you think you know.

I will never let you take it from me, Laura says.

Okay, Beth tells her. Then I'll press this anyway and take everything. She says it but doesn't think that she means it. In those seconds she asks herself if she could do it: because it's not Vic's life she's messing with, this time, but somebody else's, somebody with a boyfriend and family; and when she thinks about how much she would be taking, all she can see is Vic killing that boy. And she can imagine it as clear as day: he finds the boy there, and he reaches out his huge hands to the boy, and he crushes him, and he lifts him and hurls him, and he waits for the crack of the boy's body on the rocks. Only then does he think about what he's done. Maybe, inside, he wonders where it came from.

Maybe the Machine knows.

Beth stops. She pulls the Crown from Laura's head.

Go, she says. Laura stands, and she's woozy still, and she's got blood matting her hair, but she staggers through the flat, clutching the furniture. She doesn't say anything about Vic: in the darkness, he is almost part of the flat itself. She reaches the front door, her movements silent-movie melodramatic, limbs flung and legs crossing, and she turns.

You're a monster, she says, once more, but she's looking at Beth. She ignores the other, with its breathing and its menace; she never looked at him once, Beth realizes. And then she's gone.

Beth sits at the dining table and drinks water, and she reaches for the pills she's got in her pocket. She takes three.

You let her go, Vic says.

What would you have done? Beth asks. This wasn't her fault.

I don't know, Vic says. She'll come back now though, right? With the police. He lies back and shuts his eyes. The flat seems all the darker for it.

Beth goes to the Machine's room and lies down. She sleeps. She doesn't know for how long. When she wakes up, it's because the Machine's fans have started up again; it's eager. She deprived it, letting Laura go.

She says, I've ignored so much of you. She stands and moves to the side of the Machine and pulls the plug from the wall. I need the screwdriver, she says. Vic, still sitting on the sofa, doesn't move to help her, so she gets it from the drawer she left it in, and she lies on her back and she opens the Machine up again and peers inside it. It's so dark. She gets a torch from the kitchen and shines it inside, and the light bounces around the whole thing, reflecting off every inside surface, and she can hardly see anything. But then her eyes settle in and she sees how big it is inside; and how small the cluster of wires that make its guts is. Like a ball inside it, little more than the size of a fist. Floating, suspended by wires.

She hears something so she ducks out and goes to look. It's Vic. He's brought the bags out of the bedroom and put them by the door. He's standing in the streetlight from outside, and she can't take it, because she feels like she doesn't know him like this, so she switches the lights on in the flat. His face is as white as she's ever seen it.

I don't know, he says. We have to leave, right? So we should go. He pulls on his own fingers, cracking each at the knuckle. I'm so scared, he says.

We can't go until morning, she says. The first boat isn't until half past six.

Should we wait down there?

No, she replies. Get yourself ready, that's the right thing to do. I have things to do here. She opens the cupboards, where there are more tins of spaghetti, and takes slices of frozen bread from the freezer, and she starts the process of making dinner. We should eat, she says. So they eat together, at the table, and Vic keeps one eye constantly on the door; and Beth keeps her eye on the Machine. She stands in the doorway after they've eaten, as Vic is washing up – she laughs at that, because they're abandoning everything else in a halfway state, walking out and expecting the landlord to deal with it: the flat a diorama of the Marie Celeste, which somehow feels appropriate – and then watches the Machine doing nothing, but somehow, she thinks, doing everything.

I'm going to kill you, she says. That's going to be my last act. She goes into the Machine's room and sits close to it. There's something wrong with me, to have done what I've done. Who does it make me? she asks it. She

293

puts a hand on its cold, metal skin, and it shivers under her touch.

She remembers being a child: her dog, so sick. Her parents telling her that the car didn't mean to hit it, and that it was getting old. This – loss, her mother's word – is a part of life. Intrinsically linked, two little l-words entwined. They invited her to say goodbye, and she put her hand on its fur, on its chest (because she wanted to avoid the sodden red tea towel that covered the dog's hind quarters) and she felt it breathing and, as it died, it shivered. That's what happens. That flash-rush of coldness envelops.

I need a shower, she tells Vic. He's standing by the door.

Okay, he says.

48

The water is hot, and Beth is worried about the scab, so she washes her body first. She thinks about how people wash themselves after committing a horrific act in a movie; all going back to Shakespeare, back to Lady Macbeth scrubbing her hands. Beth lathers and washes off, and she repeats, but she doesn't seem to feel any different. Nothing changes.

So then her hair, and she holds the tips underneath the powerful flow of the tap before putting the rest of her head under. She covers the scab with her hand at first, and then, when she's sure that it's okay – as she watches the water whirl around her feet she can see chunks of thick dried blood, but nothing fresh, which was the worry, that soaking it would open it up again – she lets the whole area be washed. She knows then that the cut looked far worse than it was: it doesn't hurt, and she can feel the dried blood flaking away. She lets it, letting the bigger chunks pick themselves apart. They sit by the plug and slowly dissolve. It doesn't hurt when it's just water, and it doesn't hurt when she runs shampoo through it, but she can feel the skin there below her hair: tender and pink.

She dries herself in the bath and then stands in front of the mirror, and she rubs the towel over herself before pulling on underwear and cleaning her teeth. She looks at the pink skin on the front of her temple, so similar to Vic's own scar. The same shape. (They always marvelled that his scar somehow had the shape of a bullet. They were just seeing what they wanted to see, but there, on her head: a bullet, side-on, clear as anything.) She thinks about what to do with her toothbrush. All of this stuff can be left, she thinks. France will have toothbrushes. Spain will have shampoo.

I want to do my hair, she tells Vic. I should do something else with it.

Okay, he says. His voice is quiet.

She looks at herself. She looks better, she thinks, much better. Human, suddenly. She wonders if Laura's awake properly yet, and if the police are in her room asking her what happened. It might take them longer to get a picture of Vic, so Beth will be who they're looking for, if Laura even has a clue. They don't have long. Beth thinks about her hair, and how changing it could give them time, if they need it. Vic's clippers sit in the drawer in the bedroom, and she doesn't give it a second thought once she's plugged them in. She picks a high grade and doesn't balk as she runs it along her scalp, front to back, and watches the clusters of hair mound in the sink as they fly off. Vic doesn't ask her what she's doing, so she takes swathes out. She does the front first, and then the top and the back – though she might need Vic to tidy it for her, and she pictures him standing over her, clutching the clippers tightly in his fist – and then she moves the clippers to the side where the scab is. It's mostly gone, so she gently starts picking at it with her fingernails, pulling off smaller lumps, dragging them along the remaining hairs until they're free, and then drops them into the sink. She manages to get most of it, but there's still some left. She can see the pink of the fresh skin closer to her temples, but here, under the hair, she can't, because the scab is dark against her scalp. It is at its darkest, and she pulls her hair from side to side to try and see underneath it, but she can't, and she can't get a purchase on the scab.

She knows, but she tells herself that it's still only a scab.

So she takes the clippers and puts them on the line of her temple and pushes them along, and watches the hair come away, almost strand by strand, that's how focused she is. It doesn't hurt. It shakes: she feels the slight tremor of the device in her hands and on her head, and she thinks that this is nothing she hasn't felt before, right here, vibrating the skin on this exact spot. And then the hair is gone from there, and she can see right to the skin, to the roots of the hair: and the bruise that sits at the puckered points the hair grows out of. It runs in a perfect circle, the size of an old fifty-pence piece, and she touches it but the skin doesn't change: it doesn't go pink, and it doesn't go white. She thinks about her headaches, and how tired she's been.

She takes the clippers to the other side of her head and the hair there is gone even faster, stripped away without a pause. She can see the Crown's pad-mark even clearer here, because there's no cut to contend with. She finishes the rest of her hair and then stands back and looks at herself. Barely recognizable, at a glance. She thinks that this is somebody else. It's somebody else who did this, who wore the Crown, and what? What did she want to forget?

She goes to the living room. Vic stares at her.

What did you do? he asks.

To stop them from recognizing me, she says, but even as she says it she's unconvinced. As if something inside her willed her to do this, so that she would see. She points to her temples. Snap, she says.

What? He rushes towards her and looks, puts his hands onto her head – she can feel them, so strong and warm and large, and she imagines them squeezing, crushing her skull, some feat of terrifying strong-man prowess – and he parts her hair with his fingers and examines the marks. He knows what they are. He's seen his own, even as his hair has grown over them. His hair has grown so quickly, abnormally quickly, that they're almost covered, and he almost looks normal. What did you do? he asks.

I don't know, Beth says. I don't know.

When, though?

I don't know. She had assumed it was recent, but it could have been long ago. How long's it been since she looked at this part of her head? Nothing about her has changed: no hairstyle changes, no haircuts that she hasn't done herself. Nothing that would make her look at that part of her head, behind the temple, hidden away. She wonders if they've been there for years, even. As long as Vic's.

She tells him to go to the bedroom and get some clothes out for her – she tells him which ones – and she sits on the arm of the sofa and thinks about what could have made her do this. Desperation, she thinks: if Vic did something so bad that she couldn't live with it. Or if she did, maybe. But Vic . . . She thinks about the boy, and about Laura, and how easy he found it to shrug both incidents off as just something he did. An action, like breathing or eating. Totally justifiable.

He is simply standing in the room, not doing anything, so she has to go and find the clothes herself. She stands in front of him and dresses, and she looks at herself in the mirror by the door when she's done, from across the room. These are clothes that she hasn't worn in years, younger than she should be wearing, by a margin. She can fit into them now, after the last few weeks; and where they used to pinch her body, now there's a sag and a hang. In the mirror she looks like a different person.

Okay, she says. Not long to go now. Wait here.

She goes to the Machine. It still trembles, like it knows what's coming, but she doesn't end it yet. She flicks through the screens for the recordings, to find out more, to see if there are numbered files of her speaking on here, telling the Machine that she wants to forget whatever it was that she couldn't live with any more. But the only recordings are Vic's old ones. Vic in file form. Vic as a

299

fake man. Vic by proxy.

Something. Something outside, coming from the rim of the estate, coming closer and closer, the sound of engines and sirens that starts below the noise of the Machine, getting louder and louder, and by the time she gets to the living room she can see them as well, in the red and blue that flashes around the darkness.

49

We have to go, Vic says.

We can't, she tells him. She tells him to get into the Machine's room and to wait there: to sit on the bed and not touch anything, and to trust her. He does, or says that he does. Beth flicks the lights off and peers through the curtain down at the bollards, as the policemen climb out of their cars; and there, with them, is Laura. She clutches a rag to her head, something large and bulbous, and she steadies herself on the car door as she climbs out, then waits there a while. It's still dark: only just heading towards light. Nothing like as hot as it will be. Nothing even close yet.

Beth ducks down, hiding, because she thinks that the best way to ride this out will be to sit inside and wait until they leave. She doesn't know how this works, not really – only what she's learned from television – but they can't enter her flat, she knows that, not this quickly. So they'll wait, and when the police are gone they'll make their move. They'll get onto a ferry and get off the island. She worries then that the police will be waiting for them at the dock, but that's a problem for later. Now: they're here, down below, because Laura was assaulted, and because she'll have told them that Vic killed that boy. Beth tries to remember his name – because she wants to give him that much, rather than thinking of him as something so vague – but she can't. She can remember the way that he looked at her, certainly; and the menace in his loping, drawn-out walk; and the scar that he had, across his neck; and she wonders again what it was from, and then she remembers his dead mother – car crash? – and thinks that it must be a scar from that, a remnant. That makes her feel sorry for him: carrying it around like that. Reminded, every time he rubs it. Always there but never in view, and he can't see it, but he can't forget it either.

Beth watches them come into the estate proper, and then to the stairs, and then they're out of view – at the blind corner, in the stairwell, and then filing along the balcony. She can hear the crackle of their radios, and she can hear them asking Laura if she's all right. Beth crouches low and scuttles to the back room, to the Machine's room, and she stands in the doorway with all the lights off, knowing that they won't be able to see her.

Stay quiet, she says to Vic. He's still sitting on the bed.

The police knock on the door, not touching the bell, just hammering straightaway: the base of a fist making the whole thing thud.

Mrs McAdams, they say. She hears it, muffled through

the door, and she looks at Vic. She looks at the Machine.

Don't make a noise, she says.

The thudding comes again, and she sees the shape of one of them at the window. It's getting lighter outside: not quite dawn yet, but not far off. She sees him bend down, and she stays stock still, in that darkness. Feeling safe enough.

Mrs McAdams, the policeman says again.

Beth, Laura says. We know you're in there.

Please go away, Beth whispers. Because she needs to get out of here, and she needs to take Vic somewhere else, and start this again: working with him, keeping whatever's inside him under control.

The policeman hammers again, and then the letterbox flap lifts and eyes peer through.

Nothing, he says. No lights, no movement. They might have gone already.

She won't have gone, Laura says. Where would she go?

We can't get a warrant until later this morning, but we've got people watching all the ways off the island. They'll find her. (Beth strokes her head: her new haircut might be enough, she hopes, when she reaches the docks.) The policemen start to walk away – Beth watches their silhouettes go past the window – but Laura isn't with them.

I'm going to wait for her, Laura says.

You really should come with us, they tell her. Stern but humouring.

I'm not going anywhere, she says, and then the door is hammered again, but this time it's Laura's knock, Laura's fist. Beth! she shouts. Beth, I know you're in there! Her voice becomes clearer as she speaks: speaking through the pain that she must still be experiencing. This must matter to her. We only want to talk to you, Beth. Nothing more.

I don't know what you think I want, Beth, but I so want to believe you about everything. I only want to help you, because you're my friend. Even after all of this – after you hurt me, Beth, and threatened me with that thing, I still want to help you. Doesn't that tell you how much this means to me? She knocks again: softly, this time, with her knuckles, not the flat of her fist. The police are nowhere to be seen. And I thought that we connected, didn't we? And you told me all of your secrets, and I was there for you. I could have helped you, Beth: I could have guided you. Beth hears the turning of an engine: must be the police. They're nearly alone with Laura. Vic's body tenses, because he could finish this, she knows, but that would seal everything. That's a decision that she could never allow. She could do so, as easily as she could wipe Vic's past, but neither is going to happen. Laura taps the glass again. Please, Beth. I can help you. Let me?

We're in this together, Vic says. Beth worries that he says it too loudly, but Laura doesn't hear him.

I know, Beth whispers in reply. She walks into the near-light coming through the windows, and towards the front door. She gets as close as she dares – the sound of the engines now long gone – and she waits there. She doesn't know what she's waiting for, exactly. For something.

Beth, please. God can save you, Beth.

But I made him, she says. Laura shuffles, loud enough

304

to be heard. You told me that it was a sin, Laura. And you want to be my friend?

Where is he, Beth?

Please, Laura. Just leave us alone. I'm sorry about your head, but—

Now we have matching wounds, she says.

Yes. Beth touches her bruised head. She has that scar, and so will Laura, and so does Vic. Vic had it first: everything else is mere imitation.

So much in common, I told you. Beth can hear Laura's smile through the door. It's not too late, Laura says.

Come on, Beth says. We both know that's not true.

Where is he really?

You'll tell the police, Laura. You brought them here.

And now they've gone, Laura says, but Beth instantly knows that she's lying: her voice is too persuasive, almost patronizing. Don't worry, it says: trust me. Please Beth! Laura begs. You're all alone in there, don't you see that? You're sick. I'm only here to help you! The police are only here to help you! Beth backs away from the door. She speaks to Vic.

They're outside, she says. I don't know what to do. I don't know what to do. Vic walks up next to her and reaches out his arms, and he holds her; and she thinks that he could smother her and she might be happy for that to happen, somehow. What did I erase from myself? she asks him, and he smiles at her – she can see the corners of his mouth from where she is, wrapped up in his arms – and he replies, because he's figured it out before she has.

Who says you erased anything? Who says that you didn't put something else in?

She knows that there isn't long, so she quickly bolts the door and drags the table over from the kitchen area to put against it, together with some chairs. She asks Vic to help her move the sofa. This flat is her bastion. Fitting, somehow: years of being stuck in it, and now she accepts that this will be where it ends for her.

What should I do? Vic asks.

I don't know, she says. Make sure that they're kept out. Tell me what you can see.

He nods. Yes ma'am, he says. His army voice. She loved – still loves – that voice. She takes the tools from the kitchen drawer and she lies them on the bed in front of the Machine.

I can't let anybody else have this; have you, I mean, she says to Vic. You understand? The fans start. They start, as if she was powering it up for a treatment, but she's not; and they keep accelerating, as if she's been running it for an hour, which she hasn't; and they keep going, until the noise is louder than a shout, and the vibrations through the floor make Beth almost lose her footing. She doesn't know if this is real any more, or something else. She wishes that she could ask somebody else if they can feel this, but there's only Vic, and he's as much a part of this as the trembling casing of the Machine itself.

She presses the screen first, then flicks through the menus to the hard drive, and she goes through the sequence to erase everything. The screen's vibration is so violent that it nearly hurts her finger as she presses it:

running up it from the tip, making the joints shake. When she pulls her finger away it's like she's got pins and needles, but she's pressed the button, and she's confirmed that this is what she wants to do. The Machine may protest, but this is her choice. It's not enough, she thinks. Hard drives can be recovered. Data – zeroes and ones – lives on past anything we do to it. Vic stands in the doorway and watches her.

Can I help you? he says, but he seems sad to be saying it.

You don't want any part of this, Beth says.

Maybe not.

What happens after this?

I don't know, he says. Are you taking it all away?

Just the memories, she says. Just what it's got of you. She touches him: the vibrations inside her travel to him, and his skin seems to shake, sending him out of focus for a second. There, and yet not. You keep watching, she tells him.

She kneels on the floor and then moves onto her back, and she peers upwards into the opened insides of the Machine. She can see the wire cluster in the middle but can't reach it, not from where she is; so she starts to stretch her arm, pushing her body up into an arch and pressing her shoulder against the edge of the opening. She reaches with her fingertips, flailing them as if that might make the ball come closer, but it doesn't work. So she moves herself more, and then suddenly she's closer; her head underneath the hole, and it's large enough to squeeze inside, she thinks. So she does.

She starts with one shoulder and her head, and once they're inside, the other shoulder, and she moves herself around, stretching and finding space inside the Machine's enormity. It's bigger inside than out, she thinks, and then she manages to bring the top half of her body up and into the Machine, and she reaches up until the ball of wires is in her hands, and she can start to unwind it. It's tightly packed but there are no knots, no seals, and she manages to wind everything out until she sees the central nugget: the hard drive, a solid lump of silver metal, attached through a normal plug socket, almost: nothing complicated.

She touches it; it shivers. When she pulls the plug out, the shivering stops.

In the bedroom, Vic sits on the end of the bed and holds his head in his hands. He looks up when Beth reappears.

Is that me? he asks.

Yes, she says. She holds him out, and his metal glints in the darkness of the room.

What are you going to do with it?

I have to destroy it.

Okay, he says.

So. She puts the hard drive into her pocket. Outside the front door, more hammering: the forceful fists of the police again.

She's in there, Beth hears Laura say, and then they hammer more. Laura shouts: She's a murderer! She killed little Oliver! (Beth smiles when she hears his name. That was it. Oliver.) The police don't try and quieten her. They keep hammering.

Mrs McAdams, they say, we know you're in there. Please open the door, or we will enact forceful entry. Beth listens as other people's voices appear: the fat neighbour and her daughters, asking what's going on, their voices carrying through the walls and doors. She sees people massing outside, and hears Laura again.

She killed that boy, you know that? She's a murderer, and she tried to kill me! She tried to erase me! Beth can see her through the crack in the curtain, even from here: standing by the railing, towel held to her head, preaching. When I confronted her, she tried to kill me! She blames it on her husband, but he's been disabled by her. She thinks he's in there with her, but he's not! He's not a murderer; she is! He's in a home, a vegetable: a victim of what she has done!

I'm not, Vic says. What she says. I'm not.

No, Beth says. Of course you're not.

The police hammer, and the door starts to move slightly in the frame. One of them shouts about going to get the ram, and Beth knows what happens then: this all comes apart around her in seconds. Everything needs to be forgotten about and abandoned. She can't let them get this, all of this.

She stands, suddenly alone, with the Machine.

I started this, she says. Didn't I.

50

Beth tries to force the bedroom window open more, but it strains at the hinges. Beneath them, not far below, is the Grasslands, and she knows she could make that drop. It's not too bad. It would hurt, but she'd walk away.

Smash it, Vic says. So Beth takes the light from the bedside table and turns it around, and she rams the base at the window. It doesn't smash – the glass is far too thick for that – but the thin struts of the window buckle slightly, widening the gap. Harder, Vic says. Really give it some welly. She stands aside and lets Vic take the lamp, and he rams it over and over again, until the window is wide enough for Beth to squeeze through. Outside there are railings along the edge of the window, and she puts her hands on them. If you lower yourself down first, the drop will be less, Vic says. So warm: the railings burn to touch, and her hands sweat as they touch them. She doesn't have any other choice. She can hear the banging from the other side of the flat, and Laura's voice carrying through.

She is messing with forces that she doesn't comprehend, Laura says. Beth wonders what sort of audience she now has. How much the islanders are humouring her. They will break down the door and enter the flat, and they'll charge through the rooms looking for them, or for signs of who they are – No, Beth thinks, who she is, that's all – and they will tear her belongings apart. And will they stand in awe of the Machine? Will they stand in front of it, as hollowed and gutless as it now is, and will they know to search through it? Or will they look at its opened front and know that it's dead: that it's like Vic's body, lying in that bed, with all that makes it what it is taken from it, stolen from the inside by Beth, and left ruined, alone and blinking and reaching for purpose? She gave it up so quickly.

She thinks back to the day that Vic all but died. She stood outside his room as they told her their diagnosis: how the Machine had taken him. She had spent hours holding his hand until that point, knowing – so sure, so absolutely utterly bloody-mindedly sure – that he would pull out of it, do some sort of right turn and there he'd be, complaining of a headache and sleeping all day and rubbing at those bruises on his head, but still her husband. He would go back to talking incessantly about things that they both remembered, key events, holidays and hotels and birthday parties and other things that mattered; and those things that the Machine made up for him the first time around, people and places that didn't exist. They would come from nowhere, and he would say, I love you,

311

and he would take her hand, and he would say, Do you remember that holiday in Hawaii? On Big Island? And Beth would smile and ask him to tell her about it. That's how she'd phrase it: Tell me about it, she would say, and she would close her eyes and lie back and put her head in his lap, and sometimes he would stroke her face and her hair, but sometimes he would simply let it be, getting so carried away with the story and the words that were somewhere inside his head that he almost forgot that she was there. It didn't matter, because this was him, and he was happy. Better fake memories, than memories that tore him apart and kept him awake at night. So when he lay there, frothing and howling, she told the doctors that she couldn't see him. She asked them again if they really meant that it would be permanent and they put their hands on her shoulder.

Now, somehow, Vic stands below her, on the Grasslands.

You can jump now, he says. Drop, bend your knees. Take the fall, don't let it take you.

Okay, Beth says. She lets go. This is a trust exercise, like they made them do in therapy. How much do you trust your partner? Will they catch you if you fall? Beth goes down on her ankle, on the hard lawn – nothing to take the pressure, nothing spongy underneath to make this easier – and she falls to her side. She lies there for a second: the echo of the ram – she assumes – against her front door, coming through the whole estate, bouncing off the walls.

You have to run, he says.

I know. Her ankle is sore but workable, and she gets

going, along to the cliff edge, and from there to the outskirts of the estate. The greyness of the place is over-whelming from here: the hidden part: the stuff behind the cooker or underneath the fridge. Graffiti lines the walls of people's flats – FUCK TENBEIGH, one says, about the Prime Minister, and WHO LIVES HERE IS A CUNT reads another, and TITS is a third, with breasts drawn below it; and Beth knows that this last one was made by the boy, and she wonders when, because it looks old and faded and somehow part of the concrete, so she wonders how young he was when he actually did it – and there's rubbish, like manmade scree, piled up against the building, trainers and food packets and empty tins, all browned from the sun, all rotting and cooking under the heat. Then she sees the body of a cat: dead, partly eaten, flies swirling. She can't smell it. It's been here too long now, almost a fossil.

When she reaches the front of the estate, cutting along the cliff-side path towards the strip of shops, she sees it from the bottom of the hill. There's a crowd of people outside her flat, and all along the balcony. All with their arms raised, all watching Laura, who shouts things that Beth can no longer hear. She doesn't suppose that the words matter now: this is just to incite them, to get them baying for blood, and they're all transposing something else onto this. Nobody cared about the boy, because if they did they wouldn't have allowed him to become who he was, and yet they find it easy to make Beth a villain suddenly, and everything – the place, the heat, the sense that her life as she knows it is all ending so soon – can be blamed on her. She doesn't know what they would do if they caught her, but their arms are raised in fists, and they shout things at each other. Beth watches as Laura seems to command them, and they go into the flat past the police, and they reappear within seconds in groups of three, dragging the Machine out.

We have to go, Vic says.

Wait a minute, Beth tells him. She watches them bring it out in its three pieces, somehow separated – she had forgotten that that was how it arrived, less than whole, and that she made it what it was, physically, if nothing else – and they bring each piece to the edge of the balcony. They know what it is and what it does, because they were everywhere: the lives that they destroyed. The tabloid campaigns to ban them: OUR SOLDIERS, RUINED FOR THEIR COUNTRIES, they howled. And when the dementia patients and the Alzheimer's patients and the amnesia patients began to be affected, that was it. Everybody hates the Machine. They throw the pieces over the balcony and they shatter on the floor below, held together by bolts that aren't meant to take impact, and the black metal sheets flay off as the structure comes apart. Piece two follows, colliding with piece one, and then the final piece, the centre, with the screen and the lack of guts. All three lie crumpled, and they watch them. The people on the balcony – policemen, locals, the boy's gang, Laura – all see the figures at the end of the road. They roar.

Beth turns and runs to the edge of suicide point.

I can't let them get you, she says to Vic.

314

Then run.

I will, she says, but first. She pulls the pebble of the hard drive from her pocket and gives it to him. Go on, she says. He pulls his pose, his Adonis pose, his bodybuilder weightlifter idealized pose that she never saw him pull in real life, and his arm curls backwards and then releases, spring-loaded. The hard drive flies out and through the air, towards the water. It doesn't skim; it smacks into the gentlest wave and it's gone. No glint as it sinks.

Now what? Vic asks. She strips her clothes off. Down to her underwear. You might not make it, he says. There are rocks, and then the swim.

I can do the swim, she says.

The rocks, then.

Maybe, she says. She doesn't wait for him: she throws her arms upwards and bends her knees slightly, and then flings herself forward and out. She opens her eyes, because if she's going to hit the rocks she wants to know: but all she can see is Vic already in the water; already, that body cutting through the waves, his arms making a wake of their own, and she knows as she hits the water and it shocks her and he's suddenly gone, that she'll be swimming behind him the entire way.

51

She rushes up the lawn, because she doesn't know if they're here. She doesn't have a clue if they'll be watching this place or not. It depends on where they think she is. They might not even know that she made it off the island; this might give it away. Doesn't matter, she thinks. So little time to go. So she runs across the lawn, patting her clothes down, and she smiles at the lady at the front desk, who smiles back. She doesn't know if she recognizes her, and that's fine, or if she just notices the burn marks on her head, so visible now. Vic comes just behind her, and the woman doesn't bat an eyelid at that, but Beth doesn't expect her to. She's used to this now.

She follows the sand-coloured line, even though she knows the way, but she's always followed it, like a habit. She doesn't wait in the doorway because she doesn't know how long she's got.

Hello, she says to Vic, lying on his bed. He doesn't

answer, because he can't. She can't remember what happened the last time she was here. She was going to come and get him, and something changed. She wishes that she could remember what that was. How far she got, even: if she stood here and helped him dress and then chickened out, because it would be too much. And would it even work? And did she want it to? She puts her hand on his leg, which is thin and weak and soft. I've come back for you, she says. The other Vic – the one that she's brought with her, who is somehow a part of her and nothing else – doesn't say anything. He stands by the door and watches her, and he looks at her from underneath his eyebrows, tilted forward.

Are you okay? she asks them both. Neither can answer her, so she carries on. I love you, she says. That's why I did this. That's the only answer, isn't it? And would you want this? She sits on the edge of the bed.

They said to her, when it happened, that there was nothing left of him inside. This isn't your husband, they told her. This is a body. And it's alive, and it's learning, but it's nothing like him, and it's nothing to do with him. You asked us why so many people find it easy to divorce their loved ones when this happens. That's why. There's nothing of him left any more.

So, she says to Vic, I don't know where to go from here. But I have an idea. She squeezes the body's hand. I really do love you, she says. She kisses him on the forehead, even as his head moves of its own accord, left to right, and her lips smear on it. Okay, she says. So I should go. I'll see you soon.

317

She gets out of the room and doesn't follow the sand-coloured line back to the entrance. Instead she follows the black line. It takes her up another flight of stairs, and down a corridor, and then to another flight behind a door, and she expects this to be locked but it isn't, because who is going to break in to get to this? It gets warmer as she climbs: no air conditioning up here, and the warm air from below seeps up through the building's floorboards, and by the time she's at the top of the last staircase she's almost broken into a sweat and she's breathing heavily through both her mouth and nose.

There's a door that she opens, and there's nobody in here. There's a cordon that she steps over, and there, at the back of the room, stands the Machine. The same model, which she knows is right. It would have to have been, really. She doesn't know if it's plugged in, and it doesn't matter: because she steps to it and puts her hand onto the screen and it starts up. The screen lights up and the metal buzzes as the fans work. The dust and warmth in the room swirl around, so fast that she can see them moving, the fans behind the Machine churning them into something like a wind, and the vibrations of the metal – because this hasn't been used in so long, and somehow it's hungry, somehow – make the floorboards shake and the dust in the air shake. She knows it isn't real. Vic, her Vic, the one inside her head, watches her. He doesn't say anything, because there's nothing left for him to say. But he stands in the light coming through the windows and he watches.

She pulls the Crown down from the dock and adjusts

318

it, moving the arms and the pads. There's no lubricant here, no painkillers, nothing to make this easier. She thinks that's about right. This should hurt. So she puts the pads onto her head with the Crown itself, and they sit in the same space as the bruises, as she knew they would. She moves a chair from the side of the Machine and then thinks better of it, taking just the cushion instead, and the cushion from another chair, and puts them on the floor. When she's started she'll sit on them, or maybe lie down. Whatever feels most comfortable. After a while it won't be her choice anyway.

So then she flicks through the menus. PURGE. COMMIT. The vibrations through her fingers. One hand on the screen, the other on her chest, where her heart is. She can feel them both, pulsing together so quickly. She slumps down and starts to talk.

If they come in now, and they ask her what she is doing, she'll tell them. And if they ask her why she's trying to wrench Vic out, she'll say, Who said anything about Vic. And she'll plead with them to let her finish; and she'll ask for a room here, and tell them about her savings, and say, That should be enough. Put me with him. Let us be whatever.

This is what I want, she will tell them. And she'll pray that they let her keep on talking, lying there on the floor in agony, screaming the words out, thinking it all through, all about her and about Vic and about everything she can draw on from her entire life, and she'll beg them to not put her back in, because even though they know how to, now, they would ruin this; and she'll say, This is what I want.

Acknowledgements

Thanks to my editor Laura Deacon, Patrick Janson-Smith and everybody at HarperCollins; and to Sam Copeland, and all at RCW.

And thanks to early readers: Kim Curran, Holly Howitt and John Smythe.